Seacrest Sunsets

Seacrest Sunsets

Love Along Hwy 30A
Book Two

Melissa Chambers

Copyright 2018 Melissa Chambers. All rights reserved.
First Edition June 2018

Perry Evans Press

ISBN: 978-1-7324156-1-4

Edited by Trish Milburn
Cover image from iStock

melissachambers.com

Also by Melissa Chambers

Chapter One

Three presidents had been elected since the last time Maya enjoyed the bar scene, yet here she sat with the same well-meaning friend who'd dragged her to these sorts of places since they were too young to flash their real IDs. These days, her idea of excitement was a second glass of wine and anything on the Home and Garden Network. But her best friend from high school had other ideas.

Felicity set her wine glass down on the bar. "Relax. It's not like we're at Studio 54."

Maya glanced around the seedy little bar. "I still don't understand why we couldn't have had a drink by the pool back at the house."

"Because we're single, and there are no men back at the house."

"I'm not here for a man. I'm here for you and Sebastian. I rarely see either of you. This is our week to catch up and reminisce about our idiotic high school days, not to go to bars."

Felicity trained her gaze on Maya's heel which Maya didn't realize she had been bouncing uncontrollably. "You're wound up tighter than a spool of thread," Felicity said. "You need to loosen up. That's what vacations are for."

Maya let out an irritated sigh. "It's just hard to relax. I'm getting ready to start this new position at work. This vacation was probably a bad idea."

"You said this vacation was mandated by your boss," Felicity said.

Maya rolled her eyes, unable to argue.

"When's the last time you had sex?" Felicity asked, and Maya busied her mouth with the wine glass. "That's what I thought. You're pent-up. You need release, and not from a vibrator. From a man."

Maya considered her surroundings—a floor with so much muck caked layer upon layer that she'd had to peel the bottom of her sandals off of it as she walked, Christmas lights strung across the ceiling in late May, the walls covered in magic marker and pen with phrases like Tommy loves Crystal and Drink more, wurk less. "And you think a dive bar in Panama City Beach is the place to find me one?" Maya asked. "There were some perfectly nice restaurants near Sebastian's house in Seacrest, you know?"

Felicity cut her eyes at Maya. "The sort of guys you'd meet at one of those places would prepare your taxes or give you advice on your 401(k) plan. This is the kind of place where you can find a good, old-fashioned, blue-collar man who knows what to do with his hands." She tipped her wine glass toward the door. "Like one of these guys. Hel-lo."

Two men took a seat opposite them across the bar. The first one had to be six and a half feet tall, towering over every guy in the bar, with black, wavy hair complimented by a dark complexion. In his own right, his looks trumped any she'd seen in months…except for the guy he was with. Holy mother of God.

He stood about six feet tall with dark hair shaved close to his scalp and muscles on his arms that made Maya think he could bench press her without breaking a sweat. It wasn't that he was the best looking guy she'd ever seen, but he was by far the sexiest. He had a Mark Wahlberg quality about him, a sexual oozing of epic proportions. He scanned the room with a comfort level that said he was familiar with the place, his dark eyes commanding attention, and he certainly got it from her. Felicity rolled multiple R's over her tongue. Maya shrugged. "Pretty cute."

"Sweetie, there's cute then there's these two. Take another look."

Maya did. "Okay, so they're hot. Big deal."

Felicity relaxed her shoulders, her eyelids drooping. "I know these two don't fit your typical pocket protector, taped glasses, high-water wearing dates. But it's okay. You don't have to only date nerds. You are allowed to date guys who can lift more than a laptop."

"These guys aren't potential dates for me. They are gods." She pointed to the big one. "That one's the god of making women drool, and that one's the god of making them fall directly to their knees."

The god of making women fall to their knees locked gazes with Maya. She glanced away, heat flushing into her cheeks.

"Ooh, would you look at that?" Felicity brought her drink to her lips to cover her mouth. "The sexiest man in Panama City Beach is staring at you."

Maya tucked a lock of her thin hair behind her ear, a dreadful habit she could not break. She did it constantly when she got nervous, which was pretty much all the time. She was high strung, and the action was an attempt at self-soothing, though it never worked. "He's not looking at me."

"I disagree."

Maya shifted her gaze to him, and her stomach floundered as he looked back. He gave an almost imperceptible upturn of his full lips that was so sexy she thought she might remove her underwear and toss it at him on autopilot.

She looked away, tucking her hair again. "He's not looking at me. He's looking at you."

Felicity laughed. "Please. I know when a man's interested in me. That one is not. His friend might be though." She lowered her chin and gave the taller one a smile that demanded his consideration.

"Guys like this don't ask me out," Maya said. "Trust me. I run into guys like this at the gym every day. They have zero interest."

"It's because you hide your figure in baggy gym clothes. Who does that when they have a body like yours?"

"I'm a conservative dresser. I'm not comfortable in a sports bra and shorts up my butt."

4

"Look, you work your ass off on your body. I'm just saying it wouldn't kill you to show it off here and there."

"I thought I was doing okay tonight?"

Felicity considered her. "You only look decent because I made you leave the cardigan in the car. We're in Panama City, not Amish country."

Maya frowned at her friend.

"You should let that guy take you home." Felicity said.

"You're high. That guy does not want to go to bed with me."

"Why wouldn't he? You're hot, Maya."

"A guy like that wouldn't go for someone my age, anyway."

Felicity pointed with her wine glass. "That guy isn't young. He's our age. Can't you see the lines around his eyes?"

"I know he's around our age. But mid-thirties guys who look like that date twenty-year-old girls, not thirty-five-year-old women with presumably ticking biological clocks."

Felicity eyed her. "I don't know a twenty-year-old who has a better body than yours."

"This is not me being self-deprecating. I'm just being realistic. And honestly, even if God himself were to shine a light down from heaven and will a guy like that to have interest in me, I'm not so sure I'd reciprocate."

"Why the hell not?"

Maya let out an exhausted breath and turned to her friend. "I date Leonard from Big Band Theory, not Ryan Gosling from Crazy, Stupid, Love. I date

Clark Kent, not Superman. I date moderately attractive, endearingly quirky IT guys who work weekends for fun." She offered her palm toward the guy across the bar who made her knees buckle, and she wasn't even standing. "I don't date that."

"Sounds thrilling."

"I don't want thrilling. I want comfortable and reliable. I don't want to send my husband on a guy's night out and be checking my phone every ten minutes to make sure he's not falling for some seriously gorgeous girl he met when he was away from me." She motioned toward the guy who was interested in a game on a television screen above the bar. "Look at him. Can you imagine how often a guy like that gets hit on when he leaves the house? If I was with someone like that I'd be a nervous wreck all day long."

"You're already a nervous wreck all the time."

"See, there you go. I don't need that kind of added stress."

Felicity peered at her. "This is about your sister, isn't it?"

"No," Maya said quickly. At least that was always what she told herself. But of course it was about her sister. Being two years older than Maya, Meade had served as her role model since they were kids. The most intelligent person Maya had ever known still to this day, Meade was an absolute idiot when it came to picking a man who would not move her away from everyone and everything she loved, rob her blind, and then shatter her heart like a bomb hitting a glass wall.

"Only you, my friend, would use the word stress

in talking about that guy across the bar from us," Felicity said.

On cue, he looked over at them and quirked a smile that ensured Maya's worst fear—he heard them talking about him.

She lifted her wine glass to cover her mouth. "I think he can hear us."

"He cannot. It's loud in here." Felicity fluffed her auburn curls. "Okay, you want the shorter one, right?"

Maya turned to her friend. "Have you heard a single word out of my mouth?"

"The tall one is cuter, but the shorter guy is sexier. You're taking him."

"Oh, great, thanks." Maya rolled her eyes and took a sip of her wine.

"Excuse me, sir," Felicity said to the bartender. "Can I have a quick word?"

Maya got the uneasy feeling that always came around when Felicity took an interest in her love life. "What are you doing?"

The bartender narrowed his eyes at Felicity then walked toward her.

"The guy over there with the blue shirt and short hair," Felicity said. The bartender started to turn around. "Don't look."

He stopped mid-turn and looked back at her cautiously. "I don't know which one you're talking about. I can't remember what colors they have on."

"Okay, he's got brown hair shaved close to his head, a great suntan, and he's got a really nice, broad physique."

"Bo?" he asked.

Felicity grinned. "So you do know him. What can you tell us about him?"

"What do you want to know?"

"Like, is he a rapist or anything like that?"

"Felicity," Maya whispered.

"Bo? He wouldn't hurt a fly. Well, at least not a girl. He'd kick a dude's ass if he was asking for it."

Felicity grinned again. "Perfect. Is he married or dating any kind of psycho girl who'd be willing to chase another girl off with a gun, say?"

"Bo's not married. I don't think he's dating anyone. Hadn't really dated anybody seriously since Angela, and that ended a few years back."

"Excellent. You're sure he's straight?" Felicity asked.

"Bo?" The guy chuckled. "Yeah, he's straight." A customer called for him. He held up a finger, and then left them.

Maya pressed her knuckle against Felicity's leg. "I'm going to hurt you."

"You're going to thank me. Look how much information we've already gleaned from this one little conversation."

"I'm not going to have sex with that guy. What if he has an STD?"

Felicity looked him up and down. "I'm not sure it wouldn't be worth it."

"AIDS. You would like me to have AIDS," Maya said. Felicity lifted her eyebrows in consideration. Maya held up both hands. "Enough. You're insane. Whatever you're doing, just stop right now. Can we leave?"

The bartender handed the customer a beer and

then made his way back to Felicity. She pulled a bill out of her wallet and set it down on the bar in front of him. "I've got a twenty-dollar bill here for you if you can find out, discreetly, when the last time he had an AIDS test was."

Maya hid her face with her hand.

"You serious?" the bartender asked.

"As a 1969 Corvette Stingray." The guy looked impressed. "But you can't tell him we're asking. You've got to be creative."

"You're nuts." He started walking away.

"You want to make it fifty?" she asked. Maya jerked her head around toward her friend.

The bartender leaned in. "You're serious, aren't you?" Felicity lifted her eyebrows in response. He stared her down. "All right, I'll find out for you."

"Remember…discreetly," she said then gave him a nudge in their direction.

Maya leaned in. "Felicity, you can't give this guy fifty dollars, are you crazy?"

"It's the winnings from that lottery ticket I bought earlier. Found money." Of course Felicity won fifty dollars on a lottery ticket. That was her luck.

"Yeah, but think of what you could buy with that."

"I can't think of a better way to spend fifty bucks than to get you a worry-free, proper lay, and that guy looks like he could do the trick."

"What did I tell you?" Chase sang into his bottle.

"That you were gonna buy me a beer," Bo said.

"I am, birthday boy. I'm talking about these two

across the bar. You see them?"

Bo stared at the basketball game on the television above the bar. "I see them." It was hard to miss them. The girls that usually came in his favorite bar wore bikini tops with cut-off shorts. These two looked like they'd walked off the pages of The Wall Street Journal. At least the one with the blond hair did…the one with the body that made him breathe hard.

Chase nudged him. "Now I think I deserve a few props for conjuring up these two."

"How'd you do that? They were sitting in here before you did your little voodoo dance outside."

"I asked the universe to send my good buddy a beautiful woman for his birthday, and we walk in here and sit across from these two. I'd call that fate."

"Or Saturday night at Alligator Alley. Take your pick," Bo said.

They drank their beers, watching the game. "You want to throw darts?" Chase asked.

"Nah. You go on though."

"Mmm hmm. You're about to bust a move, aren't you?"

"Not before I bust your lip. Will you shut up?"

Chase could only sit quiet for five…four…three…two... "That one with the blond hair's got a rock hard body somewhere behind that dress. Look at the definition in her arms."

Bo drew his beer to his mouth. "I hadn't noticed." Like hell he hadn't.

"What's wrong with you? Not fifteen minutes ago you were out in the car talking about how you wished you could find the one and have eighteen kids and all that."

"Eighteen?"

Chase motioned to the two women across from them. "What's wrong with these two? That one with the grin looks like a lot a fun."

"Will you quit motioning at them? I know who you're talking about."

"Well, what's your hesitation?" Chase asked.

"They're tourists."

"How do you know?"

Bo gave Chase a look. "You think those two are local PCB girls?"

"Well, no, but maybe they live off 30A somewhere."

"If they did, they'd be over at Bud and Alley's in Seaside or George's in Alys Beach. These two got lost is how they're here. I can promise you that."

Chase considered them. "They are a little classy for this place. Maybe they're high-powered real estate agents from the 30A area."

"If they were, you'd know them."

Chase owned the biggest property management company in South Walton. If you were in real estate in the Florida panhandle and you didn't know Chase, you probably hadn't made it yet.

"Maybe they're new in town," Chase said.

"They're tourists you optimistic son of a bitch."

Chase sat up on his stool. "And you're done with tourists."

"I told you I was. I've done enough of that over the years. I'm not falling for another week-long fantasy romance where the girl goes home, and you talk a handful of times over text until the whole thing fizzles because reality sets back in for her. No thanks. I turned thirty-five today. How many more years am I going to date like a twenty-year-old, knowing there's no future? The next girl I take on a date's gonna live somewhere in the Panama City Beach or South Walton area...Destin if I get desperate."

"What about Fort Walton?"

Bo glared at him.

They sat quiet for a minute till Chase said, "They've got Bobby all huddled up there. What do you think they're wanting from him?"

"Drinks most likely."

Bobby came their way. "You ready for another one yet?" he asked Bo.

Chase leaned in. "So what were those girls all huddled up with you about over there?"

"Nothing. Just hitting me up for a free drink." Bobby leaned on the bar. "Hey, so Bo, you get a physical every year, don't you?"

Bo frowned at his bartender buddy. "Why the hell would you ask me that?"

"I was just wondering if you could recommend a doctor to me."

"When I'm sick I go to the clinic down the street."

"You been lately?" Bobby asked.

"Yeah, I went three weeks ago as a matter of fact for my insurance policy on my business. You want me to have them fax you the results?"

Bobby leaned in. "They give you an AIDS test when you went?"

Bo stared at him hard, and then made sense of the nonsense. He smiled. "Sure did."

"And?"

Bo lifted an eyebrow. "You want to sleep with me or something?"

"Fuck you," Bobby said then turned around and started wiping down the counter.

"Bobby," Bo said. Bobby walked over and placed himself back in front of Bo, tuning in. "You can tell them I got a clean bill of health."

Bobby pursed his lips and walked away.

"You son of a bitch," Chase said.

"What'd I do?" Bo wasn't able to suppress his grin.

"They didn't want to know shit about me," Chase said.

"You're the one conjuring up women so I can find the love of my life tonight."

"Yeah, but it'd be nice to be asked about my AIDS," Chase said.

"You got AIDS?"

"Fuck no, I don't have AIDS."

"Well, there you go. I asked. You're welcome."

Maya and Felicity sipped their drinks, waiting for the bartender to come back and report. After a few minutes, he eased toward them with a couple of fresh drinks.

"He got one three weeks ago through a physical he did for insurance. Clean bill of health."

Felicity clapped her hands together. "Hot damn. We have a winner."

The bartender shook his head, collected his tip,

and put it in his pocket instead of the jar.

"What now?" Maya asked.

"Now, we get their attention and get them over here. Yoo-hoo!" Felicity waved at the boys across the bar.

"Felicity," Maya said in her loudest whisper. The two men played it cool when they caught sight of Felicity. They appeared to consult on the matter, then stood and walked around the bar.

Maya gripped her knees hard to keep from murdering Felicity. "I'm going to kill you."

"Don't speak so fast." She opened her face up in a smile. "Hello, guys. We just saw you two sitting over there all by yourselves and thought we'd see if you wanted to join us. I'm Felicity and this is—"

"Marlene," Maya said.

"Marlene," Felicity said slowly.

"I'm Chase and this is Bo," the taller guy of the two said.

Felicity patted the seat beside her. "Would you like to sit over here next to me, Chase?"

Maya looked down at her drink as the god of bringing women to their knees straddled the seat next to her. "So, Marlene, why'd you need to know if I'd had an AIDS test?"

Chapter Two

Maya's face was so hot she thought it might start steaming. Her tingling chest tried to make her brain register mortification, but she was too consumed with this guy's presence inches from her. He had looked good from across the bar, but up close was a completely enhanced story. His tanned skin played the perfect backdrop to his piercing, dark eyes. As he spoke, her gaze was drawn to his full lips, and she wondered what it might feel like to kiss him hard, among other things.

She snapped out of it and attempted to string words together into a sentence. "My friend is, well, she's mentally ill."

"I've got a friend or two like that." His smile seemed intent on putting her at ease, but with her nerves, that was a tall order.

"So, where are you staying?" she asked.

"You get right to the point, don't you?"

Another shot of heat soared to her neck. "No! God, no. That's not what I meant."

"I'm just teasing you." He gave her arm a quick touch that sent goose bumps racing under her skin. "Actually, I'm staying at my house. I live here."

"You're a local?"

"I take it you're not?"

"No, I'm just down here on vacation."

He nodded like he'd heard that line a million times. "You're staying here in PCB?"

"Actually, no, with a friend over in the South Walton/30A area."

"Which community?"

"Seacrest?"

"Beautiful town. A have a buddy who lives there."

She twirled the stem of her wine glass. "I didn't realize 30A was so close to Panama City."

"Yeah, we're just down the road, but we're two different worlds as far as the people go."

She glanced around the bar. "You're right about that."

"Too redneck for you over here?"

"No, I didn't mean that." She touched his knee, and then retracted her hand quickly, her stomach fizzing a little. "I haven't offended you, have I?"

He chuckled. "Takes a lot more than that to offend me. Where are you from?"

"Indianapolis. Go Colts!" She pumped a tight fist into the space in front of her. What in the world? She didn't even like baseball.

"You a big football fan?"

Football. Jesus, where was her head? "Actually,

no. I don't really follow it."

He smiled and took a drink of his beer, gripping the bottle with his strong hand. "What do you do?"

"I'm an Operations Director for a marketing firm." She shook her head with a small smile. "Actually, I'm a VP now. I just got a promotion."

He held his beer to her glass for a toast. "Congratulations."

She grinned. "Thanks. I start the Monday I return from vacation."

"Operations. So you keep everything running?"

"I guess you could say that. It's not creative. I'm not creative."

"I doubt that," he said.

"No, really, I'm not. I'm much better at organizing and details. Gun to my head I couldn't come up with marketing copy for anything, really."

"Gun to your head, you could do it."

She messed with the hem of her dress, trying to process the conversation she was having. This guy was so typically a guy her sister, Meade, would sit and talk to, promptly fall in love with, and then he would in turn, in some way, ruin her life and whatever plan she was in the midst of.

"Bo!" A girl who stood somewhere right around five feet tall with a low-cut shirt exposing a massive chest threw her arms around him and hopped into his lap.

"Jordan." He put his hand on her arm, possibly to pry it off of him, but he'd need a crowbar for that.

"Why haven't you been in lately? I look for you every week but it's always the other guys." She scrunched up her face in an exaggerated pout. "You never come see me anymore."

"Jordan, this is Marlene." He directed the girl toward Maya.

The girl looked as if Maya was a fly that she would love to swat down if she'd only had a swatter handy. "Nice to meet you," the girl called Jordan said with a tone so fake it made this strange situation even more awkward. He lifted her up with little effort and placed her feet back on the floor. She pointed at him. "Come by soon." She left with a little bitty wave of her fingers.

He turned back to Maya. "How long are you in town?"

"For the week," Maya said, recalibrating after the explosion named Jordan. "We actually just got here today. Our friend we're staying with was tied up so we ventured out this way by ourselves."

He lifted his eyebrows. "You better be careful doing that. You never know who you might run into. Maybe even somebody who hasn't been tested in a while."

Felicity would die a slow death at Maya's hands later on for that. "You're not going to let me live that down, are you?"

He lowered his chin and gave a discreet shake of his head. She was starting to sympathize more and more with her sister's poor choices. "So why didn't your friend ask about Chase? Bobby only asked me about the test."

She hid her face in her hand at the mortifying conversation she was having. He sat silent. Finally, she slid apart her fingers and peeked at him.

"Take your time. I've got all night." He kicked back on his stool, resting his elbow on the bar, taking a swig of beer.

She gulped her wine. "My friend thinks she's being my wingman or something like that. She's crazy. You don't have to play along."

"Do you want me to leave?" he asked.

The thought was utterly unpleasant. "Well, I...no?"

"That didn't sound too convincing."

She gave him a doublewide grin. "No, I don't want you to leave. Please stay."

"Well, you don't have to beg."

Her face flushed again, causing that stupid smile she kept getting.

"So your friend there, she wants you to have a good time tonight. Any reason for that?" he asked.

"What do you mean?"

"Have you had a bad break-up or something like that? There's some reason she's trying to hook you up."

"Oh, God." The hand went to her face again. She flinched at his touch on her wrist. He placed her hand back on her leg and gave it a squeeze, causing her heartbeat to pick up speed.

"I like to look people in the eye when I talk to them. You keep covering yours."

"Sorry," she said.

"There isn't anything to be sorry about, darlin'."

His Southern-drawled term of endearment sent shivers up her spine. Every second she spent with him she became more charmed and drawn to Felicity's suggestion of a one-night stand.

Maya was not the one-night stand sort. She was the responsible, sensible one. She kept things in order. She dated guys whose idea of living on the wild side was watching TED Talks in bed. She did not fall for ridiculously sexy strangers.

The decent prospects back home were few and far between, and dating had become a necessary chore. But for the first time in years, she was enjoying engaging with a man. Sitting and talking to this guy didn't make her into her sister. She was just talking, not falling in love. She had entirely too much sense for that.

"No bad break-up. My girlfriend just thinks I'm too...conventional."

"She thinks you need to loosen up?"

"Yes."

"Do you?"

She turned her head at the sound of a group in the back of the bar by the pool tables laughing loud in unison about something, and then met his gaze again. "No. I mean, I know I'm on vacation, but it's just the first day. We've got the whole week."

"So it's too early for you to do anything out of character just yet?"

"Yes, I guess so."

"It was nice to meet you." He stood up off his stool.

Instinctively, flirtatiously?, she grabbed his arm and pulled him back down to his seat. What had gotten into her? She'd blame it on the wine, but she hadn't even broken into her second glass yet.

He smiled at her, sending a charge of electricity through her core. "So I've got no chance in hell with you tonight?" he asked.

She opened up her flirtation arsenal. "I'm still considering it." She wasn't, of course…was she?

"Oh, good. That changes everything." He clapped his hands together and rubbed them, as if warming up for something.

She raised an eyebrow. "What do you mean?"

"I mean I've got a chance. Clearly I've got to step up my game."

"How are you going to do that?"

"Let's see what I've learned about you so far. You're a good girl, one who doesn't mess around with strange guys typically. But you are on vacation, so you're feeling a little bit…untamed."

She tried to quell her smile, but to no avail.

"And you did your homework on me before you got me to walk across the bar to talk to you, which shows you're as thorough in your social life as you are in your career."

She nodded approval.

"You've got the body of a runner, and by the look of the muscle tone in your arms, I'd say you rarely miss a day at the gym, so you're clearly disciplined as hell."

Her face flushed at the idea he'd noticed her body.

"You've probably not been with too many rednecks in your time, if any, but you did drive over here to PCB from 30A, so you may be looking for a little adventure."

She shrugged, still not saying a word.

"So how'd I do?"

"Pretty good. But I'm still undecided."

"Aww, damn. All right, you know I'm clean. What else do you need to know?"

She considered him, twirling her wine glass. "How do I know they won't be dragging the lakes around here looking for my cold, dead body tomorrow?"

He dropped his head to one side. "Now that's just hurtful. You think I'm going to kill you?"

"A girl can never tell."

"Here. I know what'll make you feel better. I'll let you talk to my sister." He pulled a phone out of his pocket.

"Oh, no. That's not necessary, really."

"She lives in Franklin, Tennessee now. Moved up there a few years ago, but I'll get her back here eventually." He put the phone on speaker.

"Seriously, there's no need—"

"Hey, baby brother." A Southern accent very much like his came across the speaker.

"You busy?" he asked her.

"Nah, just hanging here at the house. You having a good birthday?"

His face turned red, and Maya smiled. "It's your birthday?"

He shook his head quickly, but clearly it was. "I've got a favor to ask of you," he said into the phone.

"Just one? Must be a slow day."

Maya giggled, liking this girl.

"I'm here at Alligator Alley with a girl I've been talking to for a while."

"Yeah."

"And she's thinking about going home with me."

He winked at Maya, who had hit yet another wave of mortification that evening.

"Uh huh," his sister replied, unfazed.

"But the problem is she's not sure if I'm a murderer or something, so I was hoping you'd set her straight about me. Let her know what kind a guy I really am and all that."

"Uh huh. Darlin', what's your name?" she asked.

Maya froze for a moment. He motioned to the phone for her to speak. "Um, Ma...Marlene," she answered, her voice coming out in a mouse-like squeak.

"Marlene?"

"Yes, that's right," Maya said.

"Listen to me, Marlene. Run. Run as fast as your feet will carry you. He's a no-good, lowdown, womanizing—"

Bo punched at the phone until it disconnected. "Well, I guess that didn't quite go as planned."

Maya giggled. She liked his sister. The call had actually made her feel even better about him. God, was she actually considering a one-night stand? She reminded herself for the millionth time that she was not her sister. She wouldn't take it past this night. Dammit, she did deserve a single night of crazy, heart-stopping sex with a guy that looked like this one. She could do that. She could control her feelings, unlike her sister. She could walk away with the good time in her back pocket and not need anything other than that. She was sure of it.

Felicity appeared in front of her. "Marlene, I'm so tired. Chase has offered to take me home. Do you mind?" She handed Maya the keys to her car.

Felicity couldn't leave her. She was Maya's safety net. Without Felicity here, none of this worked. "Wait. I'll come—"

"Oh, no. You stay here and have fun. I'm going to head out. Oh, and you'll need to drop this nice man off at his house. Chase says Bo lives just down the road. Chase lives in Seagrove, which is really close to Seacrest, so he's going to take me home. You'll take care of Bo, won't you?"

Maya glared at her friend.

Felicity plowed forward. "You two enjoy your evening, okay? Here, have the next round on me." Felicity laid a twenty-dollar bill down on the bar. "Bye now, y'all," she said with a deliberate Southern accent and scurried away dragging the tall guy with her.

Maya turned to face Bo. He gave a closed-mouth smile and a shrug of his shoulders, and with that, she quit plotting Felicity's slow demise.

"You ready to tab out, Bo?" the bartender asked for the fifth time.

Maya hadn't enjoyed a man's company this much since she could feasibly remember, maybe ever. A glance around the bar told her they were the only ones left. How had she not noticed that until now?

"I guess y'all are ready to close, huh?" Bo asked.

"For about the past thirty minutes now," the bartender said.

Maya dug in her purse for her wallet, but Bo was already handing the guy his credit card.

"No, I was going to buy you that birthday drink,"

she said.

"You did," he said.

She smiled. "I ordered it for you. I didn't actually pay for it."

He shrugged. "You win some. You lose some."

Maya lived at work and at the gym. She met friends for dinner or movies. But she never put herself in a situation where she'd meet a guy like this one. There were those vile dating apps where one could hook up, sure. But when would she ever again be presented the opportunity to have a good time with a guy who she'd gotten to know a little, really liked, didn't seem to be a psycho, and was so absolutely sexy that she couldn't even think straight looking at him?

Her stomach quaked at the idea, but she would not back down now. She had earned this opportunity after decades of always doing the right thing to counteract her sister, who wouldn't have blinked an eye at going home with this guy and then, in turn, would sign over the deed to her house to him.

"I guess you need a ride home?" Her voice came out higher than usual, and she inwardly cursed herself.

He stood up off his seat and lifted his chin. "Depends. You still think I'm going to throw you in the lake or something?"

"I think I'll roll the dice."

He grinned. "Better blow on them first."

Bo directed the girl whose name he highly suspected was not Marlene to his house. He

25

couldn't be sure, but he thought that was probably the only lie she had told him. She seemed nervous as hell at the beginning of the night, but she had come around after they got to talking. He actually thought it was pretty cute, how nervous she was. Some of the tourists down there were overly aggressive due to the copious amounts of alcohol and the desire to throw caution to the wind. That was fun every once in a while, but it robbed him of the thrill of the chase.

This girl couldn't have been more different from the ones he typically met around this town, tourist and local alike. This was a responsible, professional, highly intelligent woman. One who scared the shit out of him. He'd never been with a woman like this. She had the most interesting balance of confidence and modesty. Hell, he hadn't closed a bar down with a girl in years. He liked this one. He liked her so much he'd have to let her go.

She was here for the week. What was he going to do, spend the next few days taking her out, showing her around town, fooling around, then tell her bye next Saturday? Fuck that. He'd done enough of that in his time. He was thirty-five now. It was time to try to date someone who lived within driving distance from him, someone he could actually see in the flesh longer than a week. Right now, he had everything in check with this girl. He'd enjoyed the night with her, and he needed that to be the end of it.

She brought the car to a stop in his driveway but left the engine running. The ball was in his court to offer an invitation inside. She seemed ready. Fuck a duck was he ready. But he was a thirty-five-year-old man. He could keep his dick in his pants when he needed to.

He turned to her. "Thanks for bringing me home."

"Sure." She drew her sweet little lips together in a line and nodded.

She was pretty in a way he suspected she didn't even realize. She wore very little makeup around her crystal blue eyes, and her soft, straight hair that hung just below her chin looked too naturally blond to have come from a bottle. She had an innate beauty about her, one he hadn't picked up on right at first, but the more he'd talked to her, the more it shined through with her sweet personality.

"Hope you ladies enjoy your vacation." He had his hand on the door handle, but he couldn't pull it. What? Was he a pussy now? He couldn't just walk away from her?

"We're looking forward to getting some sun tomorrow. Do you know if it's supposed to be pretty?"

"Should be mid 80s."

"Great, that sounds perfect," she said.

They were sitting there talking about the goddamned weather when they could be in his bed right inside. All he had to do was invite her in.

"Do you know your way back to where you're staying?"

She nodded and held up her phone. "GPS."

"Good." He paused for way too long. Why couldn't he just get out of the goddamn car? "You're okay to drive and all?" he asked, knowing she was. She'd stopped drinking her wine as soon as her friend turned the keys over to her, and they'd sat there for hours.

"Oh, yes. I'm perfectly sober, unfortunately." She smiled at him, and he wanted to cave worse than a smoker wanted a cigarette.

He held his hand out to her. "Well, it was nice to meet you." She took it, and they shook on it, but neither let go, the whole time gazing into each other's eyes. He liked this girl in front of him, and he suspected one night with her wouldn't be enough. She lived in another world, one she wouldn't be leaving behind for him, so what was the point?

He gave her hand one final squeeze. "Good night." He let go, then forced himself to open the door.

"Oh," she said. "Happy birthday."

He smiled. "Thanks."

She leaned over toward him, resting her fingertips on the back of his neck and pressed her lips against his cheek, just barely catching the corner of his mouth with her kiss. He closed his eyes, drinking in the smell of her hair for the brief moment. He was such an idiot. Why didn't he walk away when Chase did?

She pulled back. "Good night."

"Good night," he said, scanning her face one last time. Of all the girls he'd said goodbye to on nights like this, he'd never felt more like he was letting a possibility slip through his fingers.

He forced a final smile, and then got out of the car.

Chapter Three

Maya lay in bed examining the intricacies of the nouveau beach art on the wall of Sebastian's guest room. She couldn't decide if she was embarrassed, ashamed, upset, or pissed off. Maybe some of each.

She had not imagined the connection between her and Bo. She wasn't one to assume a guy was interested in her. But she knew flirting when she saw it, and he'd done so shamelessly. Turned out he was all talk. Nothing but a big fat tease.

His attention had given her confidence in the connection and encouraged her to say and do flirty things she otherwise wouldn't have. Maybe that was his game—take women who obviously didn't date guys like him, pump up their egos, and then shoot them down like rabbits on a carnival game.

That wasn't it at all. He was a good guy, she could just tell he was. She never knew chemistry like that existed. She'd been in two long-term relationships, but heat had never filled her belly like it did when that man looked at her. She was getting started up again just at the thought of it.

This was just the sort of bonehead move her sister, Meade, would have made. Spend the night panting for some guy like a puppy. But Meade would have written him a blank check and laid herself over a puddle in the road for him to walk over.

Maya pulled up Facebook on her phone and went to her sister's page. There she was in a picture, cheek to cheek with some guy a good seven or eight years younger than her, hot as a fire pit. He was new. But of course he was. Seventy-eight people liked it. She hovered over the like button. She just couldn't do it.

She texted Meade.

Hey. Made it to Sebastian's house. It's beautiful down here.

She gave it a minute, and then a message flashed on her screen.

Cool. I'll try to come next time.

Maya rolled her eyes. That would never happen. And besides, it'd taken Maya five years to make this trip. She'd all but lost touch with Sebastian. Felicity was easier to keep up with since she lived closer, but Maya still didn't give her enough time. And now with Maya's promotion at work, she doubted she'd be on any vacations for a long time.

You should. Saw the pic on your FB page. Is that your new guy? The one you mentioned last week?

Yep. That's Luke.

What does he do?

Maya waited for it. It was taking a while for this response, and she could only guess why.

He's in between jobs right now, but he's got several interviews lined up.

There it was. Maya was sure Meade had set those interviews up and was equally as sure Luke would not be attending them if Meade's past taught Maya anything.

Meade texted again.

Have you talked to Mom yet?

Maya frowned and texted back.

No. Why?

I screwed up and mentioned you were in Florida when she called yesterday. She's pissy that you didn't tell her you were going. Sorry.

Maya winced. She wasn't mad at Meade. She should have told her she wasn't going to tell their mom about going to see Sebastian because then she'd comment about women traveling unescorted and then Maya would have to say Felicity was going with her, then she'd get a lecture about bad influences and how her fit body was her biggest asset and if she let up even for a week, then she'd look like Meade, and was that what she wanted?

Meade texted again.

Just tell her to fuck off like I do.

As long as Maya lived, she would never understand Meade's ability to let everything her mother said and did slide right off her shoulders. Of course, Meade was the brilliant one, the genius, the one her parents could brag about incessantly even though she was currently using her brilliant mind to deal blackjack in Vegas and not to cure cancer or improve upon spaceships.

"Details, Marlene. We're dying for details down here!" Felicity shouted from downstairs.

Maya let out a deep breath and typed into her phone.

Thanks for letting me know. Gotta go. Talk soon.

"If you don't come to us, we'll come to you," Sebastian shouted.

She flipped the covers off and made her way to the kitchen table where Sebastian had a coffee and some sort of pastry waiting for her, proving how out of touch they'd been. She hadn't eaten a pastry in years.

"Thank you, Bastian," she said.

"So?" he said.

"I hate to disappoint you two, but nothing happened," Maya said.

Felicity's expression dropped. "What do you mean, nothing happened? Do I have to direct the two of you into the bed? I thought I had made it obvious enough."

"Oh, you did. And we stayed there talking for hours. But then when I took him home, he basically said good night and got out of the car."

"You mean he didn't invite you in with him?" Sebastian asked.

"No. And I was putting it out there. At least I thought I was." Maya stared at her coffee cup, twisting it two-handed.

"Well, your idea of putting it out there is not the same as the average girl's," Felicity said.

"I know that. But I flirted, I promise I did." She

picked up the cup with both sets of fingertips then set it back down. "I even went in for a birthday kiss."

"How did that go?" Sebastian asked, and Maya gave him a look.

"It was his birthday?" Felicity asked.

Sebastian cocked his head to the side. "Who is this guy? What did you all talk about for hours? What does he do?"

"I don't even know. He mentioned owning a business, but then we got sidetracked before he told me what kind of business. That was how it was. No uncomfortable silences. We talked nonstop about everything and nothing."

"I don't understand this," Felicity said. "I saw the way he was looking at you."

Sebastian pulled the lid off his coffee. "Maybe he's gay."

"You wish," Felicity said.

Maya dropped her forehead into her hands. "Can we not talk about it anymore? It was humiliating enough the first time. I mean finally, I'm ready to stick my neck out and do something totally out of my character, and I get rejected after hours of investment in this guy."

"Okay, subject closed," Sebastian said.

Maya eyed Felicity. "What about you? How did you make out?"

Felicity waggled her eyebrows. "Very well. My guy was really fun."

"When did you get home?"

"Just a minute ago. I Ubered. He was still asleep. I didn't want to wake him."

Maya threw up her hands. "How do you do it?"

Felicity took a sip of coffee. "Do what?"

"The whole capturing men thing. It's like breathing to you."

"It's in her DNA," Sebastian said.

"What can I say? I likes the mens."

Sebastian clapped his hands in front of his chest and rubbed them together. "So, I've got a special treat for you ladies."

Maya perked up. "Oh, good. What are we doing?"

"Okay, don't shoot me, but I've got to go see the ladies at the nursing home today. I was out of town last week and didn't have time to visit Friday or yesterday. I haven't seen them in a week. I promised them I would come today. I've never been away from them this long, and I'm sure their hair desperately needs my attention."

Felicity crossed her arms over her chest. "Now, how are we supposed to compete with three elderly ladies in a nursing home?"

Sebastian rested his hand on her forearm. "It's not a competition. There's plenty of me to go around. They know you are here this week, and they understand. Just let them have a few hours today, then I'm all yours."

"Are you going to introduce us to them this week?" Maya asked.

Sebastian patted her arm. "Later in the week, I promise. I've got something for you two today. I've arranged for you to spend the afternoon at a fabulous local pool. I've got your passes right here."

"What's that out in your backyard?" Felicity

pointed toward the window revealing Sebastian's pool.

"The pool guy's coming this morning to get it ready for summer and for you two. There was an accident in it last fall, and it's been shut down ever since. I really haven't even thought much about the stupid thing since then. I meant to have it ready before now."

"What kind of accident?" Maya asked.

"Someone hit her head on the diving board. She was drunk. We never should have been out there. Anyway, old news. She's fine now. You'll meet her this week. You'll meet my whole crew. I'm having a little soiree here tonight in honor of you two. I want everyone in our circle to meet my oldest friends from home." Sebastian proffered a hand to each lady.

"Oldest? Who's old?" Felicity said.

"I thought we were your circle," Maya said.

He grabbed each girl's hand and squeezed. "You are my original circle, never to be broken."

Felicity wiggled the fingers on her free hand. "All right, gimme those passes. What time does that pool open?"

"Ten o'clock." Sebastian turned to Maya. "Are you going to eat that pastry?"

Maya scrunched up her face in apology. He was sweet for thinking of her, but there was no way she was eating that pastry. She never ate sugar. Ever. When she strayed off her path of order, bad things happened. Case in point, last night.

Sebastian held up both hands. "All right. I just thought you might be indulging since it's your

35

vacation."

Felicity swiped Maya's pastry. "Please. She wouldn't eat something like this if you told her the earth was going to stop turning tomorrow."

Sebastian went to the cabinet. "I've got your steel-cut oats right here. Is this the right brand? It says gluten-free."

She smiled. "You remembered."

"Of course I remembered, sweetie. Okay, I'm gone. Don't the two of you get into any trouble without me.¬"

"No trouble for me this week," Maya said. "That's a promise."

Maya lay face-down on the bed in her own personal guest room. She and Felicity each had their own room—better than the Four Seasons. Felicity sifted through Maya's clothes. "How do you already have everything on hangers? When did you do this?"

"Last night before we went out." Maya let her eyes droop closed.

"Oh wow," Felicity said, moving to the second-story window. "Someone's here."

Maya picked herself up off the bed and walked that way. A shirtless hard body of a guy was holding a net, the muscles on his back rippling as he stroked it through the pool. His tanned, wet skin glistened in the sunlight.

"No idea what his face looks like under that ball cap, but who gives a damn with that body," Felicity said.

"Probably best we don't see his face. It'd only pale in comparison to the rest of him," Maya said.

"It'd have to. Look at this guy. Maybe we can hook you up with him."

Maya moved behind the curtain. "Will you quit it? There's no requirement that I have sex this week."

"I've made it my mission, my dear friend. You know I like a good project. Besides, it hurts my head that you've only had sex with two guys in your life."

Maya walked over to the drawer to pull out a bathing suit. "Many times with each. You're making me out to be some Virgin Mary."

"I don't even think you can count Al," Felicity said.

"We were together almost three years."

"How many times did you have sex during those three years?"

"Plenty of times."

"Good sex?"

Maya threw a bikini at Felicity. "Will you get dressed so we can go?"

Felicity held up the bathing suit. "Damn, you're thin. I don't think I can even get a boob in this top."

"You're welcome to try," Maya said.

Felicity shrugged and headed to her room. Maya sneaked back over to the window to watch the guy working on the pool. She saw hot bodies at the gym on a daily basis, but watching this guy work and sweat, his tanned skin glistening with the movement of his muscles, was making her core light up. This was all Bo's fault. He'd unlocked some hidden desire inside of her. She'd been fine with nerdy guys until this point. But the idea of running her hands across a pair of shoulders like that was a temptation worse than the poison apple itself.

He walked around the far side of the pool and looked up directly at her window. She stepped quickly out of way, and then drew the curtains closed. Now she was that creepy old lady eyeing the pool guy. Man did she need to get her libido in check.

"Hello, gorgeous pool guy."

Bo turned to find Sebastian coming through the French doors. "Hey, man."

"Thanks for coming on such short notice. I was out of town last week and totally forgot to schedule you."

Bo checked the results of his final chlorine test. "I actually had you on the schedule for tomorrow. If I'd known you had houseguests this week, I would have come sooner."

"Speaking of my houseguests, I want to invite you to a little soiree I'm having tonight. They're good friends of mine from home, and I want to introduce them to my friends."

He thought about the girls from last night and Marlene saying she was staying with a friend in Seacrest. But those girls were from Indianapolis, and Sebastian was from Chicago.

"Who are your houseguests?" Bo asked.

"So glad you asked that. I want to introduce you to my friend Maya tonight. Did you meet her earlier today?"

"Nah, I heard somebody leaving a while ago, but I didn't see anybody."

"Well, she's fabulous, and she's perfect for you."

"For what, the week?" Bo asked.

Sebastian shrugged. "Sure."

Bo shook his head, gathering his equipment. "No thanks."

"But you haven't even met her. She's fabulous."

"I'm sure she is, but I'm not into it."

"Not into sex?" Sebastian asked, looking like Bo had a third eye.

"To be honest, no. I've screwed enough women to start a softball league. At some point, it gets old. I'm getting old, I guess."

Sebastian put his hand in the air like he was stopping traffic. "Hold up. You are my age, I believe, so stop calling yourself old."

"Fine. I'm old. You're young."

Sebastian put his hand on Bo's forearm. "What is it, boo? Are you okay?"

If some of the knuckleheads Bo went to high school with saw the way Sebastian touched him and made a fuss over him, he'd catch hell for it. But Sebastian was one of Bo's favorite people. They drove each other nuts, coming from two completely different universes—Sebastian, an effeminate gay man from Chicago, and Bo a redneck from Panama City Beach—but their friendship worked in the oddest way. Same went for all this group of friends he'd found himself in thanks to his closest friend, Blake. Blake had sort of connected the two worlds of Southern straight men and Northern gay men, tossing in a prom queen from Savannah and a free-spirited woman from New Orleans. They were as oddball as it came as a whole, but Bo couldn't think of a group of friends he'd ever had that he preferred to be with more.

Bo pulled his arm away. "It ain't nothing. Just don't want to have another week of falling for someone who's going home. Can you understand that?"

Sebastian crossed one arm over his stomach and bit on his knuckle. "Bo Harrison showing his vulnerable side. My God, can you get any hotter?"

Bo headed for the gate. "I've got supper with my parents."

Sebastian followed behind. "You have dinner there every Sunday afternoon and it's never stopped you from meeting us after when we're doing something you want to do."

"Exactly."

"Come on, I really want you to come tonight. I swear I won't do any sort of matchmaking. I just want my friends to all connect. I want to show my BFFs from home how fabulous my BFFs from here are."

Bo kept going, thinking about it. He really just needed a night to chill with Jake on the couch and catch up on whatever was on Netflix. "Next time," he said.

"I think Cassidy's coming."

Bo stopped at the gate. "She is?"

Cassidy, owner of Seaside Sweets and all-around hot as fuck forty-something, was Bo's kryptonite. He'd been enamored with her since the time he made a move on her and she clocked him in the mouth, not that he didn't deserve it. He hadn't dared try to touch her since, of course, but just being in the same room with her lit him up. He always let her come to him, and she always would, eventually, with a no-nonsense smile and a few flirtatious words before someone else would inevitably steal her away. She was by far the most interesting one of them all with her past work in the Peace Corps and her world travel prior to being a bakery owner. She was close with everyone in the group, but she didn't make it out nearly as much as all the rest of them did. He had to grab his chances to be around her when he could get them.

Sebastian grinned. "I knew that would change your mind."

"What time?"

"Six."

"Can I bring something?"

"Your beautiful self. I'll have everything else."

Chapter Four

Bo pulled up in the parking lot of one of his biggest clients. Besides owning this particular pool park, Roy owned two resorts off 30A and a water park in PCB. He had enough need to warrant his own staff of pool guys, but Roy'd had problems in the past finding good workers who knew what the hell they were doing, and after a close call with the health department, he was too rattled to go back to staffing that function on his own. That was just fine with Bo, but he knew Roy could pull the business at a drop of a hat, so he made sure he got plenty of face time with him and kept his properties pristine.

As Bo walked through the doorway, his eardrums were assaulted as the young Jordan shouted, "Bo!"

She was an itty bitty thing, all except her chest. She couldn't be a day over twenty-two, but for some reason she wasn't going to rest until he made a move on her. She'd be waiting a while for that to happen.

She scooted out from behind the front desk and jumped on him in a hug. He glanced around to make sure Roy wasn't around. This was where he kept his main office, which was why Bo always came by to pick up his check rather than having him mail it. He wanted to keep reminding Roy he was here.

Bo pried Jordan off of him. "You got an envelope for me?"

"All business today, huh?"

"You got something else in mind?"

"I've always got something in mind when it comes to you."

He was okay with a little flirtation with her, but that was as far as he'd ever let their relationship go. Six years ago, after he'd finally broken free of Angela, he'd have been all over that. But he was thirty-five now, and he'd sown all the oats he hadn't been able to throughout his twenties. He needed something deeper now. He wanted to learn from the woman he was with and grow, become a better person in general. Girls like Jordan were fun, but what then? She rubbed up against him, hand on his hip. She'd always been forward, but the last time or two he'd seen her she'd gotten downright shameless. He had to find a way to politely put a stop to that.

"Your boss is going to come in here, and I'll lose one of my biggest clients," he said.

"I'll make sure it's worth your trouble." She slid her hand down to his ass, and then moved it around to the front. He stepped away from her before he copped wood mid-day in front of God and everybody. She gave him a dirty smile and pulled an envelope out of the desk. "I saw the size of that check. Too bad you won't spend that on an amazing night out with me. You'd be guaranteed to get your money's worth at the end."

"Bo!" Roy made his way up the hallway, and Bo had never been happier to see the big ole bastard.

"Hey, Roy. Thanks for the check." Bo waved the envelope.

"Don't spend all that in one place." He offered Bo his hand, and they shook on it.

"I just wanted to check in and see how my guys were doing for you," Bo said.

"Pools look great. While you're here though, would you mind checking the filter on the kids' pool? It might be clogged with something. I had a complaint earlier. I haven't been out to check it yet."

"I'll take a look."

"You up for golf this Saturday?" Roy asked.

"I'll set it up. Seven o'clock tee time work for you?" Bo asked, happy to ass-kiss.

"I'll be in touch. Jordan, be sure and treat this man real good when he comes by. He's my boy." Roy patted Bo on the shoulder.

"I always do my very best, Roy," she said with the innocence of a schoolgirl. Roy gave a crooked-tooth smile and headed back to his office. "See," she said, "the boss man even wants me to do you right."

"Hey, old man. Come here on a Sunday to hassle

our employees?" Tyler, a lifeguard not a day over twenty slung open the door leading in from the pools and stood in the doorway, sizing Bo up. He was young, dumb, and full of—

"Come in or out Tyler. The flies are getting in," Jordan said.

Tyler stood up tall and crossed his arms over his puffed-out chest. "Hey, while you're here, I'm going to need you to check the filter in the kids' pool. There seems to be some issue with it. May need replacing."

"I'm headed that way." Any other punk kid would have gotten the finger, but this particular punk was the boss man's son. Bo was planning on riding his pool business into retirement, and he figured this kid would be his client one day, as much as that pained him. But he wasn't too proud to eat some crow now and then. The check in his hand was enough to make payroll. He was no fool.

"Hey, you box?" Tyler held both fists in front of his chest and jabbed in Bo's direction.

"No."

"Ah, chicken shit, huh? I don't blame you. I wouldn't want to fight a young guy like me if I was you."

Tyler jabbed a little too close to Bo. He was rethinking that check. There were better ways to earn money, like hauling trash or emptying sewage tanks.

"Tyler, Bo'd whoop your ass one-handed if you two got in a ring," Jordan said.

"We'll see about that." Tyler gave a series of quick jabs at Bo, just barely missing him.

The worst part about it for Bo was that it was like looking into a twenty-year-old mirror. As much as he hated getting older, he was thankful as hell for the ounce of maturity he'd gained throughout the years. He supposed he could thank Angela for some of that. He'd had to grow up fast once she came into his life. Bo opened the door. "I'll go check that filter."

Jordan glared at Tyler. "Dumbass."

"We'll set up that fight soon!" Tyler shouted at Bo's backside.

As Bo made his way through the big pool area outlined with cabanas toward the kids' pool around on the other side, he couldn't help but compare Jordan to the girl from last night. They were on two different planets. If the two were standing side by side, and he had to pick one, there wouldn't even be a contest.

The one from last night was smart, sweet, shy, strong, and goddamn sexy. That was the kind of woman he wanted in his bed. Jordan was easy. She didn't expect much of anything from him other than to be good in bed. Marlene, aside from giving a fake name, was mature and challenging. She was the kind of woman to force a man to do better, be better. The kind of woman he needed and wanted. Goddammit. Why did he have to run into her last night? Now he couldn't get her out of his head. And he couldn't have her. The worst possible combination.

Felicity shaded her eyes with her hand. "Is that our pool guy from earlier?"

Maya followed Felicity's gaze to a tall, broad guy walking with purpose toward the kid pool. Maya's heart practically leapt from her chest. "Oh my gosh. I think it's him."

Felicity took off her sunglasses. "The pool guy?"

Maya backhanded her on the arm. "No. The guy from last night."

Felicity's face broke open in a grin. "You are right. That is him, isn't it?"

"This can't be happening. We've got to leave." Maya shoved her magazine into her bag.

Felicity held her hand up. "Sit tight. He can't recognize you in that hat and those glasses." She had a point. "Damn, did he look this good last night?" Felicity asked.

This was what Maya got for even considering veering from her natural order of things and dipping a toe into those forbidden waters.

"I didn't realize how hot he was. Look at those legs. Look at the muscles in his calves. I bet he's a runner. Plenty of stamina."

"Can we change the subject please?" Maya asked.

"I think this one's worth a second try."

"Felicity," Maya said with a warning tone.

"Yeah, we're not done here." Felicity started waving. "Hello!" Maya sank deeper in her lounger. "Hello, big guy," Felicity waved some more.

Bo did a double take, slowing his stride, and Maya's heart pounded against her chest, her face flushing with heat that wasn't coming from the sun.

"Come on over. That's right, come on." Felicity motioned the man to them.

This was why she didn't hang out with Felicity that much. She always pushed Maya's limits. "I will kill you painfully while you're sleeping tonight," Maya said through clenched teeth.

"Oh, goody. He's coming. Ready for round two?"

Panic surged through Maya's chest as Bo approached them. She'd been basking in humiliation since he shut the car door last night. The only saving grace had been she would never have to see him again, and now he was headed right toward her, and not on his own accord, but because her deranged friend had motioned him over. Like there was any way he could avoid Maya now.

God, was it possible he was even better looking than she remembered? Sensuality bled from him with every assured step he took. His muscles bulged out of the sleeves of his T-shirt, and heat filled areas of her where the sun didn't shine.

"Well, hello," Felicity said to Bo as he approached them. "Do you remember Marlene from last night?"

"How could I forget Marlene?" he asked with a grin that could melt a glacier. Maya gave a half-hearted smile, wondering when the brutality would end.

"You here for a swim?" Felicity asked.

"No, actually—"

A young male lifeguard passed by waving his fists in the air like an idiot. "Tuesday afternoon. Me and you." The guy stopped and eyed the ladies. "See, now these two are more your scene, dude." He started jogging backwards and turned around just before he tripped over a lounge chair.

"Is that douche a friend of yours?" Felicity asked.

He glared at the guy. "No." He closed his eyes and shook his head, and then turned back to them. "You ladies have a good day for it today out here."

"Pull up a chair and sit with us," Felicity said.

He hesitated, considering Maya. She would not force him to sit down and muddle through awkward conversation with her. He was finished with her, and she wouldn't hold him hostage here. She diverted her eyes down to her magazine and flipped a page.

"Thanks, but I've got to get going." He pointed in the direction of the children's pool.

There it was. The answer to everything. His wife and kids were over there, and he was coming to see them. Or maybe he had partial custody, and he was here to make the switch. He hadn't mentioned a thing about kids last night, but why else would he be headed to the children's pool? Maya flipped another page and tried to focus on a tampon advertisement.

"Good to see you again, Marlene."

Her heart fluttered at the personal address. She barely glanced up from her magazine. "Mmm hmm." She wanted to dive into the water and never come back up.

"Y'all take care, now."

Felicity looked at her then back at him. "Okay, you, too."

He turned and walked toward the children's pool. As soon as he got out of earshot, Maya turned to Felicity. "Are you happy now?"

"What? That was harmless. At least from his end. You were positively rude."

Maya gritted her teeth. "I was positively mortified."

"Oh, now quit. It wasn't that bad. We seriously never have to see him again. We won't come back here this week."

"He lives in Panama City. What in God's name is he doing here?"

Felicity fanned herself. "Who knows."

"I bet he's a dad and his kids are over there."

"Maybe, but that doesn't mean he's married. He is at that age when couples start getting divorces more frequently."

"He looks about our age."

"Yeah, so?"

"So you're saying we should have already been married by now and on our way to divorce court?" Maya asked.

"Not me. You know I'm never getting married. But you can skip right past your first divorce and pick up one of these guys out there who's ready for renewal."

Maya eyed her friend. "Do you ever see the negative in anything?"

Felicity drew her eyebrows together. "Why would I want to do that?"

Maya's heart warmed. Felicity was the polar opposite of her—laid back, relaxed, and completely uninhibited. And she'd been trying for over two decades to help Maya loosen up. They were unlikely friends, but Maya knew of nobody else in the world who cared for her more, and who truly wanted happiness for her.

"I love you."

Felicity sat up and looked at Maya like she'd lost her mind. "I've known you twenty years, and you've never said that to me."

Maya flipped another magazine page. "I'm on vacation. Anything can happen."

Bo hadn't seen that coming. He thought he'd never see her again. He wished he hadn't. She looked damn good in that bikini. But she was having none of him. Uneasy and irritated weren't really emotions a guy was looking for when gauging a girl's interest. He was losing his touch.

As he pulled a T-shirt out of the drain of the kid's pool, he considered whether he should go back and give it another try with her. But to what end? She'd be gone by Saturday. He couldn't cave on this, no matter how drawn he was to her.

He rung out the shirt and headed back toward the front. He glanced at the two women. Marlene's friend waved at him, wiggling her fingers. Marlene sank down lower in her chair, clearly not interested. With the clarity of the light of day, she was probably thanking God she hadn't slept with him.

He walked into the front office where Tyler was sitting on Jordan's desk while she typed into her computer. "Filter needs replacing, doesn't it? I told you it would," the punk kid said to him.

Bo heaved the wet T-shirt at his chest, and the surprise of it threw him off balance and knocked him off the end of the desk. "All set." He winked at

Jordan. "Stay good."

"Don't count on it," she replied.

The wet T-shirt slammed against the door as it closed behind him.

When Maya and Felicity walked through the front door of Sebastian's house, savory aromas filled the air. They found him busying himself with caterers. "Ladies, you have exactly one hour before the guests arrive. Go, go, go. Get your showers."

"I told you we were staying too late," Maya said.

"I know, it's just that place was too fabulous to leave. My God, Sebastian, that looks incredible." Felicity grabbed for a crab cake.

It'd been years since Maya had eaten anything fried. She turned and headed up the stairs.

"Oh, Maya," Sebastian said. She turned back to him. "Wear something fabulous."

She lifted a brow. "Why?"

"I've got a great guy coming tonight who will be perfect for you."

"A set-up?"

He nodded.

"One of your friends?" she asked.

"Did you see the pool guy today?"

She rested her forearm against the bannister. "Yeah, we saw him for a minute out the window."

He waggled his eyebrows. "Hot enough for ya?"

"I just got a glimpse of his shirtless back. But yeah, hot didn't begin to cover that back."

"Well, you're in luck," he said.

"You want to set me up with your pool guy?"

"Yes. He's not only hot, but a really great guy. I

think he'll be perfect for you, and maybe not for just a fling."

"Now how's that gonna work with me in Indy and him here?"

He waved her off. "These things tend to work themselves out. Just get ready, and show some skin. You work hard enough for it." He grinned at her. "Something tells me tonight is going to be your night."

Chapter Five

Sebastian greeted Bo at the door with a huge smile. "So glad you could make it. Come on. I want you to meet my friends from home."

As they made their way through the house, Bo scanned the room for Cassidy, but she wasn't around. They walked out the French doors to the pool, and Bo spotted her at the far side by the diving board talking to Blake and her niece, Seanna. Bo would meet Sebastian's friends and talk for a while, and let Cassidy spot him…wait for her to come say hello. Maybe tonight would finally be the night she'd cross over that threshold from seeing him as a dumbass redneck to looking at him as someone she might consider going on a date with.

Sebastian led Bo to Desiree, who was talking to a tall, thin woman with straight, chin-length blond hair, and his heart took a beat off course for a second. He could only see the woman from the back, but he knew that hair, and he knew that body. His face opened into a smile.

Sebastian set his hand on her shoulder. "Maya, I want you to meet my good friend, Bo." Sebastian turned her around to face him, and his chest warmed at the sight of her face.

"Hey, Marlene."

Maya stood in utter and complete shock.

"Marlene?" Sebastian asked. "Wait a minute. Is Bo the guy from…"

The blood rushed out of her face, while her stomach tied itself into knots a Boy Scout couldn't undo. She stood frozen as an ice sculpture.

"So it's Maya?" Bo extended his hand. "I'm Bo. It's nice to finally meet the real you."

Sebastian drew his hand to his mouth. "Oh my God. What are the odds?" He pointed at Bo. "You know, I thought for a split second it could possibly be you, but then Maya said the guy from last night said it was his birthday."

"It was my birthday," Bo said.

Sebastian put his hands on his hips, and then pointed at Bo, addressing Maya. "We were together for Blake and Seanna's welcome home party earlier last night and he didn't even mention it."

"I thought your houseguests might be them, but then I remembered you were from Chicago," Bo said.

"I am. I was for a while. I lived there eight years, before I moved here. But I grew up in the Indy area with Maya." He put his arm around her and squeezed.

Bo stared at her, a little grin on his perfectly plump lips, and fizzy soda water pumped through her blood stream.

"Okay, I think I'll leave you two alone now." Sebastian patted them both on the back and walked away. Maya turned to Sebastian, willing him to come back, but he was already off.

"Well, that's disappointing. I never knew anyone named Marlene before," Bo said.

Maya pieced herself back together. "Um, how do you know Sebastian?"

"I'm his pool guy. And we run around with the same group of friends."

She widened her eyes. "You're the pool guy?"

"That's right."

"So that was you here earlier today."

"I was here earlier. You should have said something if you saw me."

"I didn't know that was you."

He smiled. "Was that you up in the window?"

She rubbed her forehead, feeling every inch of the voyeur she had been.

"I guess this is actually our third time today to run into each other." He lifted an eyebrow. "You stalking me?"

Her heartbeat sped up. That was the last thing she wanted him to think. "No," she said with no reserve of finality.

"I'm just teasing you, darlin'." She lost feeling in her knees at the Southern-drawled pet name. "Did you get plenty relaxed today at the pool?"

"Yes, it was nice. Were you there with your kids or something?"

"My kids? I don't have any kids."

Relief washed over her. "I saw you going to the kid pool. I thought you might be there with your family."

He frowned. "You thought I had a wife and kids?"

"I couldn't think of why else you'd want to go to a kid pool."

He smiled a little and raised an eyebrow. "You were trying to figure me out, huh?"

"No, not like that. I mean, I kind of wondered why you would...never mind."

"I'm the pool guy for that pool, too."

She nodded, the pieces falling into place. "The business you said you owned. It's for pool cleaning."

"Yeah, I was there picking up a check, and the boss man asked me to look at a clogged filter."

"I guess you never told me what you did."

"Guess not. You never told me Sebastian was the friend you were staying with."

She tossed a hand in the air. "It never came up."

"I guess we were busy talking about a lot of stuff last night." He looked around. "Didn't Chase drop your friend off here? I can't believe he didn't tell me once he figured it out."

"No, she Ubered home," she said, then cleared her throat, "this morning."

He nodded, having the decency to look contrite. He glanced around and took a drink of his beer, then met her gaze. "So any chance of you telling me why you didn't give me your real name last night?"

There was no chance in hell. The truth was

Felicity had piqued Maya's interest in the idea of a one-night stand. In order to allow herself to even consider something so out of the question, Maya would have had to become someone else. But she found the name change to be the only lie she could tell.

"I was just being silly. I had no idea I'd ever see you again."

"I didn't think I'd see you either. But I'm glad I was wrong."

Maya's stomach wiggled, and Felicity sidled up to them. "We've got to quit meeting this way."

"I was just getting ready to head to the police department and file a stalking complaint," he said with a wink at Maya, sending her stomach a little further into orbit.

"I think Maya's the one who needs to file," Felicity said. "She was here at Sebastian's first. So that was you earlier today, cleaning the pool. Sebastian filled me in."

"Y'all should have come down and said hello."

"We certainly should have."

Chase stepped up to the group, hands up in the air. "I swear to God I'm not following you."

Felicity smiled at him. "It's a pleasant surprise, isn't it?"

"Absolutely," Chase said, pulling her in for a hug. He looked at Bo. "Did you put this together?"

"I thought about it a second, but it didn't make sense because I always thought Sebastian came from Chicago," Bo said.

"That's what I thought, too," Chase said.

It was no surprise to Maya that Sebastian hadn't

mentioned much about Indianapolis. That was where his family was, and they didn't speak of Sebastian's family.

Felicity narrowed her gaze, going back and forth between Maya and Bo. "With all that time you two spent at the bar, how did you not put any of this together?"

Maya bit the inside of her lip, feeling caught. They'd been flirting shamelessly. Past the first ten minutes, they didn't talk about their occupations or friends. When they weren't talking about what they'd do if they had three hours in Paris or what movie scene they'd pay to get caught in, it was all innuendo and exchanged grins. The whole night had been like foreplay.

She couldn't be sure, but it almost seemed like Bo's face was looking at hot as hers felt. He shrugged, holding Maya's gaze. "Guess it didn't come up." His lip quirked up just enough for them to share a secret, wordless exchange.

"Mmm hmm," Felicity said. "So what were you talking about all that time?"

"Politics," they said in unison.

After a couple of hours, the crowd thinned, leaving just a handful of them gathered around the coffee table in the living room. Bo noticed for the first time Cassidy wasn't around. He had been so caught up with Maya he hadn't even given Cassidy a second thought.

Ashe eyed Desiree. "Truth or dare?"

Desiree glanced around. "Oh, okay, we're doing this?"

Sebastian shrugged. "Sure we are. Choose."

"All right. Dare. Why not."

Ashe put a finger to his chin and raised his gaze to the ceiling. He settled back on Desiree and smirked. "Sing us a sexy song."

"Ooh, good one," Sebastian said.

Desiree sat thoughtful for a moment, messing with one of her braids. She tossed it behind her back, cleared her throat, and then sang a beautiful song Bo barely recognized. Desiree's voice was sweet and tender but with just a hard enough edge to keep it interesting.

Growing up on the Redneck Riviera, which was whiter than a damn Garth Brooks concert, Bo had not had many black friends. Desiree was always exposing him to things outside of his white-bread world, but never made him feel naïve or dumb. He appreciated her for that.

"Wow," Maya said, her eyes wide. She held out her arm, showing the goose bumps that populated it.

"That was incredible," Felicity said.

"What was that song?" Bo asked.

"Nina Simone, straight boy." Ashe rubbed his hands together, grinning. "'Feeling Good'."

Desiree smiled back at him, the two of them sharing a moment. Desiree had said once that Ashe was her soul mate. Bo found that interesting since Ashe was gay, but what did he know?

Maya glanced over at Bo with a big smile, the song seeming to unhinge something in her. It was pretty goddamned sexy.

Ashe stood. "Did I see a bottle of red hot liquor in the kitchen?"

Sebastian held up one finger. "You know that's not mine. Who brought it?"

"I brought it," Chase said.

"That stuff is funky, funky," Desiree said.

"Want some?" Ashe asked, making his way back into the living room with the bottle and a stack of small, plastic cups.

"Okay." Sebastian held out his hand. "Any of you who mess with this nastiness gives me your keys first. You're spending the night." Chase and Ashe handed their keys to Sebastian, who eyed Desiree, and she pulled her keys out from somewhere within the folds of her skirt. He shifted his gaze to Bo.

Bo glanced at Maya, who was stifling a grin and looking down at her lap. No way in hell was he leaving her right now. "All right, what the hell." He handed Sebastian his keys, who gathered them possessively to his chest and walked to his bedroom. Ashe set the cups down on the coffee table and poured shots all around.

"It's been ages since I took a shot of liquor," Maya said.

"It's not gluten-free!" Sebastian yelled from the other room.

"Do you have Celiac disease?" Desiree asked.

Maya waved her off. "No. I just try to eat natural."

"You should see the way she eats," Felicity said. "It's nauseating. All vegetables and health food. I can't remember the last time she ate a dessert."

"It shows." Chase said, and Bo glared him down, a twinge of jealousy biting at his chest.

Sebastian rejoined the group. "Whose turn is it?"

"Mine." Desiree trained her gaze on Bo. "Is there any dare you won't do?"

Bo shrugged. "I doubt it."

"Then make him do a truth," Sebastian said.

"Don't I get to pick?" Bo asked. Desiree lifted her eyebrows. "Okay, truth," Bo said.

"When's the last time you were in love?"

Color seeped into Maya's cheeks, which made Bo's stomach uneasy in a good way. He shifted in his seat, considering. These people didn't know Angela. He'd met them after she'd walked out of his life. He wasn't trying to hide his relationship with her, it was just a part of his past. And once she was gone, he moved forward full-steam-ahead. Those were dark days, and he had no desire to relive them.

"Oh, my goodness. Bo Harrison has been stumped," Sebastian said. "Hand me that book of world records."

Bo narrowed his gaze at him. "I'm going to answer. I'm just thinking about it."

Maya was interested in her plastic cup, running her finger around the rim.

"I don't know. I used to think I had been when I was younger. But I find myself redefining all kinds of stuff these days."

Desiree lifted her eyebrows. "Really? What's your current definition of love?"

"I thought I just had to answer one question."

"Two answer minimum," Sebastian said. "House rules."

Bo glared at his friend. Everyone kept their gaze

directed toward him like he was getting ready to give up the location of a buried treasure.

He scratched behind his ear. "My past relationships haven't always been...healthy. Love didn't play the biggest part. I'm not doing that again though. I want someone who'll help make me a better person, and I want to do the same for her, somehow." He'd failed miserably at that last part with Angela. He fidgeted with a string on his jeans. He'd said too much. He'd always been a talker. Couldn't help it.

Desiree put her hand over her heart. "Bo, that is so beautiful."

"Oh, it was not," Chase said. "He's as full of shit as the day is long."

Bo punched him in the arm, and Chase held up two fists, a smile wide on his face. Chase wouldn't hit Bo or anybody else to save his life. He was a gentle giant—the life of the party. He didn't have a hateful bone in his body.

Maya stared at the leg of the coffee table, a trembling hand tucking hair behind her ear. Damn did she make his stomach do funny stuff.

Ashe held up his pointer fingers and glanced around the group. "Good luck to whoever has to follow that."

Desiree nodded at him. "You're up, Bo."

He turned to Maya, who had her gaze trained on her feet tucked around the other side of her body. "Maya," he said.

She jerked her head around and met his gaze, her face opening in a grin, then she cut her eyes away. "Okay."

He was so used to girls who came on strong and left nothing for interpretation. She made him feel like he was back in middle school, all nerves, passing a girl a note that indicated boxes to check for yes and no.

"Truth or dare," he asked.

"Truth," she said as if on autopilot. "No, wait…dare."

He nodded toward the table of desserts. "Eat one bite of one of those."

She shifted her gaze between the dessert table and him. "But, I don't eat dessert."

"It's just one bite," Desiree said.

"She's freaking out because she hasn't had anything sweet in ages," Felicity said.

Sebastian stood and walked to the table of desserts. "Oh, for Christ's sake, Maya. You can run fifty miles tomorrow to make up for it. Here, try this one. It's Cassidy's chocolate mousse cake." He forked a bite of the cake, set it on a small plate, and placed it in front of Maya.

She stared at it like it was an alien's eyeball. Bo picked up the fork, and she fixed her stare on the dense piece of chocolate cake. He eased it toward her, and she parted her lips, barely. He drew his finger to her bottom lip, pushing down slightly to part her lips farther, then brought the fork up to her mouth.

She closed her lips around the fork, and he eased it away, gazing into her eyes. She held the bite of cake in her mouth for a moment then recognition flooded her face. Her eyes got big, then they got small, closing while she chewed the cake.

The room remained silent, everyone seeming fascinated with watching her eat chocolate for the first time in God knew how long. She chewed slowly, relaxing her body against the back of the chair like she was on the verge of an orgasm.

Hell on a stick. If a piece of chocolate cake could make her look like that, he could only imagine what he could do to her if he worked some tricks with his tongue.

She swallowed, and her face glowed with satisfaction. She opened her eyes and looked at him. He held her gaze while a smile made its way across his lips.

"Damn, anyone else need another shot?" Ashe asked.

"Me!" the rest of the room yelled in unison.

Chapter Six

Bo crunched another potato chip, watching Maya out of the corner of his eye. He offered her the bowl again.

"No thanks," she whispered, watching the movie—or trying to.

"They're fat free," he said.

She jerked her head toward him. "Really?"

"No," he said, putting another one in his mouth. She pursed her sweet lips at him, and he rattled the bowl. "Just have some. You can run it off tomorrow."

"I've already got chocolate cake to run off, thanks to you," she whispered.

"You didn't have to take the dare."

"Yes I did. I'm the new girl here. I didn't want to look like a wuss."

Chase, positioned on the couch behind them, let out a snort in his sleep. Maya turned to Bo, and they cracked up. She nodded at Chase, sprawled out on the couch that was too short to contain him, his feet dangling off and Felicity crashed out up against his chest. "We should totally wake them up and tell them to go to bed."

"You ever woke up an eight-hundred-pound gorilla?" Bo asked.

Maya gave him a cute grin, lifting an eyebrow. "You have experience sleeping with Chase?"

"Lots of it. He's been known to sing power ballads in his sleep."

"You don't know that."

"I do, too."

She grinned at him, and then turned to the television. Sebastian sat up straight. "I dozed."

"For like half an hour," Bo said.

"I'm going to bed," Sebastian said. "You two should, too. There's empty bedrooms going to waste."

Maya's expression fell, and she sat up straighter, gluing her eyes to the television.

"I think we're gonna finish the movie," Bo said.

Sebastian tried to focus on it. "Is it still on?"

"Yeah," Bo said. It was The Godfather. He'd bet a hundred bucks Sebastian couldn't tell it'd been over for the past fifteen minutes and the second one had started, at least not in his current groggy state.

"Mmm," Sebastian said and glanced over at Ashe, who was crashed out in the big chair, feet up on the ottoman and cradling Desiree to his chest. Sebastian waved them off and stumbled to his bedroom.

Maya looked over at Ashe and Desiree, who

looked content as a pile of sleeping puppies. She turned back to Bo. "So are they…a couple?"

He bobbed his head from side to side, considering the question. "In what way?"

"Well, I thought he was gay, but they seem like more than just friends."

"They might be for all I know. Maybe they love each other in a way we can't understand."

She looked at him thoughtfully, like she was seeing a part of him for the first time. "That's kind of beautiful."

He shrugged and ate another chip.

She nudged him with her shoulder. "You seemed to have a little connection with her. Did the two of you ever date?"

"No, but I did drive her home to New Orleans for her aunt's funeral last year. Ashe was supposed to take her but he came down with the flu." He smiled remembering. "You should have seen the looks on her family's faces when they saw me coming. She was holding my hand to make me feel comfortable, and they about shit their pants, thinking a redneck like me was dating their beautiful, artistic daughter."

"I'm sure that's not true."

"Oh, I'm sure it is. To this day I've never seen a group of people look more wary or relieved when she set them straight, but they warmed up after a while."

"You know you're not nearly as redneck as you like to think you are."

"Hush your mouth, woman."

She giggled, making his heart light up. "Did you

go to college?"

"Yeah," he said.

"Where?"

"Florida State."

"That's nothing to sneeze at. What did you study?"

"Business."

"How long were you there?" she asked.

"Five full years including summers, but in my defense, I got my MBA as well."

She gave him an impressed look, and he was a bit ashamed of himself for letting that little brag slip out, but he couldn't help wanting to impress her.

"So have you ever had a job besides your pool cleaning business?" she asked.

"Well, yeah, lots of them, in bartending and construction work, that sort of thing. But nothing in the business world." He cleared his throat. "And the business is actually a little more than pool cleaning."

"Oh?" she asked.

"I've got a pool supply store in PCB."

"Really?"

Her wide smile made his neck heat up. He adjusted himself in his seat on the floor. "Yeah, you should come by sometime this week and say hello. If I'm there I'm usually in the back, but just ask for me."

She nodded, still smiling. "I will."

Ready to move the focus away from himself, he nodded at Ashe and Desiree in the chair. "One of us should take a picture of them. They look pretty cute all snuggled up like that."

She looked at them. "You know, I think I can see the attraction to Ashe. He's sort of sexy in an Adam Lambert kind of way."

"The singer?" Bo asked.

"Yeah. I'm totally inexplicably attracted to him. He's openly gay and absolutely nothing like any guy I've ever dated or been attracted to, but I see his picture, and I'm like…" She put her hand over her heart and closed her eyes, mouth open. Damn he wanted to kiss her. She opened her eyes and looked at him. "What?"

"Nothing."

She grinned, tucking hair behind her ear. "Who's your unexplainable celebrity crush?"

He thought about it and got a little embarrassed. He glanced at her and then looked away.

"Who?" she asked.

He looked down at the bowl of chips, unable to contain his smile.

She shoved him playfully. "Who?"

"I don't know her name."

"Well, what's she been in?"

"I don't know. She was in The 40-Year-Old Virgin."

She thought about it, squinting off in the distance. She pulled out her phone and typed into it, and her face lit up. "Catherine Keener?" She showed him her phone, and his face got hot.

"Yeah, that's her."

She smiled. "I love her. You're into her?"

He shrugged, breaking a potato chip in half.

"She's quite a bit older than you."

He shrugged again. "I don't know."

"That's sort of hot, Bo."

"What is?"

"That you're into older women."

"How's that hot?"

She grinned, readjusting herself on the floor.

"Is the floor hurting your butt?" he asked. "We can kick Chase and Felicity off the couch. Send them to bed."

"No, it's fine." She looked over at Desiree and Ashe again.

"Go poke them," Bo said.

"Bo," she whispered, nudging him.

"I didn't mean anything sexual by that. Get your mind out of the gutter, darlin'."

Her eyes went wide, and she broke out in a closed-mouth grin. "I didn't think you did," she said through clenched teeth.

She was about the most fun person he'd ever hung around with. "Go poke 'em," Bo said again.

"I'm not poking them."

He picked up a napkin and wadded it up. She grabbed his hand, and a jolt of electricity shot through him.

"Do not throw that at them."

"Of course I wouldn't." He tossed it over his shoulder, and it bounced off Chase's forehead. She shook her head at him, but she seemed to be having just as much fun as he was. He nodded at the almost empty bottle of liquor. "Wanna do another shot?"

"God, no. I had to choke down that other one."

"Wanna play a game?" he asked.

She eyed him. "What kind of game?"

"The first one of us to utter a sound has to do

that last shot."

"No way. I'll lose," she said.

"Why do you say that? We haven't even started."

She picked up a napkin off the coffee table and tore a piece off of it. "Because I'm so bad at awkward silences."

"No you're not," he said.

"I didn't say I knew how to fill them. I said I'm bad at them." She gave him a look. "Wait, have we had awkward silences?"

He chuckled. "Not a one since I've met you. I just meant you seem thoughtful sometimes. You take your time choosing your words, and you don't seem to notice there's silence in the meantime."

"I do?"

"That's just my observation."

"Nobody's ever told me something like that."

He shrugged. "I don't know. It's just what I see."

She stared at him a minute. "Okay. Let's do it."

"You want to?"

"Yeah. Let's do it."

"All right. You ready?"

"Yep." She inhaled a deep breath and let it out her nose while staring at the table. He looked at her, and she finally met his gaze, smiling, but then zipped her lip. He pinched her arm, and her eyes went wide and she shook her head. He pinched her again. And she looked at him again, shaking her head quickly. He went for her a third time, but she grabbed his hand and held up her pointer finger on the other hand.

He let silence sit between them for a little while longer, then he picked up a chip and put it in his mouth, crunching it. She put one finger to her nose and pointed at him with the other. He shook his head, indicating it didn't count. She let out a breath like she'd been holding it. "You made a noise."

"I did not. That was the chip making that noise."

"That counts."

"It does not. I said the first one to utter a sound. I did not utter a sound." He grinned. "But you did."

She closed her palms over her eyes. "Oh, God, I totally fell for it, didn't I?"

"Yep," he said, pouring the shot in her cup.

When she looked back at him, a little bit of her mascara had smudged, but he liked it, so he didn't tell her. He handed her the cup. "Time to pay up."

"You're not a nice person. You know that, right?"

"I never claimed to be."

She glanced down at the liquid and then up at him. "This stuff is really disgusting."

"Oh, yeah."

She narrowed her gaze at him. "You're really going to make me do this, aren't you?"

"I can't make you do anything."

"But you'll shame me if I don't."

"That's possible."

She winced, putting it up to her mouth. She was just about to tip it back when he stopped her. "I'll split it with you."

"You will?"

"Mmm hmm."

She smiled. "Thank you."

"What are friends for?" he said, and her smile wavered a little. That was certainly an idiotic word to use, especially since he'd never flirted harder with anyone in his life.

She put the cup to his mouth, and he opened for her. She poured the liquor in and kept going till it was all gone. She pulled back, eyes wide. "You drank my shot."

He swallowed down the cinnamon-flavored liquor, wincing at the burn on his throat. "You're gonna pay for that."

She jumped up. "I've got to powder my nose. But I'll gladly pay you Tuesday for taking my shot today."

A girl like that who could make a Popeye joke. He was so in over his head. She went up the stairs so he hit the head in the downstairs hallway. He found some toothpaste in the drawer and sloshed it around in his mouth. When he came out, Chase and Felicity were heading up the stairs, so he sat on the couch where they'd been lying.

When Maya came back down the stairs, she had on a T-shirt and a pair of sexy little shorts with lace on the bottom. The mascara smudge was gone, and her hair was smoothed out. "Sorry. I had to get comfortable." She sat down on the couch, sort of next to him, but too far away.

"Don't be sorry."

"I was going to tell you before that I would steal your keys back for you if you wanted to go home, but after you hogged my shot of red hot..." She clucked her tongue against her cheek and shook her head.

"I hope you know my throat's still burning from that."

Desiree let out a whimper followed by a sigh, and then snuggled back into Ashe's chest. He knew he should wake them up and let them go to a real bed, but having them there in the room with Maya and him took some of the pressure off. He was having a lot of fun, and he didn't want to do anything to ruin it.

Maya looked over at him, lowering her voice. "You deserved it for tricking me."

He pointed at the television. "Shh, we're missing the movie."

She shot him a look that called him out on his bullshit, and then sat up tucking her legs behind her. He pulled the blanket off the back of the couch, and then tossed the cushions off. He scooted back, lying down, and patted the spot in front of him. "Come here."

She gauged the situation a second, eyeing the spot.

"I promise I won't snore in your ear like Chase."

She smiled. "Promise?"

He nodded. "On Chase's future grave."

She widened that smile and lay down in front of him. Covering her with the blanket, he let his arm drape over her, a sense of home that he'd never felt before with a woman washing over him.

They watched the movie, this time without saying another word, her breathing taking on a slow rhythm that lulled him right to sleep.

Chapter Seven

Maya fluctuated in and out of the strange state between sleep and consciousness. Her brain was trying to wake her up, but she wasn't ready. She needed more sleep, but her pillow was too firm, and it was making her face sweat. Or was that drool?

She forced her eyelids barely open, and a stubbly chin came into focus. She froze as she realized not what, but who she was lying on. She lifted up a bit to reveal a small puddle of drool pooled on Bo's shirt.

She cringed, reaching for a stack of napkins on the coffee table. She delicately sopped up the drool, but it was hopeless.

"Hey," he said, his voice low and gravelly.

She looked up at him wincing. "Sorry," she whispered.

He looked down at the spot on his shirt and smiled, closing his eyes again. "No problem."

The last thing she wanted to do was leave the warmth of his body, but she needed to brush her teeth and people would start getting up soon. She peeled herself off of him and tiptoed across the room to the stairs.

After brushing her teeth and fixing her hair back to presentable, she put on some real clothes and headed back down.

Desiree wiped underneath her eyes, her crocheted sleeve falling down her arm. "I can't believe we slept in this chair the whole night."

"We should have woken you up, but you looked comfortable," Bo said.

Desiree smiled. "So did the two of you."

Maya's ears burned and she chanced a glance at Bo, who quirked a smile as he stacked cups on the table. Maya went to help him clean off the table, and they both grabbed for the bottle of liquor at the same time. "Go ahead," she said.

"You'll end up making me take it anyway, won't you?"

She shrugged with a little smile and let him take the bottle. They carried all the trash to the kitchen, and Maya indicated the counter. "Just set them there. I'll rinse it all before I put it in his recycle bin. He's got a whole system in place."

"I'll help you," he said.

"It's a one-woman job."

His eyebrow went up. "And you can handle it?"

"Absolutely, I can."

He smiled. "All right. I better get home. My dog's probably crossing his legs right about now."

Her phone rang in her pocket, and she grabbed it

from habit. "This is my boss. I'm just gonna…" She went to hold up a finger to indicate for him to hang on, but at the last minute she held up her hand awkwardly as she stepped out onto the patio to take the call.

"Ken. Hi," she said.

"So sorry to bother you on vacation, Maya. This will just take a second though. I'm trying to access the system through the admin logon, but it's not taking the password. Hang on."

She waited impatiently while he carried on a conversation with someone. She glanced through the window to see Bo walking toward Sebastian in the living room. She wasn't ready for him to leave. They needed to give a proper goodbye that hopefully ended with a kiss.

"Sorry about that. So do you have the new password?" Ken asked. She started to give it to him. "Hang on. Spinning wheel of death. How's it going? Where are you? Florida?"

"Yes, it's great. Do you want to just take down the password on a sticky note?" She knew what his desk looked like on a given day. She'd be lucky if he could find anything to write with much less to write on.

"Hang on. It's coming up. Christina!" he shouted at his assistant.

She inhaled a deep breath, pinching the bridge of her nose. She wished he would let her talk to Christina. She'd find a sticky note and a pen.

"Okay," he said. "I'm ready." She rattled it off to him. "Great. I know you're on vacation, but would you mind hopping on this conference call at ten? I

78

don't care if you do it from the beach. I just need your input on the implementation of the Smith-Sneed initiative."

Bo waved at Sebastian and then locked eyes with her a brief moment before holding up his hand in a final wave and heading out the door. She closed her eyes, that familiar stress of work bearing down on her shoulders. "Yep," she said.

"Great. Christina will send you the call-in info."

She ended the call and then started to head back inside until her phone buzzed again, this time with a far worse fate…her mother.

She clenched her eyes shut and figured now was as good a time as any to take her medicine. She answered the call. "Hello, Mother."

"From sunny Florida, I hear," she answered with that snippy, slightly shrill voice that sent Maya to the moon.

"Yes, as a matter of fact. I didn't mention it because I didn't want you to worry."

"Oh, is that why, now?"

"How are you, Mother?"

"Same as I was when we had lunch Friday and you failed to mention the fact that you were going on vacation. How's Sebastian?"

"He's wonderful."

"Being the perfect host, I assume."

"Of course."

"Taking you to a lot of good seafood restaurants?"

She cringed, gritting her teeth. "Lots of fresh fish and salads."

"Good. Sounds wonderful." Silence sat between

them for a moment while Maya rubbed her forehead, then her mother said, "Do you remember Sondra Bloom from school?"

"Mmm hmm."

"I was just talking to her mother, Helen, the other day. Sondra's getting a divorce." She laid the information down like a trump card, and Maya could see what was inevitably coming next. "Infidelity...on his part of course."

"Mmm hmm," Maya moaned.

"So I invited Helen to have Sondra sub for our tennis group, and she did. So Sondra comes walking onto the court, and I was shocked at her weight. She was unrecognizable."

Maya dug a knuckle into her own forehead. "I'm so sorry, Mother, but Sebastian needs help with breakfast. Can we talk later?"

"Of course. Have fun...but not too much fun, okay?"

"Okay. I'll see you." She ended the call, her heart rate instantly calming. Maya had been prone to anxiety her entire life, but the attacks had eased up drastically once she moved out of the house and away from her mother. It'd gotten so bad when she was in high school that she'd actually hyperventilated a few times. She hadn't done that in decades, thankfully.

She padded back inside which was empty of everyone including Sebastian, so she headed over to the kitchen sink and washed out all the cups and bottles. She filled Sebastian's tea kettle with water and put it on the stove as Chase and Felicity shuffled down the steps. "It was good to see you again, Maya," Chase said.

"You, too."

Felicity turned to Chase. "I'll see you tonight." Maya lifted her eyebrows discreetly, but Felicity got that look in her eye and Maya cringed. "Hey, Bo and Maya should come with us tonight."

"Oh, no," Maya said. "That's okay. Sebastian and I are going out."

"Well, if you change your mind," Chase said, and leaned down and kissed Felicity quickly. With a wink, he said, "See you."

Once he was out the door, Felicity turned to Maya. "Well?"

"Well, yourself?"

Felicity waved her off. "We didn't do anything. We were dead to the world after all those shots. Besides, it's not like I'm gonna be banging the headboard against the wall with all of you in the house. That would have been weird, and rude."

"Do you like him?" Maya asked.

"I do," Felicity said like she was sort of surprised about it. "He's really fun. So easy to be around. What about you?" She got that deviant look in her eye.

"We just fell asleep on the couch together."

"Did you kiss him?"

Maya frowned. "No. Should I have?"

"Well, if you wanted to, yes."

Maya slid the chair back from the kitchen table and sat. "Okay, I know you're going to fuss at me about being anti-feminist or something, but I want to be kissed. I don't want to have to do the kissing. Is that so nineteen-fifty-five of me?"

Felicity joined her at the table. "Of course not, sweetie. There's nothing wrong with wanting the man to take the lead. It's not necessarily my style, but if it's what you prefer, that's okay."

"What I would prefer is to be kissing him. At this point, I'm not even sure I care who initiates it."

Felicity narrowed her gaze. "What do you think his holdup is? I mean he clearly likes you. Any moron can look at him with you and see that."

"It feels that way," Maya said with all the conviction she felt.

"Well, how did you leave it this morning?"

Maya rolled her eyes. "Nowhere. Stupid Ken called me as we were getting ready to part from one another."

"That goddamned job of yours."

"Felicity," Maya said, feeling that protective slant toward her job. It was like a family member. She could talk bad about it all she wanted, but nobody else could.

"No, I'm just saying. It's like the place couldn't function without you. They have zero boundaries. What did he want?"

"Just a password." She'd leave out the ten o'clock conference call she had to jump on.

"Well, Bo knows how to get in touch with you if he wants to."

"So you and Chase are going on a date tonight?" Maya asked.

"Yeah, is that okay?"

"Of course it's okay. Go, have fun. Bastian and I will do something. I'll make him take me somewhere good for dinner."

"Where is he?" she asked, looking at his open bedroom door.

"I assume he went to the market to get breakfast stuff. I'm going to make some oatmeal." Maya stood. "Do you want some tea?"

"I'll hold out for the hard stuff." Felicity turned on the television and started flipping.

After a while, Sebastian came through the front doorway with Ashe in tow. "One bite of these cinnamon rolls will change your life."

Maya lifted a spoon of oatmeal to her lips. "I'm feeling guilty enough about the cake. Don't get near me with those things."

Sebastian handed her a bowl. "Don't worry, freak. I picked you up some organic fruit."

"Oh. Thank you." Maya pulled off the top.

Felicity reached into the bag. "I, on the other hand, will have a life-changing cinnamon roll."

Ashe took a seat at the kitchen table with them. "So, who's got a story to tell?"

"Felicity's saying nothing happened with Chase and her," Maya said.

"It was the shots," Felicity said. "We're in our mid-thirties. You can either have shots or have sex, not both."

"What about this morning?" Ashe asked.

"With everyone in the house?"

Ashe shrugged and then gave a wide-eyed grin. "He's a tall, cool one, isn't he?"

"Fabulous kisser," Felicity said.

"You know who else is a good kisser?" Sebastian asked.

"Who?" Felicity asked.

"Bo."

Maya looked up from her fruit. "What?"

"You heard me." Sebastian took a bite out of his own bowl of fruit.

Felicity scooted her chair closer. "Look who's got a story now."

"You've kissed Bo?" Maya asked.

"It's true, I was there," Ashe said.

"What? How?" Maya asked. Was he gay? He wasn't gay. But that would answer why he hadn't kissed her yet. Her stomach knotted.

"May I?" Ashe asked. Sebastian gave a single nod, and Ashe leaned in. "It was last fall. We'd all been to a big Halloween bash, and then we went to Wooley's in PCB afterward."

Felicity held up a hand. "Wait. What is PCB?"

"Panama City Beach," Maya said. Felicity lifted her eyebrow and Maya pursed her lips at her, but couldn't help a smile.

"A gay bar in PCB," Sebastian clarified.

"Bo got asked to dance by a queen, and Sebastian started ruffling his feathers about being a homophobe," Ashe said.

"Bo's a homophobe?" Felicity asked.

"Oh, no. Sebastian was just giving him a hard time. Anyway, to prove his point, Bo walked over and laid a big kiss on Sebastian's lips. We all about fell out."

Sebastian gazed off into the distance. "That man has the softest lips I have ever felt in my life. Am I right or am I right, Maya?"

Maya sat in shock. How was this possible? This man who had woken places in her core she didn't know existed was going around kissing gay guys, but wouldn't even kiss her.

"Well?" Sebastian asked.

Maya took interest in her fruit. "I wouldn't know."

"What? You mean he hasn't kissed you yet?" Sebastian asked.

"No, he hasn't. Apparently he's fine to kiss a gay man in front of a group of people, but he can't kiss me in the privacy of a car or in this house, or anywhere else for that matter."

"That's just weird," Ashe said. "The way you two were carrying on last night was exhausting. It was like perpetual foreplay."

Maya froze. "You mean last night when we were playing Truth or Dare?"

He gave a slow shake of his head. "No, when you thought you were the only ones awake."

She winced. "So you heard…everything?"

"Maybe not everything, but enough. He leaned in. "Would you like me to give you a little performance later?"

Maya closed her eyes tightly as heat engulfed her body. She rewound the night like a tape recorder, remembering comments about Adam Lambert and Ashe being sexy and what his relationship with Desiree may or may not consist of.

She rubbed her temple. "I'm just a little mortified right now. I'm going to head upstairs to prepare for my conference call."

"You're working today?" Felicity asked.

"Just a call. I'll be off in a half hour, and I'll be all yours."

As she headed up the stairs, Ashe stood and belted out what Maya was pretty sure was an Adam Lambert hit. "Oh, God," she said, covering one ear with her free hand and vowing never to speak words ever again.

Chapter Eight

Felicity took a twirl. "Well, what do you think?"

Maya finished up the last of her work emails, but emails were like termites—they just kept on multiplying. She shut her laptop. "Beautiful, absolutely beautiful. Your hair looks good like that." It hung around her shoulders in a tousled, easy, beach girl kind of way. "Sebastian did a fantastic job."

Felicity cradled the auburn waves with her hand. "Really, you think?"

"Absolutely."

Maya was happy for Felicity. She seemed to be having a good time, and she deserved it. But Maya couldn't help a twinge of disappointment. She hadn't heard a peep from Bo today. Not that she was expecting to, but she'd hoped.

Felicity checked out the window. "So, where are you and Sebastian having dinner?"

"He said he's taking me to a local place here in

Seacrest."

"Uh huh," Felicity said, her eyes glued to the window.

"Will you relax? I'm sure he'll get out of the car and come to the door for you."

"Mmm hmm." Felicity walked toward her.

"Are you okay? You seem nervous."

Felicity waved a hand. "I'm fine."

"Sebastian, come on," Maya said. "I'm getting hungry."

"You've been on your computer," he shouted from the bedroom.

It was true, and it'd also gotten her suckered into another conference call for the next morning. "I'm off now."

"Miracle of miracles." Felicity took another look out the window, and then perked up. "They're coming!"

Maya eyed her. "They? Whose they?" Sebastian came out from his bedroom with his comfy clothes still on. Maya looked him up and down. "What are you doing? Why aren't you dressed?"

Felicity squared herself in front of Maya. "Okay, don't be mad."

Maya's stomach churned. "Felicity, what did you do?" She bolted for the window. The big, black truck she had seen in Bo's driveway that first night was sitting there.

"I told Chase I wasn't comfortable going out with him alone, that I didn't know him very well, and that I really wanted you to come, and asked if he could bring Bo."

The blood drained from Maya's face, and she

clenched her fists. "You didn't." She nodded. "Jesus, Felicity. I'm sure that was real believable seeing that you've had sex with him, and he slept in the bed with you last night."

"I'm just trying to help things along."

"I don't need you to do that. If he was interested, he would call or text me. He knows where I am."

"This is the last time I interfere. I swear. I just think there's something there we're missing. If we don't get to the bottom of it tonight, I promise I'll drop it."

Maya frowned at her, but the car doors shutting outside sent her into motion. She rushed to the bathroom and checked for lipstick on her teeth, smudges on her face, and bats in the cave. She smoothed out her hair, and then looked down at her dress. No wonder Sebastian had been so particular with the outfit she picked for the night.

Maya came out of the bathroom and stopped in front of the two of them who stood side by side, a guilty as sin, united front. "You both suck." The doorbell rang.

Sebastian drew the corners of his mouth outward. "Smile!" He scurried to the front door and opened it. "Hello, straight boys. Come in."

Chase wrapped his arms around Felicity. "Hey." He turned to Sebastian. "You okay with us taking them for the night?"

"Of course. Take away. We're sick of each other already."

Bo approached Maya. "You look good." He went to give her a hug, and she stiffened. He stopped. "Are you okay?"

"Can I talk to you a minute?"

He frowned. "Sure."

Maya walked toward the French doors and through to the pool area, Bo in tow. She turned to him. "I'm sorry about this. I had no idea you were coming until like two minutes ago."

"You don't want to go?"

"No, that's not what I'm saying. I just, I didn't want you to think—"

"I'm not thinking anything, trust me. It's been a long, busy day."

"Well, if you're tired, and you just want to go home and crash, I'll totally understand."

"Look, if I didn't want to be here, I wouldn't be here. You look really nice. Let's go out and eat."

Her fueled anger toward her meddling friends softened. "Okay."

"Come on." He opened the door for her, and she went back inside, relaxing a little.

"Everything okay?" Chase asked.

"It's all good. Let's go," Bo said. "Sebastian, you want to come?"

"No, you kids go, have a good time. Don't do anything I would do."

"No worries about that," Chase said with a smile.

"Damn. Well, you know where I am if you change your mind," Sebastian said. Chase winked at him and ushered Felicity out the door.

Maya glared at Sebastian, and he put his fingers to either side of his mouth and pushed his smile up farther. Bo offered him a hand, and Sebastian took it and shook it. "Later, man."

Sebastian held his hand for a moment. "You, on

the other hand, can do whatever you want with that one."

Bo opened the door to the restaurant, letting them all walk in. Local artwork and photography covered the walls. Maya's eye was caught by a black and white picture of a little girl in a white dress running toward a sailboat. A price tag hung at the bottom of it. She slowed and took a closer look. She grabbed Bo's arm. "Bo, look at this. Is this our Ashe?"

"Yeah, he's really good. I've got his stuff up at the shop."

She lifted an eyebrow, impressed at his good taste. She wanted to see those pictures and his store, but she didn't want to seem too interested, especially since he was pretty much hijacked to come on this date.

Chase and Felicity sat on the same side of the booth, so Bo and Maya slid in opposite them. Gazing at the menu, Maya decided to suck it up and order something as is without asking if it was organic, gluten-free, or low in butter or oil. Chase ordered a bottle of Sauvignon Blanc, and she was happy for them to bring on the wine. Her nerves could use it.

"So we found out a fun fact about Bo today," Felicity said, her eyebrow going up. "Is it true you kissed Sebastian?"

Chase perused his menu. "I knew you were gay."

Bo huffed a laugh. "That's true. The kiss. Not what he said."

"Bullshit," Chase said.

"No, they're right, I did."

Chase looked genuinely confused. "Are you serious?"

"He was giving me a hard time about being homophobic, and I couldn't think of any other way to convince him I wasn't."

"There were other ways," Chase said.

Bo smiled. "It got a laugh, anyway."

"How have I not heard this story?" Chase asked.

"'Cause you're always working."

Maya grinned. "They were at a gay bar, and Bo had been dancing with a drag queen."

Bo looked over and gave her a look. "She asked. I didn't accept."

"Well, that's just rude," Felicity said.

"Are you calling me a homophobe now?"

She shrugged. "Let's see where the night goes. If it takes us to a drag bar, you can redeem yourself."

He glanced over at Maya with a closed-mouth grin. "I'm actually good right here." Her stomach did a quickstep.

"Well, your kiss left quite an impression on him," Felicity said.

Bo shrugged. "Of course it did."

"How about you? What did it feel like kissing a dude?" Chase asked.

"You want to find out?"

Chase threw his napkin at Bo.

The girls laughed. Maya couldn't help but be a little turned on by the thought of these two hunky straight men kissing…passionately…touching. A look from Felicity indicated to Maya that she wasn't the only one thinking it.

"Chase, what do you do?" Maya asked.

"I've got a little property management company. We manage houses and condos up and down 30A."

"By little, he means the biggest one in the area," Bo said. "And he's building a hospital right now."

"A clinic," Chase corrected. "I'm part of an investment group. We're dipping our toes into a few things."

Felicity looked a little prouder to be his date. She motioned between the two guys. "So how do you two know each other?"

"We've got a mutual buddy, Blake," Chase said. "You might have met him last night, but they weren't there long. He's newly coupled up and can't stay out of the bedroom for too long."

"That sounds atrocious," Felicity said. "Not the bedroom part. The couple part."

"You not into the couple thing?" Chase asked, his expression impassive.

"I find it binding, like someone's mummified me."

Chase chuckled. "I'll be sure to keep that in mind."

Felicity motioned across the table. "Maya's better at it than I am."

Maya tucked hair behind her ear, feeling a little put on the spot. Bo looked over at her, considering her. He seemed like he wanted to say something, but the server appeared. While everyone placed their orders, Maya thought about what it'd be like to be Bo's girlfriend, coming home to him every night, eating dinner together, watching TV, lying in bed with him reading. Who was she kidding? Like she'd ever read another book if he were beside her in bed.

He nudged her. "Maya."

"Hmm? Oh, yes. The red snapper, please." She handed her menu over and smiled at Bo, and then repositioned her fork.

Chase and Felicity started talking to each other, so Bo looked at Maya. "You were way off just now."

Her cheeks warmed. "I was thinking about work."

"Must be a damn fun place to work judging by the smile on your face."

She gnawed on her bottom lip, knowing she was busted but kind of liking it.

They walked across the street where Chase and Felicity disappeared down a public beach access walkway. Bo led Maya to a gazebo with a swing facing the ocean in a park area. Even as slammed as he was at work, her face had been popping into his head all day. He'd been trying to figure out what his next move was when Chase had called him and asked him to take Maya out with him and Felicity. The proposition had been like an arrow, directing him toward her.

Maya gazed around at her surroundings. "This whole place is so quaint. I've never seen anything like it."

"The communities along 30A are one of a kind, that's for sure."

"Where are the cheesy T-shirt shops and fast food chains?"

"Not allowed. Only mom and pop places."

She rested her hand on the swing's chain. "I

can't imagine anyone who's ever vacationed here without dreaming of living here at some point."

He considered her, unrealistically getting his hopes up. "Have you?"

"Thought about living here? Oh, no. I mean, sure, the thought popped into my head, but I couldn't. It's a nice thought, but I've got my job back home and all." He nodded. That hadn't been the answer he was hoping for. Damn, he hadn't even kissed the girl yet, and he was testing her to see if she'd move there. Dumbass.

He turned to her. "So you work at a marketing company, right?"

Her eyes went wide. "That's a good memory. I don't even remember telling you that."

"You did, when I first met you."

She nodded. "Mmm. I was a little nervous when I first met you."

He narrowed his gaze. "What are you like at work?"

"Different than how I am with you." She smoothed a stray hair behind her ear.

"How are you different with me?"

"I'm not nervous at work. I'm actually very much in charge and full of authority, if you can imagine that."

"I can definitely see you being like that." He couldn't help a smile. "You don't seem too nervous around me anymore."

She turned beet red and looked away from him. "More like giddy. I'd die if my work people saw the way I act when I'm with you. I wouldn't be trusted with sensitive company secrets, that's for sure." Her gaze swept over him with that same playful smile they were always giving one another.

A warm, summer evening breeze blew some stray hairs out of her face, the roar of the ocean their background music. Never had there been a moment better manufactured for a kiss. And Jesus Christ did he want to. He wanted to do more than kiss her. He dreamed of exploring every inch of her body with his tongue. But something ate at his gut.

She let out a breath. "Sebastian got a huge kick out of letting Ashe tell us the story about the night you kissed him."

"Figures," he said.

"He thought it was hilarious that he'd kissed you, but I hadn't."

He turned to her, fighting his gut. "You want me to kiss you?"

"No," she said, shaking her head, but her smile told him otherwise.

"You don't want to kiss me?" he asked.

She giggled. "No."

He was such a stupid idiot. This girl who he was becoming dangerously attracted to was sitting right here beside him, hinting for him to kiss her, and he wasn't allowing himself to go there. What if he just kissed her? A kiss didn't have to lead to sex or any kind of commitment, week-long or not. A kiss was a kiss. Simple as that.

She scratched her cheek. "So, what do you do when you're not working, usually?"

Their conversations earlier in the week had been pure teasing and flirting, but his refusal to make a move had shifted them into small talk. He was more clueless at this moment than when he was at fifteen years old asking a girl out on his first date.

"Pretty much what you've seen me doing this week. What about you?"

"I work a lot. I go out with girlfriends sometimes. Date a little, I guess."

Of course she did, but he couldn't help a pang of jealousy at the thought of her on a date with some other guy. "You do online dating?"

"I have, years ago. I put that whole experience up there with dental work. Have you ever done it?" she asked.

He shook his head. "Nah. Seems like a lot of work—filling out online profiles about yourself, posting pictures, weeding through people's profiles. The whole thing sounds exhausting."

"That's exactly what it is."

"How do you typically meet guys?" he asked, his curiosity getting the better of him.

She shrugged. "Randomly. Occasional blind date." She rolled her eyes. "God, I think I have one scheduled for next Friday."

He liked that she seemed to think it was a chore, but still, the thought of some guy taking her out didn't sit well with him.

"I don't mean to sound ungrateful," she said, "it's just that it usually doesn't go well. People have good intentions, but they think just because you're single and some other guy is single that you're going to be this perfect match."

He grabbed the wooden bar behind him, stretching his arm. "I've been there, too. I've gotten to the point when someone offers a setup, I kindly decline."

She considered him. "I may do that next time."

He wanted her to do it this time, with the date she had scheduled next week, but that was pointless. "You work out, don't you?" he asked.

"Yes, I do that quite a bit."

"It shows."

She motioned at his arm. "Well, clearly I'm not the only one of us who works out. What do you do?"

"Weight training and running basically," he said. "What about you?"

"I do weight lifting classes, yoga, running…"

"It's working."

She smiled. "Thanks. Yours is working, too. Oh, God. I meant to tell you. Ashe totally was awake last night when we were whispering about him."

"You mean when you were saying how hot you thought he was?"

She clenched her fists. "Oh, crap. I was so hoping it wasn't as bad as I remembered."

He chuckled. "What'd he say about it?"

She lowered her chin at him. "He serenaded me this morning with an Adam Lambert song."

"I'm sorry I missed that."

Felicity and Chase walked down the public beach access ramp toward them.

"They weren't down there for long," Bo said.

"Yeah, I figured we'd be here for an hour."

"You all ready to get back?" Chase asked.

"You're ready to go home?" Bo asked.

"Yeah, if you don't mind. We're both pretty tired," he said, his arm around Felicity, but clearly they wanted to do more than sleep.

Maya gave Bo a look that said she took the hint, too, and they all headed to the truck.

"Thanks for driving," Chase said, helping Felicity down from Bo's truck.

"Thanks for paying. Where are you taking us tomorrow night?"

"Mickey D's," Chase said with a wink, and he and Felicity were off to have the wild monkey sex Maya was now just about desperate for. Damn Felicity. Maya had been fine without sex for a while now, hadn't even given it much of a thought until Felicity started putting these nutty ideas into her brain.

Bo glanced over at her, his hands on the steering wheel, but not going anywhere yet. "Can I take you somewhere?"

He could take her anywhere on the planet. "Where?"

"Do you trust me?"

She grinned at him. "Maybe. Are they going to find my dead body in the woods tomorrow?"

He squinted, closing one eye. "Not tomorrow."

"Well then sure. Let's go."

Hints of masculine body wash and leather filled the dark cab of Bo's truck, lit only with the neon lights of the dash as they drove down Chase's wooded street. The satellite radio was tuned to the grunge channel, Soundgarden's "Hands All Over" permeating the car. She'd never heard it and wasn't typically a fan of grunge, but she'd never think of Soundgarden the same way again. He turned it up.

He must have liked that song. She did too, now.

He pulled a handful of chocolate mints out of his shirt pocket and offered them to her. She had seen a bowl of them at the restaurant but hadn't dared to grab one—sugar. She shook her head, and he put them back in his pocket, unwrapping one and popping it into his mouth.

After they drove a little way down 30A, he pulled up to what looked like a high-end neighborhood and powered down the window at a guard station.

"Hey, Bo," the security guard said. "You here to check the pool?" he asked with a grin.

"We'll just be minute," he said.

"Mmm hmm," the guy said, and the arm lifted.

"Thanks," Bo said with a smile, and they were in.

Maya pointed back to the guard. "Should I feel cheap?"

He took her hand and laced his fingers inside hers. "You could never seem cheap."

She smiled. "Good answer."

He parked in a small lot at the back of the neighborhood that opened up to the beach. "You okay to walk in the sand?"

"Mmm hmm," she said, a flock of butterflies letting loose in her belly. If this wasn't a recipe for a kiss, she didn't know what was.

They kicked off their shoes just where the pavement met the sand, and he held out his hand for her to take, his thick fingers spreading her thin ones.

The cool, powdery sand massaged her feet as she walked. "Oh my gosh. That's better than a pedicure."

"You haven't been to the beach yet?"

"No. This is my first time."

"First time this trip, or…"

"First time I've ever been on these panhandle beaches, actually."

He gave her a look. "Are you serious?"

"Yeah. I mean I've been further south like to Naples and Miami, but growing up, my family usually vacationed on Lake Michigan, or we traveled to Colorado or Santa Fe or to one of the coasts."

He nodded, his brow furrowing a bit.

"Where did your family go on vacation?" she asked.

He shrugged. "We didn't, really. I guess it was too expensive for my parents."

She felt a little guilty for her upper-crust upbringing. "What about you? Where have you traveled as an adult?"

"I've been to New Orleans a few times, Austin for South by Southwest. Ever since Shayla's been in Nashville, I've used my time away from work to visit her there. I don't know. I don't really travel much. It's not like I'm gonna escape to the beach."

She huffed a laugh. "I guess not."

They reached the shore, and Maya inhaled a deep breath of thick, salty sea air. He lifted an eyebrow. "You want to feel the Gulf of Mexico on your feet?"

She smiled. "Definitely."

They stood just outside of reach of the water, her hand becoming clammy with nerves, or was that his? She started to step forward, but he squeezed her hand. "It will come to you. Just give it some time."

She glanced up at him, her heartbeat starting to really speed up. She'd been waiting only days, but damn if it didn't feel like she'd been waiting for him to come to her for a lifetime. She stepped forward and then met his gaze. "I don't have much time here."

He turned toward her, his Adam's apple bobbing up and down as he swallowed, his expression serious as he scanned her features.

She took his other hand. "What are you waiting for?"

"Right now, I don't have a goddamned clue." He took a step toward her, forcing a wave of heat to rush through her core as he cradled the back of her neck and brought his mouth to hers, pressing his soft lips against hers as a bolt of electricity shot through her body. He parted her lips and gave her his tongue, tasting like the chocolate mint he'd just sucked on, making her wrap both arms around him to get more of his body close to hers. She couldn't get enough of the taste of him, or of his body that'd she'd had on her brain in high-def all week long. She moved her hands over his muscled back, wanting desperately to slide them inside his jeans, having to strain to keep herself in check. It was their first kiss, and it was on a beach where anyone could walk up at any moment. But her body was buzzing with want for him, making it nearly impossible to restrain herself.

His strong hand eased down to the small of her back, and a fluttering sensation unleashed in her belly as his arm wrapped around her, bringing her body in closer to his. She'd never been kissed by anyone so sure of his hands, knowing exactly how to touch her and make her body melt as easy as butter.

She released her mouth from his, needing to breathe, her body so worked up she thought she might lift off the beach if he wasn't holding her to the ground. She stretched out her neck as he left kisses in a trail down to her collarbone, giving her a sense of utter powerlessness over her own freaking body.

He paused at the curve of her neck, groaning into her skin. He wrapped his arms around her, pulling her flush against his body, just holding her there to his muscled chest like he was taking possession of her.

Pulling away, he met her gaze, his brow furrowed like he had questions for her, or something to say that she had a feeling she wasn't going to like. He brushed the hair out of her face, smoothing his hand over it. "I need to take you home."

The words cut through her core like a serrated knife. "Yes, of course. It's getting late. You've got to work tomorrow, I'm sure."

He didn't nod or agree, but took her hand and walked her to the truck. They rode to Sebastian's house wordlessly, Bo with his elbow on the doorframe, biting on his thumbnail as he stared, laser-focused on the road ahead of them. He pulled up in the driveway and turned off the engine, staring at the steering wheel like he was on another planet in his mind.

She had no idea what he was grappling with internally, but she felt the desperate need for self-preservation. She shifted back into control-mode in her head, taking charge of her situation and emotions in a way that put everything into order for her.

She reached over and squeezed his knee, forcing the kindest smile she could muster. "Thanks for coming with me tonight. I had fun." She opened the car door, and as she was getting out, she clenched her teeth as he said, "Maya, wait."

She wasn't going to make this into a thing. He'd taken her on a date, under obligation to a friend and not by his own desire. He'd kissed her when she'd all but begged him to, and now he was dropping her home and not taking her to his bed. These were the facts of the case. Only an idiot would try to read any further into why he wasn't reciprocating her desires.

He walked around the front of the truck, and she met him there, giving him what she hoped was an easy smile. She would not let him see her disappointment. He stared at her like he was getting ready to give her the answers she really wanted, and she held her breath as she waited for them.

"Do you want to go running with me in the morning?" he asked.

What she wanted to do was punch him in the gut. "Running?" she asked, because what the hell?

"It's a great way to see the area up close. We can hit a few different communities if you want to do a long one."

No. The answer was no. She could only take so

much of this torture. The days were ticking off the calendar, and he wanted to go running.

He looked at her with those dark, intense eyes and those stupid lips that had just been on her neck and her mouth. She was upset because he was moving slow. To some people, this would be considered gentlemanly. To her it would be considered polite and well-mannered if she didn't want him so freaking badly and only had days left to spend with him.

She inhaled a deep breath, lifting her eyebrows. "Sure. What time?"

"Seven? Does that give you enough time to sleep?"

Of course it did. She had all freaking night to sleep now. "Perfect. Where should I meet you?"

"I'll come back here. I won't ring the bell though so I don't wake up Sebastian."

"I'll be out here at seven."

He moved in, cupping her shoulders, pressing his lips against hers once, twice, giving her his tongue and then taking it away from her as he finished the kiss with a sweet peck.

"Night," he said, lowering his chin, smiling at her, and then kissing her again like the sun wasn't coming up tomorrow.

He pulled away from her and was backing out of the driveway before she could pick herself mentally up from the pavement.

Chapter Nine

Bo drove down 98, making his way to Seacrest and
Maya. In his brain, he'd planned on taking her
home after he dropped Chase and Felicity off, but
his heart had other plans. He didn't want to sit at a
crowded bar with her though, and they had nice
beach chairs that they seemed to leave out half the
time at that neighborhood. His plan had been to sit
there in those chairs for just a little while and watch
the waves come in with no one around…just spend
a little more time with her, that's all he wanted. But
they didn't even get that far before he lost every bit
of control he'd worked so hard to keep all week
around her.

Running. He asked her to go goddamned running
of all things. She'd looked at him like he'd lost his
mind. He had. She did that to him.

He'd struggled so hard all the way back to
Sebastian's house, willing himself to tell her

goodbye and to have a good rest of her trip. He was going to walk away, and he was just about strong enough to do it until she squeezed his knee, and a shot of lust went through him like a firework. So he'd asked her to go running. Because he was smooth like that.

He pulled up in front of Sebastian's house and waited for her to come out. She eased out the door wearing black running shorts that sat high on her long, lean legs with a white spaghetti string tank top. He wanted to say screw it to the running and push her right back in the house straight up to her bedroom.

"Hey," she said with a bright smile, her eyes still a little sleepy with the early hour. She walked toward him and he held out his arms, bringing her in for a hug. He kissed her, trying to contain himself considering the morning hour, but damn was it hard.

She pulled back from him, squeezing his biceps. "I'm all stretched out, but go ahead if you need to." He hated he'd missed that.

"I'm good," he said.

"All right then, local guy, lead the way, and I'll try to keep up." The grin on her face told him she was no rookie.

They made their way up Sebastian's street to 30A. Bo usually ran by himself, but having her beside him was so natural, like they'd done it a hundred times. He had started out slow, not knowing how fast she wanted to go, but she seemed to be pulling him along, running a step ahead of him. He was up to his regular pace, but he still seemed to be dragging along behind her.

She ran like a gazelle, her lean legs stretching out in long strides, her breathing remaining steady and quiet. He was practically struggling to keep up, but he didn't mind. He enjoyed the challenge.

They ran past the palm trees that lined the entrance of the town of Alys Beach, and he led them through the neighborhoods so she could see the Mediterranean-style houses of 30A's most exclusive community. He showed her private cabanas and pristine pools flanked by palm trees. They ran on the wooden boardwalk through the nature preserves and over the lake. Maybe she'd fall in love with it enough to make her want to move there.

He led them back toward 30A to the Alys Beach playground near George's restaurant. She followed him as he ran up the grassy hill, the path winding around it. He collapsed at the top, and she sat down next to him, barely breathing hard at all.

She lay back on the hill. "My God, Bo. You've overloaded me with beautiful today. I loved that run. I felt like I was somewhere in Greece."

"Good," he said.

"Do you run here a lot?"

"Not as much as I should. Hell, sometimes I end up on the treadmill at the gym. Seems kind of ridiculous after that though. I keep a few pools in this community. You should see the inside of some of these houses."

She shielded her eyes from the sun. "I don't know if I'd want to. I'd be jealous. I can't imagine the kinds of lives these people live."

"They've got their own set of problems like

everyone else," he said.

She turned on her side, resting her head in her hand. "Do you have any good gossip on any of them?"

He thought for a minute. "Rumor has it there's a woman who lives just down the street here runs a prostitution ring."

"Really?"

"No, but it'd make a good rumor if we wanted to get one started."

She lifted her eyebrows and widened her eyes. "Ooh, let's do it."

Her blue eyes shined with mischief, doing that weird thing to his stomach again. He leaned toward her to kiss her, but she backed off. "You can't kiss me now. I'm all sweaty and stuff," she said.

"I don't care about that." He leaned back in.

"Seriously, I'm probably stinky now."

He rested on his side, with his hand on her flat stomach. "What if I like stinky?"

She scrunched up her cute little nose. "See, you're just gross."

He moved his hand slowly, back and forth over her stomach. "Disgusting." He went in for another kiss, but she rolled away before he could.

She made her way down the hill, and he went after her. She ran across the playground fast, but he felt like he was nineteen years old again with renewed energy. He caught up to her and grabbed her from behind, flinging her around in a circle. She gave a playful squeal as he swung her legs around and repositioned her in his arms, holding her like a groom holds a bride. He lay her down on the grass then pinned her wrists down with his hands, hovering over her, and from the look on her face, she didn't mind being caught.

He pressed his lips against hers, tasting the salt on her skin. Something about them having just run all those miles side by side, being outside in nature, bodies sweaty and warm, made him more primal for her than ever. She'd led him most of the run, but she didn't seem to mind letting him have control of her now. Man, what he'd like to do to that long, lean body of hers.

"Mommy, look!" a child's voice called out. "They're doing it!"

A mother ushered her kids back to the playground, shooting Bo an evil look like he'd just corrupted their young son. Give it some time, he thought, her precious baby boy would be doing the same thing to some girl one day. Bo rolled off of Maya.

"Do you see what you've done now?" Maya asked. "Children scarred for life."

"I think I'm the one who's scarred. I might have pulled something trying to catch you." He shook out his leg.

"Old men tend to get those kinds of problems."

"I guess young ladies like yourself don't have to worry about that kind of stuff. I turned thirty-five the night I met you. How many years younger than me does that make you?"

"Lots and lots."

"All right, it's going to be like that?"

She eyed him up and down. "If I tell you will you promise not to hold it against me?"

He outlined a cross with his finger on his chest. "Promise, hope to die, all that crap."

"We're close in age. I'll just put it that way."

"How close?" he asked, not letting up.

"Really close."

He nodded. "I'll accept that. So you don't have any aches or pains?"

"None I'm going to tell you about." She hopped up and headed back toward 30A, walking, thankfully for him.

"So what does Sebastian have you doing today?" he asked.

"I don't know. I just get dressed and let him lead the way. Actually, I think he wants to show me a few of your friends' shops. We're stopping by Seaside Sweets to meet Cassidy, and then we're stopping by a gift store of someone's."

He smiled. "Marigold's shop."

She raised her eyebrows. "That name got a reaction out of you. Is this one of your girlfriends?"

"No," he said with a huff of a laugh. "Not at all. We're just friends, but she's a hot mess. She keeps us all on our toes."

"You're a tight little group, aren't you?" she asked.

"I guess so, as oddball as we all are together."

"So has anyone in the group ever dated each other?"

"Not that I know of, but Marigold and Chase act like they're going to half the time. I think they're both just such huge flirts that they gravitate toward one another."

She nudged him in the side. "Have you ever

111

kissed any of the girls?"

He grinned and pointed. "There's the Seacrest town square coming up."

"You're avoiding the question."

He pulled her over in front of the big, white lifeguard chair that displayed the community name. "Come here. I'll take our picture." He held out his phone and snapped a picture of their smiling faces. He hadn't seen himself look that happy in years. "What's your number? I'll text it to you." Sly, he knew, but it was easier than having to get it from Sebastian.

She took his phone and typed her number in, and then handed it back to him. "I'll let you off the hook, today."

He reached down and kissed her in response. She was so damn easy to kiss. He walked her over to a palm tree, letting her rest against it while he kissed her some more. He had to make up for lost time somehow.

She pulled away from him, smiling. She was tall, so they were almost face to face, but he still had a couple of inches on her. "I liked what you said the other night at Sebastian's house, during your truth confession," she said.

He tried to remember exactly what he'd said. He got nervous, so he decided to blow up the moment. "I was drunk."

She smiled and then pulled away, heading back toward the path. "Have you ever been married?"

The truthful answer was no. He hadn't been married, but it felt deceitful not to mention Angela since they'd been together for so long. But damn, he didn't want to dredge up that past relationship. There was nothing about it that brought happy memories to him, and Maya was only here for the week. The last thing he wanted was to spend time discussing the most miserable time in his life.

"Nah. But I gave my high school girlfriend a promise ring. Turned her finger green."

She put her hand over her heart. "Oh, I love those things. I had a couple of friends who had boyfriends give those to them in high school. I bet she wore it with pride."

"Or with gangrene. What about you?" he asked.

"If I had one, I would definitely wear it proudly, even now."

He bumped her hip. "I meant have you been married."

She smoothed hair behind her ear. He noticed she did that when she seemed a little nervous about something. This was the first time she'd done it all day. "No, never married."

Silence sat between them like a stump. Bo nodded in greeting at some bikers who passed by them on the sidewalk. "You're leaving Saturday?" he asked her.

"Yes, Saturday."

"You're going to just miss my sister, Shayla."

"The one I talked to on the phone on Saturday night?"

"That's the one."

She smiled over at him. "I liked her."

"She's not as charming as she seems."

"I doubt that. She's kind of like you, isn't she?"

He furrowed his brow at her. "How so?"

"I don't know. You definitely sounded alike. Not just your voices, but your temperaments."

He huffed a laugh. "People do say we're a lot alike. Do you have any brothers or sisters?"

"I have a sister," she said, her mood changing.

"You close?"

She inhaled deeply. "That's a hard question to answer. I love her. I really do. It's just that she has this terrible habit of making really poor choices, and it's so hard sitting by and letting it happen, keeping my mouth shut."

"You can't talk to her about her choices?"

She shook her head emphatically. "Oh, no. That makes it ten times worse. Learned my lesson the really hard way there."

"My sister and I probably say too much to one another. I don't think either of us has ever let an opinion go un-muttered."

"That's nice," she said with a genuine smile.

"We've figured each other out though. We're so damned predictable to one another that we know when to keep our mouths shut and not even start something we don't want the other one's opinion on."

They stopped while a car turned into a condo complex ahead of them, and she huffed a laugh. "I can't imagine."

"What's that?"

"You being predictable."

"You think I'm unpredictable?"

She held her finger and thumb together. "Little bit." She started walking again, and he followed her.

"How's that?"

"Never mind," she said, again with the smoothing of her hair behind her ear, but this time, he wasn't going to let up.

He nudged her side. "You've started something now. You've got to finish."

She gave a playful roll of her eyes and slowed down on their path, stepping over to the side and holding onto the back of a bench. "Okay. I guess it's just that the first night we met, you were very flirtatious." She held up her hand quickly. "I was, too, completely, but then when I was dropping you off…" She trailed off, giving him a look.

He wasn't sure, but he bet his cheeks were coloring. Good thing it was hot and they'd been running, or he'd be busted. "I didn't make a move," he supplied.

She lifted an eyebrow in response.

He gripped her hip, rubbing his thumb over her stomach. "Well, I guess I screwed up then, didn't I?"

She crooked her finger inside the pocket of his shorts, their bodies hovering close. "You're just confusing, Bo."

Hearing her say his name in that sweet, almost-whisper made his chest light up with tingles. He ran his hand over her neck and behind her head. As he went in for another kiss, she scooted away. "Are you ready to run yet, old man?"

He smiled at her, wanting her worse than he'd wanted any woman in a long time, maybe ever. "That's just hurtful."

She took off fast, and he struggled to keep up

with her for a minute, then they fell into step with one another. When they got to Sebastian's street they slowed down. He walked her up to the front door, his breath catching back up with him. "You're not easy to keep up with."

"I don't mean to leave you behind," she said with that grin of hers that he could eat for breakfast.

"What time are you going shop-hopping?"

"I'm not sure. I've got a work call at ten-thirty."

He lifted an eyebrow. "Be sure and have some vacation on your vacation."

She held her arms out to the sides. "This was an awesome vacation activity."

"Can I call you later?"

"Sure," she said, tempering a smile.

He leaned in for a kiss, and she didn't stop him this time. He rested his hands lightly on her shoulders and pulled her to him, covering her salty lips with his. His mind wandered to what other parts of her body tasted like, waking up his cock. It'd been so long since he'd had sex he felt like a twelve-year-old kid out of control of his body. He pulled away quickly before he embarrassed himself. His gym shorts were loose and unforgiving. Luckily, his face was already red from the run, so the evidence of his embarrassment wasn't so easily spotted.

"Have fun today," he said.

"Okay." She gave him a final smile, and then went inside.

He got in his truck and sat there a minute. She'd basically just called him a chicken for not making his move the other night. He needed to talk to a

116

friend. He'd been giving Blake space since he'd gotten back to town from Kansas City. Blake was busy with the move back, working on plans for the new clinic with Chase and being batshit crazy in love and all. He was staying in one of Chase's rentals in Seagrove just down the road. Bo wondered if he might have a minute for him. He texted Blake.

Where are you?

Home. Where are you?

You got a minute?

Sure.

I'll be there in five.

Maya opened the door to find Sebastian and Felicity at the kitchen table. "Still mad at us for orchestrating that date?" Sebastian asked. Maya gave him a loving eye roll and kicked off her shoes. He forked a piece of melon from his bowl. "I was in a huff because I thought you went running without me, then I checked out the window and saw a big black truck out there on the street. So my first instinct was to assume the two of you were shacked up in the bedroom."

"That was your first instinct?" Maya asked.

"But then, Felicity informed me that your door was open, and you were gone. So with my car, Felicity's car, and the sexy redneck's truck all here, we pieced it together. The two of you went running together."

"A regular Nancy Drew," Maya said.

"Please tell me you've been kissed by this man by now?" Sebastian asked.

"You're a day behind. He kissed me last night."

"Finally." He sipped his coffee.

Maya took a seat at the table. "But I had to pretty much ask for it."

"I'm sure he was kicking and screaming," Felicity said.

"And this morning on the run?" Sebastian asked. "Did you stop anywhere for a little nookie?"

Her cheeks warmed at the memory. "A few times."

"Sounds like a fabulous way to get your exercise in," Sebastian said. "So I think our day has fallen apart. I have a work thing that's popped up at twelve, and I know you've got your call at ten-thirty. Will you hate me if I have to punt today?"

"Of course not. I'll just hang with Felicity."

She scrunched up her face. "Actually, Chase is taking me out on a boat. This is the only day he can do it. He's tied up with work the rest of the week."

Maya blinked at Felicity. "This is unprecedented for you. You better be careful or you're going to have to call this a relationship."

"Bite your tongue. Seriously, it's not. He's just really fun, and we have a good time. We're almost like kissing cousins or something."

Sebastian pointed with a strawberry on his fork. "That's just effed up."

"No, I'm serious. We're just hanging out. We have sex, and it's great, but it's just fun. It's totally low maintenance and free of expectation. I think I've found my ambivalence match."

Sebastian jerked a thumb at her. "That's the stuff of romance novels right there."

"I didn't come equipped with the love gene and I'm okay with that, just as long as I can have fabulous sex."

"On that note," Maya said, "I'm going to shower."

"Hey," Felicity said. "So are we forgiven for last night?" Both of them looked at her with raised eyebrows.

She narrowed her gaze at her two friends she adored. "We'll see how the rest of the week goes."

Blake stood in front of the refrigerator, staring inside. "Man, I need to go to the store."

"I don't want anything to drink. I just wanted to say hi a minute," Bo said.

Blake joined him at the kitchen table. "I can't believe we haven't had the chance to do anything since I've been home. It's like everything's on fast forward. I've been working on these initial plans, and I have changes I think legitimately need to happen, but it's throwing everything out of whack. I want to get my head around it before I present it to Chase and the team. Seanna and I are meeting with Sebastian for lunch to try to make sense of it. Have you ever worked with him on anything financial?"

"No. Should I?" Bo asked.

"Oh, yeah. I think he's one of the smartest guys I've ever known."

Bo would keep that info in his back pocket. He knocked twice on the table. "I'm gonna get out of your hair. I just wanted to say hi." He stood up.

"No, man. Sit. I've got a minute. I've got all damn day if you need me. What's going on?"

Bo stared at him and then reluctantly sat, feeling silly about coming to his doctor friend who was opening a new medical center about his girl troubles. "It's not anything. I'm just…I don't know." He scratched his ear while heat crept up his neck.

"What is it?" Blake asked. "Everything okay with Shayla?"

"Yeah, she's fine."

"Will she still be here Saturday? I want us all to hook up before she goes back. Let's get that on the calendar."

Bo didn't think he'd seen Blake talk this much since he'd known him. "I'll get with her about a good time when she gets here. I just…I've been sort of seeing someone this week."

A light bulb went off over Blake's head. "That's right. Chase mentioned you two went on a date with a couple of girls. Sebastian's friends, right?"

"Yeah."

Blake backhanded him. "That's great. Tell me about her."

Bo picked at the placemat in front of him. "Well, she's from Indianapolis for starters." Blake nodded, and Bo eyed him. "You know how I am about that."

"Yeah, I know, but this is different."

Bo frowned. "How do you know?"

"Because you're sitting here telling me about her. That alone says that you're into this girl more than I've seen you into anybody through the past few years."

Bo looked down at the table. "That's not totally off-base."

"Have you slept with her yet?" Blake asked.

Bo met his gaze. "No, but I've spent time with her every day for the past four days. I just finished running with her. That's why I stink so bad."

"I'm used to your stench." Blake grinned, and then his expression turned back serious. "What's got you holding back?"

Bo looked around the room for his balls. "What's the point?"

"Well, one point is to see how it goes, see if it's more than just a passing attraction."

"This is different. I've never felt like this after such a short time. I'm into her, man. She's smart and successful, and she takes immaculate care of body, way better than I do. She's confident, but there's no bravado there. She's the real deal. She makes me want to do better so I can impress her. She's exactly what I've been bellyaching about wanting to find."

Blake nodded, taking it all in.

"Doesn't matter though. She's headed out of town Saturday morning. She won't even get to meet Shayla." Bo picked up the tip of the placemat and dropped it back down.

"I've got an idea," Blake said. "How about you take the pressure off. This is just a moment in time. It doesn't have to hold the weight you're giving it. Do you think she wants to have sex?"

"Yeah," he said. "She called me out for wussing out on her about it."

Blake sat back in his chair. "Then just go for it. Have fun. Don't overthink it."

Bo stared at the table, vaguely aware of some

sort of complicated music in the background. "What are you listening to?"

Blake narrowed his gaze. "Have you dated anyone seriously since your ex?" he asked, ignoring Bo's question.

Bo thought about it. Six years had passed since she'd walked out of his life. Surely there'd been someone he'd dated who he'd developed real feelings for. He scratched his head. "I've had some relationships since her."

"Serious ones?"

He'd spent a few months hanging out with certain women, but those relationships had remained casual, until they hadn't, at which point he would usually back out slowly. "Not particularly."

"You a little nervous about stepping into something serious?" Blake held up a hand. "You'd have every right to feel that way after what she put you through."

Bo didn't want to think about that time in his life. "It's not that."

"Are you sure?"

"Maya's going home Saturday. That's the issue here."

Blake lifted his eyebrows. "Is it?"

Bo pursed his lips at Blake, starting to get frustrated. "That's not what this is about."

"Okay," Blake said. "Then just walk away."

Bo felt himself recoil.

"Well, what's the point?" Blake asked.

Bo narrowed his gaze. "Is this one of your Jedi mind tricks?"

"There's ways to keep in touch with this girl

when she leaves. We have these things called cell phones now."

"It's not the same as being with someone. I can't move there. I've got my business. And she can't move here, because she's starting a new job. This is stupid we're even talking about it." He stood up again.

Blake leaned back in his seat. "It's not stupid. It's just complicated. Just relax into this for now. Deal with one day at a time. We'll figure out the next steps later, okay?"

Bo eyed him. "Like you don't have better things to do."

"Are you fucking kidding me? I owe you about ten grand in therapy bills from when you talked me through this same shit with Seanna." He held up a hand. "Different circumstances, thank God, but you know what I mean."

Bo smiled. "Yeah. I think it worked out okay for you though. Are we still all set for tomorrow?"

Blake waved him off. "Oh, no man. I'll get Chase to come with me."

"Hell no. I'm going with you. The time away will help me clear my head. We'll be back Thursday, right?"

"Yeah. Of course," Blake said.

"All right," Bo said, clasping Blake's shoulder. "Thanks, man." He headed for the door.

"Oh, wait. I've got something for you." Blake disappeared into his bedroom and came back out with a box. "For you. I don't need them anymore." He grinned like a kid on Christmas.

Bo held up the box of condoms. "Are they extra-large?"

"Of course they are," Blake said. "Don't get lost in them."

Bo flipped him off and headed for his truck.

Chapter Ten

Maya sat out by Sebastian's pool holding a novel. She'd tried to read the same page for the past twenty minutes, but she had zero focus. She finally gave up and lay back in the chaise, soaking the late afternoon sun into her skin. She took in the moment and the fact that she was on vacation. As her co-workers were wrapping up their days and fighting five o'clock traffic, she was poolside in one of the quaintest little beach towns she'd ever seen. All she was missing was someone to share the experience with.

Felicity was still out on the boat with Chase, and Sebastian had mysteriously left the house a half hour prior. He'd told them before they'd even arrived that he was going to be tied up on Tuesday night, but he wouldn't say why or what he was doing. Maya suspected he had a date. He was so tight-lipped about his love life. He didn't want anyone knowing a thing about any boy he was seeing until he was serious about them. Smart, but boring. Talking about your crush was half the fun of having one.

Thinking about crushes, hers would not get out of her head. He was the reason she couldn't read her novel. Thoughts of his body, his lips, his charm, filled her head and gave her a perm-a-smile.

Her phone chirped, and she was almost irritated by its interruption of her thoughts of him. She pulled it off of the table next to her and readied herself for a text from Felicity letting her know when she'd be home.

Her heart skipped two beats as his name appeared with a message.

Hey. I was just thinking about you. Are you being good this afternoon?

She bit her lip, her belly doing the shuffle.

I've got the place to myself. I'm getting ready to dance on the kitchen table with the lampshade on my head. Want to join me?

She took a long, deep breath, and waited for his response.

Really?

The perm-a-smile was now hurting her face.

Really. :)

I'll see you in half an hour. Don't get too crazy before I get there.

I'm out by the pool. I've got my bathing suit on.

Be there in fifteen minutes.

She grinned and scurried into the house and up to her room where she checked everything in the mirror. She wanted to look good but didn't want to overdo it. She sprayed herself with coconut body spray and checked her hair and makeup, then went back down to the pool to impatiently await his arrival.

The groan of his engine moved closer until it cut off, making her heart flutter in her chest. She attempted to look cool and collected, nonchalant. Har har.

As the lock on the gate jingled, she casually flipped a page in her novel. He walked toward her sporting long, royal blue swim trunks with white trim and a plain white T-shirt. The man singlehandedly redefined the word blazing.

She pretended to finish a paragraph and set her bookmark in its place. "How are you?"

"I'm good. How'd you get the place to yourself?" He took the seat next to her and tossed his bag aside.

"Felicity's out with your buddy again, and I think Sebastian's on a date."

"I heard Chase was taking Felicity on the boat today. We better keep our eye on them. They're bound to wind up in Vegas or something."

"Oh, you don't have to worry about Felicity. She's a serial soloist."

"That's right. I forgot about the comment about her feeling mummified."

Maya shook her head. "That's Felicity."

He narrowed his gaze at her. "What about you? Do relationships make you feel good or like you've got on an itchy sweater?"

Her heart warmed at the idea of him asking. Not that she was reading anything into it. That'd be stupid. She adjusted herself on the chair. "I guess it depends on the guy. I've had two long-term relationships. Looking back now though, they seemed more like friendships with occasional sex."

"You ever been engaged?"

She hesitated. "No."

He flicked a bug off his knee. "You sure about that?"

"Well, with Al, my most recent ex, we always talked about it like it was inevitable. 'We'll go there for our honeymoon,' or, 'Let's wait to get the king-sized bed when we buy a house once we're married.' But he never asked, and I never really wanted him to, honestly."

"Why did you stay with him? Sex too good to leave?" he asked with a grin.

She got a chuckle just at the thought of that. "No. It was very scheduled. Saturday nights were date night, every week. We'd come home, pull the comforter back, get in, and go through the same routine. I timed it once. The whole production took five minutes and twenty-four seconds from start to finish."

He frowned. "Damn. That's harsh."

She giggled. "I can't believe I just told you that." She met his curious gaze and wondered why she didn't just keep her mouth shut more often. "What about you? Have you ever had five-minute sex?"

"Fuck no."

She smiled, rolling her eyes. "Of course you haven't."

"What's that supposed to mean?"

She motioned at him. "Look at you. Of course

you don't have five-minute sex."

A grin tugged at his lips. "What's wrong with me?"

She gave him a look. "Don't even try the coy thing with me, Bo." He smiled in concession and gripped the bar above his head. She swore he did that to show off his muscles...like he needed to. "Tell me about your last relationship," she said.

"Mmm," he grunted, closing his eyes.

"I don't suppose someone like you has relationships."

He opened one eye. "Of course I do."

"Long-term?"

He closed the eye again. "Not recently."

"How come?" she asked, though she hated it when people asked her why she was still single. "Don't answer that, actually."

He turned to meet her gaze. "Why?"

"Because I hate it when people ask me that question, like the default is to be married and have kids, and if that's not the path you chose, there must be some logical reason. How about it just never happened."

"That was going to be my excuse."

She studied him. "Would you ever want to be married?"

He dropped his arms down to his sides. "Yeah, actually I would."

She could have been wiped away with a feather duster. "Really?"

"Yeah. Is that weird?"

She laughed. "It's actually the opposite of weird. So now I really do want to know why you're still single."

"I thought you hated that question."

"Yeah, but if you wanted to be married, you totally could be."

"Well, I don't know about that. I'm not married, am I?"

"No, but you're…" She trailed off, realizing she was getting ready to have diarrhea of the mouth. "Never mind."

He sat up. "I'm what?"

She swung her legs to the side of the chair. "Wanna get in?" She headed that way before he could protest.

She sat on the side of the pool, dangling her feet in. She heard the rapid footsteps behind her and ducked as he jumped in with a big splash. He emerged from the water with her ankles in his hands. He set each of them on his shoulders, and then wiped the water out of his eyes. He wrapped his arms around the bottoms of her legs and let her hold his weightless body. She lifted him up out of the water and dropped him back in, smiling.

He pushed away from her, and when she folded her legs down, he came back over and rested his chin on her knee. "I never got married because I never found the right girl."

"Are you picky?" she asked.

"Maybe. I don't know. It's hard down here. The population of PCB is really small. All those people running around don't actually live there. I feel like I've already dated most everyone who does."

She lifted an eyebrow. "You get around, don't you?"

He spread her legs open and moved in between them, firing up her core. Wrapping her legs around his back, she brought him closer to her.

"I've never dated anyone like you," he said, his words taking her by surprise. That was her line.

"What do you mean, like me?"

He shrugged, floating away from her but hanging onto her knees. "Professional, really smart and driven, refined."

This was how he saw her? She wished she had a pen so she could write down all the words he just used to describe her and analyze them later. Why was her phone so far away? She furrowed her brow. "Thank you."

"I didn't really mean any of that as a compliment. It's just how I see you."

She was really curious now. "What are the girls you usually date like?"

He shrugged. "Well, these are tourist towns we live in. The locals work food service and retail. I mean, I've dated plenty of smart women, and sweet women, sometimes both qualities at the same time. But I'm a pool guy. The classy ladies don't usually want much from me past a fun night." He squeezed her knees with a smile. "Is that all you want from me? Sex that lasts longer than five minutes?"

She wasn't sure how to respond to this. From the second she saw him, she thought he naturally held all the cards because of how monstrously sexy he was, but for the first time this week, she realized she may be more in the driver's seat than she had thought.

She always felt in control of the relationship

when she dated the nerds back home, but she could take those guys or leave them. And there were plenty of them to choose from. She had a lot to offer a nerdy guy—good, stable job that paid well, her own house in a nice neighborhood, a trim body that she worked extremely hard to maintain. She never thought she was the prettiest girl in the room, but she always took very good care of herself, making sure all areas of her body that shouldn't have hair didn't, having her nails manicured weekly, keeping her hair trimmed every six weeks, and generally making herself presentable at all times.

She knew she had those superficial things to offer Bo for the week, but she didn't have a big rack of boobs like that young girl who hopped in his lap at the bar that first night, and she didn't have long, sexy, beach hair. Her hair was way too baby fine for that. She guessed she hadn't thought about what she had to offer him, but he'd just made her feel like she had more than she realized.

She hopped down in the pool with him, but once she got there, she lost her nerve. Should she tell him that he was the most interesting man she'd met, and she wanted way more with him than sex, even if just in theory? And was that what she wanted?

He wrapped his arms around her waist, and she rested her hands around his shoulders. "You're a pool-cleaning business owner. Don't sell yourself short."

He cupped her behind and hiked her up onto his waist. "What are you down here looking for, darlin'?" he asked, his voice low like a growl.

She hadn't been looking for anything but a week

of catching up with Sebastian and Felicity until she met him. Her boss had made her take this vacation. When he'd offered her the job, he'd disclosed how much extra pressure would come with the VP title, and that'd been just fine with her. Work was her life. She'd been ready to jump in right then, but he'd insisted she take a break and get rejuvenated to avoid burnout. Yet he continued to call, but that was beside the point.

What was she doing talking like she wanted more than sex from Bo? She had a job back home, one she'd put in over a decade's time for. She was getting everything she'd worked for not to mention a huge salary bump. This was what vacations did to people. They made them lose sight of what was important.

She pulled away from him. "I'm so rude. I didn't offer you a drink." She climbed up the ladder and grabbed her towel. "What do you want?"

He pulled himself up out of the water onto the side of the pool, his muscles working with the effort. Look away from the muscles.

"Drinks are one thing I'm not picky about." He reached for her arm, that single touch sending a jolt of want through her body. "I can go though, if you want to hang solo?"

The idea of him walking away sent a small panic through her chest. "No," she said in a rush. "I mean, I'm just thirsty. I don't want you to leave."

He gauged her, searching her eyes, and so she reached up, snaking her hand around the back of his neck and giving him a kiss. "I'll be right back, okay?"

He nodded, and she headed off. She found some berry-flavored seltzer water and some vodka and poured drinks into plastic cups. Alcohol was good. She didn't make a habit of it mainly because of the calories and how it slowed her metabolism, but when she did indulge, it always helped calm her nerves.

She exhaled a deep breath, recalibrating, and headed back out to the pool. He lay on the chaise lounge, his knees open to the sides, his hands behind his head, eyes closed, full lips relaxed, the sun casting a shimmer on his wet chest. She'd never seen a more beautiful and sculpted body than that one, and she'd definitely never touched one. Al ran with her, but he was skinny. He didn't lift. David was a little pudgy, but she'd liked that. His imperfect body made her feel secure. She wanted to be the more attractive one in the couple so the men she was with wouldn't be as likely to cheat. God knows women weren't lined up to be with either of her exes. How would she feel about being with a man who could walk out the door and have women drool over him? Not could…would.

He opened his eyes and held out his hand. "Thanks."

She sat, taking a long drink before setting her cup down. "So, you mentioned your sister is coming to town Saturday."

"Yeah, you'll just miss her. She's coming down for a few days of vacation, visit the family."

"Is she younger or older?"

"Older by eleven months, but we were in the same year in school."

She thought about how their birthdays must fall, since his was just this past Saturday. "So how did you end up in the same grade?"

"My mom held Shayla back from starting kindergarten on time. She said it was because Shayla was too small, but I don't think that was it. She'd always treated Shayla and me like twins, dressing us in matching clothes she made and all that. I think she held her back because she didn't have a clue what to do with me by myself for a year. Shayla and I were attached at the hip." He smiled. "Shayla says it was because I cried like a baby when my mom told me Shayla was going to school and I wasn't."

She couldn't grin hard enough thinking of little four-year-old Bo crying. "Is she married?"

"Nah, but she's in a relationship now."

"Do you like the guy?"

"He seems all right. I don't know him all that well since they don't live here."

She cradled her drink in her hand. "You miss her?" she asked, knowing the answer.

"We talk every day, but I do miss having her here to aggravate."

"That sounds so nice, having a family member you're so close with."

He turned toward her "You mentioned your sister already, but tell me about your parents."

Maya's heart strained like it always did when she talked about her family. "My dad's a lawyer. My mother is his paralegal. Lots of structure, lots of expectation."

"You didn't want to follow in their footsteps

with the law?"

"That was my sister's job. I didn't want to do the same thing."

"How come?"

She wiggled a little, trying to get comfortable in the chair. "My sister's really smart."

"So are you."

She loved how he said that with such certainty. "Thank you, but Meade's much smarter. She's got the IQ of a genius. I mean, she can't help it. It's not like she asked to be the smartest person in the room. But I just…" She clenched her hand into a fist, and then shook her head. "Sorry. Never mind."

"What?" he asked. "Tell me."

"She does this thing with men—boys, I should call them. She's this brilliant woman with every possible opportunity in her reach, but then a good-looking guy comes along and she just dissolves. She's a feminist's nightmare. I mean, she could be out there curing cancer or balancing the national budget, but she's currently living in Las Vegas of all places, working at a casino dealing cards and dating some new guy who is undoubtedly living with her and taking whatever little money she has." She shook her head. "I'm sorry. I didn't mean to unleash all that on you."

He sat up and faced her, his feet on the ground between them. "Hey, don't ever apologize to me for talking about something that's important to you. Do you hear me?"

She nodded, staring down into her cup, her heart ridiculously warmed by him.

"Go on," he said.

She scratched her eyebrow, glancing at his concerned expression. She'd never had a straight guy so interested in what she had to say. It made her feel okay to continue. "It's just really frustrating. I have to work ten times as hard as she does. I always have. So I'm over here working sixty-hour weeks for a decade to finally make VP, and Meade isn't even trying. But mind you, she could walk out of that stupid casino today, and with very little effort have any job on the planet she wanted." She glanced at him to make sure he still seem interested, and he did, so she kept going. "When she was in law school, one of her professors set up this special interview with the Air Force. She'd scored so high on some test that they were ready to fast-track her to work in some top-secret department. Then just before she was set to enlist, she met Rob." She shook her head, rolling her eyes. "I just can't understand it."

He took her hand. "That's gotta be hard. You love her, and you want what's best for her."

"I really do. I mean, don't get me wrong, I get tired of having to be the responsible one—the one who gives my parents something they can feel okay talking about when people ask them how their girls are, but I really do want her to live better. I beg her to move back to Indy all the time. If I could just be with her more, I could help her." She narrowed her gaze, thinking about Meade and her choices. "I've never said this aloud before, but sometimes I wonder if there's not some mental illness there." She slid her gaze to his concerned one. He didn't give her a reaction, just his full attention. She gave a humorless smile. "Sort of like a mad scientist, you know?"

He nodded. "I think there's a lot of undiagnosed mental illness out there. Not that I think that about your sister. I don't know her, of course." He narrowed his gaze at her. "Have you ever thought that maybe she's the fuckup because she can be?"

Maya furrowed her brow, taking him in.

"I mean, you're pretty on point, Maya. You've got a stable job. You're in immaculate shape. I assume you have a nice house or apartment?"

She shrugged in concession.

"Maybe that's as much for her to live up to as her brainpower is for you."

She flinched at the idea of Meade's poor life choices having something to do with her success. Agitated, she got up and walked to the pool, drink in hand. "Is Shayla your only sibling?"

"No, I have a brother."

"Oh," she said, a little surprised since he hadn't mentioned him yet. "Does he have a family?"

He followed her over there and sat next to her on the side of the pool. "Parker is ten and Kaden just turned eight." He smiled to himself, watching his feet wade in the water.

"Are you crazy about them?"

"Between Shayla, my parents, and me, they're spoiled plenty. Cindy and Dale get upset with us for giving them too much."

"Do you ever take them out?"

"Oh, yeah. See, I'm the fun uncle who gets to take them to the monster truck rallies and the racetrack, make sure they grow up good and red."

She smiled. "Do you want them? Kids?"

He set his drink down and lifted himself up, dropping down into the pool. "Get in with me," he said.

Her unanswered question hung between them. It was a pointless thing to ask. In fact, their whole conversation was pointless. Why were they taking such care to get to know one another? Were they both just stalling? Because she didn't feel so much anymore that she was the cat in this cat-and-mouse game they'd been playing all week.

Dropping into the pool and resting her elbows on the side, she opened her hands. "I'm all in."

He gave her a closed-mouth grin and backed away, resting against the other side of the pool. "You sure about that?"

Her body had no clue how to process the frenzy this man incited within her. She grabbed an inner tube that floated by and pulled it over her head. "Tell me about your family. What were you all like growing up?"

He shrugged, taking a sip of his drink, licking his lips as he swallowed. "I had a good childhood, other than the fact that we didn't have a lot of money. I ate plenty of potato chip and tuna fish casseroles as a kid." He winced at the memory.

She put her hand to her mouth. "Tuna fish and potato chips in a casserole?"

"Poor people food. We also ate a lot of rice and beans." She had to look away, thinking of all the elaborate restaurants her family had gone to when she was growing up. "But we were pretty happy, at least when Dale and I were getting along, which

139

was never, come to think of it."

"What's your mom like?"

"Tough. Shayla's just like her. She'd come after our behinds with a spatula if we acted up, which was pretty much every day. We'd fall in line after a couple of whacks." He grinned.

"You were spanked?" Maya asked, a little mortified.

He walked to the float and grabbed it, holding it steady. "You've never been spanked?"

"No." She cleared her throat. "What about your dad? What was he like?"

He frowned. "That's a story for another time, but he's good now."

She wondered what was going on there, but knew better than to push. "Do you see them a lot?"

"Every Sunday for supper."

She so wanted to be a fly on the wall for one of those dinners, or even better, attend one. "So who was the one who instilled all those manners in you?"

He pointed at his chest. "I've got manners?"

She pinched his arm. "You know you do. All that door opening and stuff."

"If my mom caught me letting a lady open her own door she'd tan my hide, even today. Made Dale and me practice all the time on her and Shayla." He chuckled. "Shayla would stick her tongue out at me right after she said thank you."

She smiled. "I'm sorry I won't meet her."

He nodded, looking down at the float between them, silence hanging there. He squinted at her. "Could you stay till Sunday?"

Her stomach soured. "We can't. Felicity has to get back for her mother's birthday, and I've got a company picnic on Sunday at my boss's house." Her face warmed. "It's actually sort of in honor of some big changes at the firm, one of them being my promotion. Not totally about me though, of course."

"But enough about you that you've got to be there."

She nodded, grossly disappointed.

"Man, this must be a really big deal. That's awesome."

She smiled, appreciating his sincerity. "Thanks." She pulled the float off of her. "So how did you become friends with Sebastian?"

"Through Blake. You met him the other night, right?"

"Briefly, yes. He's a doctor, right?"

"Yeah," he said with a proud smile that left her curious.

"So how do you know him?"

"I know Blake through Chase, who I've known for a while. I handle all the pools at all the properties he owns and manages around 30A and PCB."

"How does Blake know Chase?"

His brow furrowed, his mouth set in an O like he was trying to choose his words wisely. She had just been teasing him, acting like she was quizzing him, but now she was curious.

"Blake used to do work for Chase."

"Medical work?"

He squinted, thinking. "Not particularly. He's multi-talented. He can fix damn near anything."

141

"And Desiree and Ashe?" she asked.

"Friends of Sebastian's."

"And Cassidy and Seanna?"

He had to think about it. "Through Sebastian? Or maybe Blake. One or both of them knew Cassidy through the bakery she owns, Seaside Sweets. Seanna just came around last fall. She's Cassidy's niece."

She smiled, taking his hand and threading her fingers through. "You've got a really unique group of friends."

He pulled her closer to him. "You don't have to tell me that. I'm sure you've got your own interesting group of friends back home."

She did have friends in Indy, people she'd called friends for more than a decade. But she only saw each of those people once every six months or so, probably less than that if she was being honest with herself. Most of her friends had husbands and kids now. Their lives had taken different paths. She hadn't had a tight-knit group like the circle of friends here since she was in high school. She was too busy.

"I mostly hang out with people from work." She realized how it sounded as she said it. She had a life outside of work, she just couldn't seem to figure out what that life consisted of at the moment.

"So you know Sebastian from high school?" he asked.

She huffed a laugh. "Yeah. This is funny. I totally had a crush on him."

Bo frowned. "On Sebastian?"

"Let's just say my gaydar wasn't fine-tuned back

then. It didn't last long. I figured it out after I asked him to the Sadie Hawkins dance, and he wanted to shop for matching outfits together."

He looked up at the sky in thought, holding their clasped hands out to each side, pulling her in closer to him. "I guess Sebastian's a pretty good-looking guy, now that I think about it."

"I think he looks like Brad Goreski without the glasses."

"Who?" he asked.

She shook her head. Of course Bo wouldn't know who that was. He backed her up, trapping her with his hands on the edge of the pool on either side of her. Her heart skittered with his close proximity to her, their bodies already half-naked in their swimsuits. She twitched a little nervously. "I think you look a little like Channing Tatum," he pulled away, eyebrow raised as she ran her thumb along his shoulder, "but sort of with the swagger of Mark Wahlberg." She bit her lip and met his gaze.

He slid his hands over her hips and up her waist. "Well, I'll try to keep up. But don't expect to see me dancing like either one of them anytime soon." He lifted her and set her on the side of the pool, water sliding down her legs as he ran his hands from her knees up her thighs.

Want on a level she had never experienced before surged through her core as his hands drew closer to her center. He teased her, moving them from her knees, up her thighs, and back to her knees, each time getting a little closer. He spread her legs apart and moved in close to her, easing his hands around to her back as he traced kisses on her belly. She arched instinctively, leaning back, giving him an open canvas to work on.

She rested on her elbows while he trailed kisses down her thighs, nibbling at her skin, and then soothing the spots with his tongue. She'd never done anything like this. These moments were reserved for bedrooms with lights out, not broad daylight out in the open. And God knew a man had never evoked intrigue and arousal inside of her like this one.

He worked his way back up to her stomach and nipped at her bathing suit bottom. He curled both fingers inside the straps on her hips and tugged on it. She lifted each side so he could get the bottoms off, and glanced around, feeling more exposed than she ever had.

He looked up at her. "Nobody can see here. That's an eight-foot privacy fence."

He was right. Unless someone came back there, they were safe, but that wasn't the issue. She put her fingertips to her temple. "I know. It's just that I've never done this outside."

"You want to go inside?" he asked.

She would die if Sebastian came home to her locked away in his guest bedroom with Bo. Did she think it was better for him to find them in his pool?

She closed her legs, pressing her knuckle against her forehead. "I'm not chickening out, I promise."

He frowned, looking a little concerned, or maybe hurt. "I'm sorry if I came on too strong."

"No!" she said, grabbing his shoulders. "You have not come on strong enough, believe me. I'm glad we're to this point. I just feel a little exposed out here in the sun and all. And Felicity may be home soon."

He stepped away from her and took her hands. "Come here. Hop down."

She slid into the pool and pulled her bottoms back up. Taking her into his arms, he just held her there, rocking back and forth a little. She closed her eyes, resting her cheek on his shoulder, letting their wet bodies meld together.

"I want to be with you, Maya," he said, his tone low and genuine. "But I don't want you to be any kind of uncomfortable when that happens, okay?"

She squeezed him tighter to her, threatening to give away how much she cared about him. "I'm not uncomfortable with you at all. I promise."

He pulled away from her. "Why don't we both get showers, and then we'll go get something to eat in PCB. And after that, if you're up for it, we can go back to my house."

She smiled. "I'll definitely be up for it."

Chapter Eleven

Bo was on his third round of Solitaire as he waited for Maya to come downstairs. He hoped like hell he hadn't spooked her off earlier. He was no stranger to messing around with a girl at a pool, or in the Gulf of Mexico for that matter. But he understood why it freaked her out and was pissed at himself for putting her in that position. He had to do better next time.

His heart ballooned as she walked down the steps in a black and white sundress that showed off her smooth shoulders and arms. He stood. "You look beautiful."

She smiled. "You cleaned up well, too. I'm glad you brought those clothes."

"I didn't want to drive home wet."

"Yeah, hate it when that happens." She laughed a little, and his stomach did that fizzy thing again.

He put her in his truck, and they headed down

30A toward PCB. He liked it in South Walton, but Panama City Beach was his home and he was looking forward to letting her see a little of his town.

She pointed. "Oh, look. Is that Pier Park?"

"Yeah. You want to go there and eat?"

"You probably wanted to take me to some place only the locals know about."

"I just want to take you where you want to go."

She scrunched up her little nose. "I kind of want to go there."

He wheeled it into the parking lot and found a place. Holding her hand as they walked past the shops seemed like the most natural thing in the world, like they could have done it a thousand times before.

"How about here?" she asked.

"You do know that's a pub, don't you?"

She shrugged. "I can eat pub food for a night."

"Really? You won't resent me in the morning for taking you there?"

She crossed her heart. "Promise."

"All right." He held the door open for her, and kept holding it for a couple of girls who were coming out.

"Bo," one of them said.

He blinked Jennifer into recognition as she brought him in for a hug. "Hey," he said into her hair. Jennifer wasn't someone who gave him a good feeling, but he'd known her since high school and she was sort of a PCB staple. There was no avoiding her.

She tapped him on the chest with the back of her

147

hand. "What are you doing? Come with us. We're headed two doors down. We're meeting Sam and them. They'd love to see you." She looked him up and down. "And so would I."

He looked over at Maya, who had walked a few steps away from him. He had no desire to mix those two worlds, but he didn't want Maya to think he was ashamed to introduce her to people he knew. "I'm here with someone." He held out his hand, motioning Maya over, and she stepped toward him. "Maya, this is Jennifer and Tiffany. We went to high school together."

Jennifer looked Maya over. "What, are you here on vacation?"

"Yes," Maya said.

Jennifer nodded with a hint of an eye roll that he hoped Maya didn't catch, but there was no missing the look she gave Bo, like he was the biggest cliché on the planet. She got a wicked smile on her face. "I saw Angela last week. She's working over in Destin. Asked if I'd seen you. Wanted to know if you'd gotten married yet." She shook her head, hand on her hip. "Girl couldn't catch a clue with a net."

The last thing on earth he wanted was to be talking about Angela at that moment, especially with Jennifer, who had the biggest mouth in the panhandle, and right in front of Maya. He had such a small amount of time with her, and digging into his distant past wasn't something he wanted filling that space. He put his hand on Maya's lower back, starting to guide her away. "Good to see you both."

"You leaving this weekend?" Jennifer asked

Maya.

Maya frowned. "Um, yes."

Jennifer scooted toward the door, giving Bo the eyes. "Call me next week."

She made the request like it was something he usually did. He hadn't called Jennifer since he was fifteen years old. She was just marking her territory or something pointless like that. He was usually proud of who he was and where he came from, but it was moments like that he wished he didn't live where the whole town knew his business.

The hostess sat them and handed menus over with an extra-long gaze at Bo before heading off. He leaned in toward Maya. "I'm sorry about that at the door. She's not a close friend."

"That's okay." She smiled, but he could tell she was curious. She opened her menu, but then in a second she asked, "Who's Angela?"

His gut churned, and he scratched his eyebrow. "My ex."

"Oh," Maya said, still looking over her menu. He said a quick prayer to anyone who'd listen to please let that be the end of that conversation.

"How long were you together?"

That was the one question he didn't want to answer. "We were together in college." That was true, but enough guilt built up in his gut that he had to clarify, "And after."

Bo'd never been happier to see a waiter in his life. He took his time having the poor guy repeat what they had on tap and making conversation about local versus imported beer, hoping to distract from any further discussion of Angela.

After he left, Bo met Maya's gaze. "I'm really impressed that you didn't get a salad."

She leaned across the table like she was giving away government secrets. "I love fried oysters. I bet I haven't had them in a decade."

"You're on vacation. You should have whatever you want."

"I shouldn't really. I've been so regimented for so long, I'm not sure what would happen if I jumped off my train."

He'd asked her earlier what she was here looking for, and she'd very blatantly avoided the question. But he wanted an answer. He'd have to find another way to ask it. He glanced around the place. "I want the record to reflect that you picked this spot for this date. I was going to take you to a fancy place. I'm sure that's what you're used to." She sipped her water, giving away her answer. "Where's the last place you went on a date?" he asked.

"Oh," she said, staring off in the distance like she was thinking. She rolled her eyes. "Trust me. This is better."

"What happened?"

"This guy I used to work with asked me out. I never date anyone at the company. But he'd moved on, and I kind of did like him, what little I knew of him, so when he called, I went."

Bo hated him already.

"He wanted me to meet him at Chili's, which was okay, but it was half-off margarita night and he got wasted."

"He drank margaritas?"

She chuckled. "He drank so much that he, well,

let's just say his body rejected them."

"There at the table?"

"All over the bar. Poor bartender had to clean it all up."

Bo shook his head in disgust. "Unbelievable."

"Oh, believe it."

"I hope you left his ass there."

"I called a couple of the girls from work. Luckily, one knew where he lived, so the bartender and I got him in a car. I felt terrible for that poor driver. I gave a huge tip."

He considered her, knowing that look in a woman's eye. "Did the bartender ask you out?"

She looked up at him quickly. "How did you know?"

"'Cause you smiled a little when you referred to him."

She rubbed her thumb over her water glass. "You're really perceptive."

"So what happened to him?"

"Oh, he never called me again."

"I meant the bartender."

"Oh." She looked down at her placemat. "I don't know."

"Did you go out with him?" he asked.

"No."

"How come?"

She inhaled a deep breath and scrunched up her face. "I can't go there."

He frowned, not taking her for a snob. "Really?"

She grabbed his arm across the table. He liked how familiar she was getting with him. "No, not because I thought I was better than him or anything like that. God, no. It was just that he was really nice-looking."

Bo was confused. "That's a problem for you?"

She sat up tall and straightened out her dress. "Well, yeah. I mean…I don't date hot guys."

All he could do was laugh at that one. "Boy."

She grabbed both his arms that time. "No, this is coming out wrong. I usually don't date hot guys. Obviously, I'm making an exception this week." He let her off the hook with a grin, and she let go of his arms.

"What's wrong with hot guys?"

She made a little moaning noise. "Let's just say I'm more comfortable with nerdy guys." She met his gaze. "I really didn't want to disclose this fact about myself, by the way."

"How come?"

"Because. You don't know the person I am at home. I kind of like the mystery of that."

He narrowed his gaze at her. "Are you hiding something from me, Maya?"

She bit on her pointer finger. "No," she said quietly. The server set two beers down in front of them. "Thanks," she said.

He nodded at it. "Are you gonna be able to drink that?"

She picked it up by the handle. "Absolutely. I'm at a pub. I'm not ordering wine." She took a sip and then winced a little.

"Do you want something else?"

She shook her head, closing one eye. "Nope."

He sat back in his chair, holding the handle of his beer mug. "So what does a nerdy guy have that I don't have?" He wasn't as rich as Chase, but he did well, and she made him want to do better.

"You scare me a little."

He frowned. "Like how?"

She gave him a look, and then leaned in. "Call me next week," she said, sounding more like Jennifer than he cared for.

He closed his eyes, realizing he shouldn't have thought he could get off that easy. He met her gaze. "You have to know I'm not into her."

"Honestly, I don't think you are." She glanced around. "You don't seem to know other women are alive when you're with me." She nodded at the bar. "Have you seen these two?"

He turned to find two girls sitting at the bar, each glancing at him and looking away. "I hadn't noticed them."

"They've been staring at you since the little scene at the door earlier. And what about that hostess?"

He rolled his eyes. "I did notice that."

She tossed up her hands. "How do you manage it all? It must be exhausting."

"There's nothing to manage."

"Do you know how many women stared at or hit on Al when we were together?" She held up her thumb and finger in the shape of a zero.

"Five-minute guy?"

She gave a hint of a grin. "Yes, five-minute guy."

"All right, so you're with a guy like me, and you have to worry about other girls looking at him, but then at least you get to go home and have decent sex."

"Do I?" she asked, eyebrow raised.

He ran his tongue over the back of his teeth. "Fuck yes."

The waiter appeared with their baskets of food. Maya inhaled a deep breath, then gave the guy a huge smile. "Thank you."

He smiled back at her. "You're welcome."

After the guy got out of earshot, Bo leaned in. "You're one to talk."

"What?" she looked genuinely perplexed, which was really damn cute.

He pointed to their waiter at a table a few down from theirs. "He was just smiling at you."

She rolled her eyes. "Bo, that guy is like twenty-five."

"So."

"So, he doesn't see me like that."

"How the hell do you know?"

She rolled her eyes again and popped in an oyster.

He leaned in. "Let's get something straight. You're fucking hot. I don't know if five-minute guy or whoever the hell else you've dated has ever told you that or not, but believe me, I've dated enough girls along the Florida panhandle to assemble an army, and I've never been prouder to have a woman on my arm than I am tonight." He took a hard bite of his chicken tender and stared at her while he chewed.

She, on the other hand, had stopped mid-chew during his rant. She sat up straight, tucking her hair behind her ear, smoothed her napkin out in her lap, and then went for her purse. He stared at her curiously, eating a French fry. He was about to ask if she was mad at him when she grabbed their waiter who was walking by.

She handed him a card. "Please run this card for all this stuff here, quickly." The guy nodded and headed off. She picked up another oyster from her basket and pointed at Bo's chicken tenders with it. "Eat fast. We're going to your house as soon as he gets back."

Chapter Twelve

A large, black and tan dog met them at the door to Bo's house. "Go on," Bo commanded, pointing to a sliding glass door across the living room. "I'll put his food outside. Give me just a minute."

She took the opportunity to scan the room and check out his bachelor pad, taking in another piece of him that she was excited to get to see. It fit what she knew of him—older, comfortable-feeling home with a big, cozy sectional sitting in front of a flat screen that stretched farther than the TV stand. Her attention was drawn to a photo in a frame on a shelf by the couch—a younger version of him dressed in a tux with his arm around a stunning, black-haired girl in what looked like a bridesmaid dress wearing a no-nonsense smile on her face. Maya took a step closer, noticing how alike the two of them looked. She wondered if it was Shayla.

He shut the sliding glass door, and she jumped a

little, feeling sort of caught, though she wasn't being sneaky. "That was Jake. You can meet him later." He drew her in to him pressing his lips against hers, opening her mouth with his.

She let him lead the way, melting into his kiss. He ran his hands down her back, resting them on her bottom, and walked her backward toward the hallway. He finally broke away and took her hand, leading her to his bedroom where he wasted no time pulling her dress off over her head. She stood exposed to him, nothing on now but her matching strapless bra and thong. Instead of feeling exposed like she had at the pool earlier, a strong sense of pride in her body and raw sexuality came over her. He stood back, taking her in, and then he ran his hands over her waist, her hips, and her breasts. "You're so beautiful."

She smiled in response, pulling his shirt over his head. Running her hands along his broad chest, she leaned in, trailing kisses over his neck, which had traces of his clean scent despite their time in the bar and grill. He groaned and guided her to the bed, fooling with her bra closure as they went. Hovering over her on the bed, he kissed her mouth then started a trail, leaving tiny traces of his tongue over her neck and down to her chest. He lifted up, pulling off her loose bra, and then both hands were on her breasts, circling her nipples with his thumbs.

A shot of heat surged through her, forcing her to moan with anticipation as he took her breast into his mouth, running his warm tongue over her nipple. She grabbed his strong back reflexively and ran her hands up and down it, indulging in the rippling muscles. He gave her nipple a final sweet kiss, then moved to the other one for a repeat performance. He gave it the same treatment then headed down to her stomach, hovering over her, tracing her flattened belly with his talented tongue before moving down farther, which she wasn't so sure about.

Back in her twenties when she was with David, he'd gone down on her often, but never well. She made a few feeble attempts to guide him along, but he seemed to lack staying power and would give up just when she was finally getting somewhere. Eventually, she'd detoured him away from the area to avoid the frustration.

Al had never made an attempt to move in that direction. Curious, she confronted him about his avoidance of that particular form of foreplay. He'd merely told her it wasn't for him. She certainly wouldn't force him, and since her previous partner did it so poorly, part of her was relieved to not have to bother with the disappointment.

She wanted this night to be perfect and she had no problem with orgasms through intercourse, so she veered him away from the area, not willing to take the chance on any sort of letdown this evening. She grabbed his arms and pulled him back up toward her mouth, then took his hand and guided it back down there. He responded, finding his way to her with ease. She moaned as he made contact. It'd been so long since a man had felt her there. His touch was brand new, like this was her real first time, even at her age.

"You feel good," he whispered in her ear, which released even more heat in her.

He rubbed her right where she loved it, not on the spot, but just above it. The anticipation of the contact just below drove her even crazier than if he was touching her directly.

He cupped her whole area with his thick hand and then slipped a finger inside of her, making her squirm. He easily found her spot, tickling it, making her grip his back hard. God in heaven did this man know what he was doing. She was afraid she wasn't going to last long, and she wanted to save herself for him inside her.

She tugged at his jeans. "Take these off."

"I was going to take my time with you."

"Please don't."

He kissed her lips sweetly, and then moved off of her. Sitting on the side of the bed, he pulled off his jeans and boxers and then opened the drawer to his nightstand.

"Wait, before you do that. Can I see you?" His body was ridiculous, and she didn't know how many chances she was going to get to be with him. She wasn't missing out on a thing.

He gave her that grin of his. "What do you want to see?"

"Lay down beside me," she said through an uncontrollable smile.

He turned to her, and her mouth dropped open. She reached for it, wrapping her hand around the bottom and easing up toward the tip. It took a while to get there.

A jolt of excitement shot through her body, then realization set in. How was he going to get that thing inside of her? She raised both eyebrows. "I

MELISSA CHAMBERS

don't even know what to say."

He chuckled. "Don't be afraid of it."

"I've never seen one that…I mean, the ones I've been around…"

He smoothed her hair back from her face. "Don't freak out, okay?" Clearly, he'd dealt with this kind of panic before, seeming unfazed by her reaction.

"I'm sorry. I'm just a little, taken aback."

"It's okay if you don't want to—"

"No! I want to."

"Are you sure?"

"God, yes."

He lifted an eyebrow, gauging her. "Are you ready now?"

She nodded. "I'm ready now."

"Okay." He ran the back of his hand in a line down her chest between her breasts, and then sat up and readied himself with the condom.

She lay on her back, and he crawled over to her. He pulled her thong down her legs and tossed it away. Hovering over her, his broad chest inches from hers, he said, "If you want to stop at any time just tell me, okay?"

She swallowed hard. "Okay." She laid her hands over her head, opening herself to him.

"You look so beautiful lying there." Her chest tingled with his words.

He guided himself to her, wiggling the tip around a little, looking for a way in. It was a tough sell. She couldn't blame herself. After having been closed for business for a year and a half, her opening wasn't yet ready for something the size of Texas.

"Push harder," she said.

He pushed a little harder, getting a bit farther, and also generating a loud yell from her.

"I'm sorry," he said.

"Don't be."

"Here, I think this'll work better." He wrapped his arms around her back and rolled her on top of him. It'd been many years since she'd been on top, Al having enjoyed missionary exclusively. She was starting to wonder why she let that relationship go on as long as it had.

He placed both hands around her behind and helped guide her on top of him. She decided this would be like ripping off a bandage. She'd need to go for it, hard and fast, so she sat down forcibly on top of him, which in turn unleashed a scream so primal his dog outside responded with a howl.

"Shit, Maya. Are you—"

"Good," she said through clenched teeth. "Fine."

He rubbed her back. "Sweetheart, we don't have to—"

She covered his mouth with her hand and moved up and down on him, the pain easing with every pump until it started to feel like pleasure. She'd never been so utterly filled in her life, like he was in every part of her body imaginable and then some. He closed his eyes, resting his head back on the pillow, and she grabbed his thick shoulders, speeding up, which he seemed to respond to favorably. The harder she worked, the more the pain eased, making way for the bliss. She dug into his shoulders, and they moved together, their bodies picking up one another's rhythm easily.

She grabbed both of his hands and pushed them into the pillows on either side of his head, the muscles in her arms tensing. She sped up even faster as the pressure built inside of her, begging for release as every single inch of her core was engaged with him. He exhaled a deep breath as he twitched inside of her. The idea of him releasing himself put her over the edge, the long-forgotten feeling of climactic euphoria, not at the hands of her vibrator, surging through her body.

She collapsed onto him, exhausted and relieved all at once. They both lay there catching their breath, their chests heaving in rhythm. Finally, she rolled off of him.

He kissed her sweetly. "I'll be right back." He disappeared into the bathroom. When he returned, he handed her a towel, always so thoughtful of her needs. He lay on his back and cuddled her into the nook between his shoulder and his arm. "I apologize," he said. "I didn't last very long. It'd been a while."

"For me, too. And I'll be honest, I'm not sure how much longer I could have lasted."

"Are you okay?"

"Yes, but I may walk funny tomorrow." She gave him a playful pat. "You could have warned me when we were talking about sex earlier today."

He chuckled. "And exactly how should I have phrased that?"

She kissed his chest and repositioned herself so she could see him, resting her head in her hand. "Have other girls ever had problems with it?"

He smiled, staring at the ceiling. "I had a girl

walk out on me one time when she saw it."

"You're kidding?"

"Nah, but her best friend called me that next day wanting to hook up."

"Did you?" she asked.

He scratched his head. "New subject."

She pinched his arm for good measure. "So what number am I on the list, 543?"

"Ah, so close." She pinched him harder. "Nah, nothing like that," he said. "What about you? What number am I?"

She smoothed over the spot where she pinched him. "New subject."

"Then tell me how long it'd been till now," he said.

She rolled her eyes, too embarrassed to say. "Why?"

"I'm curious about you. I can't help myself."

His interest gave her the confidence to come clean. "My last relationship ended about a year and a half ago." She mumbled out the last part of the sentence. He nodded, a grin making its way onto his lips. She shook him. "Don't laugh at me."

"I'm not laughing. Trust me."

"What about you?" she asked.

"What about me?"

She gave him a look. "I fessed up. It's your turn."

He gave a little groan, his face coloring a bit. "I don't know. It's been a while."

"Like days, or weeks, or…"

He gave her a sneaky smile. "Longer than days."

"So, last week?"

"Longer than that."

She lifted an eyebrow. "Week before last?"

"I'll put it this way, I honestly don't know, so the last time couldn't have been too memorable."

She outlined the muscles on his six-pack with her fingertips. "You must have so much opportunity though."

"Just 'cause I have opportunity doesn't mean I want to take it. The mindless screwing gets old after a while, and my hand works just fine." Heat ran to her face, and she had to look down at the pillow thinking about Bo masturbating. He tickled her. "Did I embarrass you?"

"No. That's perfectly natural." She cracked up mid-sentence.

"I've got something to ask you now."

She lifted her eyebrows. "Okay."

"Why wouldn't you let me go down on you?"

She was surprised she didn't break out in hives from hearing Bo say those words. They both killed her with embarrassment and turned her on like mad. "That's never worked out for me in the past. I just wanted this time with you to be good."

He sat up. "What do you mean you just wanted it to be good? What makes you think I wouldn't have been good at it?"

"No, I'm sure you're wonderful. But my first ex didn't do it well, and my second ex didn't do it at all, so I've kind of lost interest in it."

"Is this a challenge?"

"No," she said, patting him on the chest, trying to make him lay back down. "Definitely not."

He stared at her. "You know, the fact that you're

so opposed to it makes me want to do it even more."

She considered him. If any man could do it right, she supposed it was him. "If you want to mess around again another night this week, we can try it."

"What about right fucking now?"

"Oh, God no. We just had sex."

"So?" he said.

"So, I'm not letting you down there after we've just had sex."

"How come?"

"Because we had a condom down there."

He cupped her with his hand. "I'm sure you still taste wonderful, darlin'."

She let her head fall backward, a shot of warmth climbing through her body. "Does that pet name work on every girl?"

He grinned, tickling her most sensitive spot. "Pretty much. Come on. Let me go down there."

She bit her lip, closing her eyes. "Not tonight, but what you're doing, you're going to need to either stop now or keep going till you're finished."

He gave her a final squeeze with his meaty hand, and then pulled away from her, leaving her desperate and frustrated. "Roll over onto your stomach. I'm not done with you, tonight."

She did what he said, trying to hide her grin, but he didn't miss it. He hadn't had this much fun in bed in a decade. He straddled her, leaning down to trail kisses over her neck and shoulders, appreciating the imperfections in her creamy skin as he went—the freckles and little moles. He ran the backs of his fingers over her arms, which lay in a diamond shape around her head, and then eased the palms of his hands over her shoulder blades and down to her waist. Her body meant something to him. She worked hard on it, and he wanted to treat it with the care and respect that she did.

He ran his hands over her toned ass, grazing past the slit, which made her twitch. He knew better than to go near there tonight, but if he could convince her to stick around, eventually, all bets would be off.

He moved to her thighs, cupping them with each of his hands, easing to the backs of her knees, and all the way down to her ankles. He worked his way back up, spreading her thighs apart as he made his way to her center. He eased his body down onto hers, positioning himself between her cheeks. Holding his weight off of her with his forearms, he slid his hands under her biceps and covered her with his body. Her eyes were closed, and her mouth widened in a grin.

"I love that," she whispered.

"Any chance you're ready for me again?"

She nodded, the smile on her face growing.

He pulled off her and reached into the drawer for another condom. He expected her to flip over, but to his delight, she didn't. He readied himself and then pulled her hips upward. If touching her body hadn't made him rock hard for the second time during the evening, the sight of her on her knees ready to take him certainly would have.

Careful to find the correct way in, he eased himself to her. She groaned as he entered her, but by the arch in her back, and the movement of her body, he suspected this time was going to be better all the way around.

He gripped the tops of her thighs for support as he pushed his way into her, immersing himself in her warm, tight flesh. She lay her head down on the pillow, showing him her beautiful profile, the little bump in her nose giving her face character. The buildup inside of him rose as her expression registered the feeling of his cock inside of her, showing him exactly what he was doing to her. He tried to last longer this time, wanting to show her he could do better for her, make her want to come back to his bed.

She gripped the pillow, her expression turning desperate, and before he knew it he was moving faster, pounding into her, hard. The moans and heavy breaths she held blew out suddenly, making him work harder for her. He wanted to be the best lover she'd had and make her never want to be with another guy again.

She let out a loud groan as her body started to tighten, which was all he needed to finish the job. The buildup released inside him, sending waves of heat and sensations through his body. He caught his breath as he held her ass tight against him, not wanting to leave her body or stop looking at the beautiful sight that was her ass.

He eased himself away from her and headed for the bathroom. When he got back, he found her still, face down, her eyes closed. He lay down beside her on the side of the bed he didn't normally sleep on, but he'd be damned if he'd ask her to move a muscle. Her long, lean body splayed out on his bed was a sight he didn't want disturbed. She looked like something somebody would have painted.

He wrapped his arm around her back and tangled his leg up in hers. She would be gone come Saturday, but tonight she was his, and he was going to make sure he took advantage of every second she spent in his bed.

The next morning, Maya sat in the passenger seat of Bo's truck typing into her phone, her expression stern and unforgiving.

"Everything okay?" he asked.

"Yeah, sorry. Just work." She kept typing and scrolling. He waited for her to finish, and then started to say something, but it dinged again. Her thumbs flew over the keypad, her mouth moving as she typed, making him smile.

She finally put the phone down in her lap, frowning as she looked out the window. He reached over and took her hand, squeezing. She turned to him like she forgot he was there, and then smiled. Her phone dinged again. Was this what her life was like? Was she always on her phone? He looked at his a fair share, but he had no problem tossing it on the counter when he got home and not picking it up until the next morning. But his business was pool cleaning and supply. Nobody ever had an actual emergency in the pool cleaning business.

"Hmm," she said, giving her phone a curious look.

"What?"

"I've got a lunch date."

Surely she was teasing him, but it didn't stop his

chest from heating up a little. "Oh yeah?"

"Your friend Seanna."

"Really?" he asked.

"Yeah, she wants to take me to lunch today. From what I can tell, it's just going to be her and me."

"Hmm," Bo said, wondering what Seanna was up to. Not that she couldn't just ask someone out to lunch, but what was the point of getting to know Maya? She was headed back up north on Saturday. He guessed he could ask himself the same question.

He pulled up in Sebastian's driveway and then walked her to the front door. Her eye makeup was smudged, and her typically straight and orderly hair was messy. But still, she somehow got more beautiful every time he looked at her. Besides, he liked the state she was in now, fresh from his bed.

He gazed into her eyes, and she squeezed his hands. "For sure the best date I ever had."

"Damn. And I was just hoping to beat out the barfing guy from Chili's."

"Mission accomplished."

He pulled her to him. "I want to see you again, but I can't tonight."

She gave a slight frown. "Okay."

"I'm going out of town for the day with Blake. We're driving to Baton Rouge for a piece of medical equipment. We've got to pick it up first thing in the morning." She gave a nod and smiled, but not quite so much in the eyes. He swung her hands a little. "I'll be back Thursday, and we can do what we talked about last night." He'd been highly disappointed that she wouldn't let him down there.

No way was she getting out of town without him knowing how she tasted.

She grinned, looking off to the side. How was she able to make him feel twenty years younger with a smile?

They both went in for a kiss and then held each other in a hug that felt like the world was ending. He pulled away and lifted an eyebrow. "Be good while I'm away."

She shrugged. "Of course."

"What are you doing today, after your lunch?"

"I think the beach. I'll have to consult the schedule for confirmation of that."

He looked her up and down. "You got any one-piece bathing suits?"

"I have one. It's for swimming laps."

"If you go to the beach, wear that one."

She pursed her lips with a suppressed grin. "I usually wear a bikini to the beach."

"How about a one-piece today?"

She laughed. "I think the guys will contain themselves."

He was only half joking. Of course he wasn't some asshole who would dictate what his girl wore. But the idea of other guys ogling the woman who was starting to feel very much like his wasn't sitting with him well. He ran his hands over her arms. "Wear whatever you want. Your body's too beautiful to hide if you don't want it hidden. But remember whose bed you're going to be in tomorrow night."

She pulled him in close, pressing herself against his cock. "How could I forget that?"

He groaned. "You're killing me. Death by desire."

She grinned so wide for him. "Be careful on your trip."

"I'll call you when I get back. Hell, I'll call you when I'm there."

"Sounds good." She pulled away from him and held up a hand in a wave as she left him there half hard again. A day and a half was all he had to be away from her, and he wasn't sure how he was going to do it. He was in for a rough ride come Saturday.

Chapter Thirteen

Maya found Seanna at a table in the open-air seating of the restaurant, staring out at the ocean, holding a glass of wine. She looked so elegant sitting there with the white tablecloth, the bottle of wine in the carafe, and the arrangement of white hydrangeas. Her dress was smart for business, but she made it look sexy with her tussled beach hair and her substantial chest. Maya glanced down at her own B-cups, which were locked up tight in her crew-collared shirt.

She stepped up to the table, almost a little nervous to meet her. Everyone loved her so much, and Blake and she were like this power couple within the group. The two of them together were almost too much pretty to take in at once. "Seanna?"

She turned around with a huge smile when she saw Maya. Talk about lighting up a room. "Hello, thank you so much for meeting me." Seanna tossed her arms around Maya, giving her a tight hug. Maya sort of stood still, patting her back. She wasn't a hugger. Seanna motioned across the table. "Have a seat, please. I hope chardonnay is okay. I texted you, but you were probably driving, obviously."

"Yes, sorry. I did text back, but it was just a second ago."

Seanna picked up her phone. "Yep, there it is. Had it on silent." She tossed the phone in her purse and zipped it up, then she pulled the bottle out of the carafe and poured Maya a glass. The brand was high end.

"You're a wine aficionado?" Maya asked.

"Oh, no. Well, I'm learning. Chase is. You've met him, I've heard. He's my boss. He thinks the correct wine order can make or break a deal." She held up her hand. "Not that there's a deal going on here today. But he did insist on picking up the check, so be sure to order expensive." She leaned in. "I'm gonna." She winked, and Maya started to understand her popularity within the group. She was so easy to be around, even for someone like Maya who wasn't always the first to warm up.

"So what do you do for Chase?" Maya asked.

"Well, lots of things. We're sort of fine-tuning my title. He's gotten too big for his company. It's growing fast and branching out, and he needed someone to be his right hand and be able to take meetings for him and that kind of thing." She glanced around the place and then met Maya's gaze, eyes wide. "I'm in over my head to be honest. He's trusting me with some really important stuff. If it weren't for Sebastian these past few months, I wouldn't have been able to do it. He's brilliant, right?"

Maya huffed a laugh. "He was class valedictorian in high school."

Seanna tossed up a hand. "Of course he was. So you live in Indianapolis, where you all grew up?"

"That's right. And you just moved here last fall?"

"Yes. My Aunt Cassidy lives here. I've been staying with her. I know she's ready to kick me out though. I'm almost ready to move in with Blake, but honestly, we just haven't had the time to physically move me."

The server came over, and Seanna opened her menu. "Sorry, we've been chatting. How do the mushrooms and the scallops look for appetizers?" she asked Maya.

"Good," Maya said, impressed by the way she took charge.

"We'll start with those and order in a bit." She turned to Maya. "Are you in a hurry?"

"No, not at all."

"Great." She smiled at the waiter, and he nodded with his exit. "So tell me all about yourself. What do you do?"

"I'm an operations director at a marketing firm." VP. She should have said VP, but she didn't want to correct herself now. She had to get used to saying that. She'd earned that title.

Seanna looked pleasantly surprised. "Oh, really? Now, what does that entail?"

Maya wasn't sure if Seanna was really interested

or just being polite, so she gave her the short explanation. "I sort of organize the place. I run the traffic department and oversee production in the art department. We've got a hundred employees, so the job is fairly high-level, probably more than I'd like it to be, honestly. I love getting my hands dirty."

"Oh really?" Seanna asked, sounding unusually interested.

"Yes," Maya said. "I'm a bit of a control freak. The higher level your job gets, the more control you're forced to let go of and have confidence in your staff. Finding people you trust to manage departments is key."

Seanna's eyes widened, and she set her elbow on the table. "Girl, it's why I have this job. Chase trusts me for some odd reason. He's even put me in charge of hiring for the new clinic he's building. Can you believe that?" Seanna sort of eyeballed her as she picked up her wine again.

Maya wiggled in her seat. "Wow, that's a big job."

"I know, right? I mean...I don't have any experience in hiring. My background is in construction management. I know how to build stuff, not hire people." She narrowed her gaze. "So what qualities do you look for in a great hire?"

Maya tucked hair behind her ear, starting to wonder if she was on a roundabout job interview. "Well, it really does depend on the position. I think managing expectation levels is key, definitely the salary budget makes all the difference in the world. Have you Googled any of this?"

Seanna sat back. "Oh, yes. Of course. I will. But

honestly, I'd love to make one fantastic hire, a person who would run the whole operation and then do all the hiring for me." She shrugged, looking less casual than Maya suspected she was going for. "An operations person, sort of like you."

The server appeared with their appetizers, and Maya took the moment to process what Seanna was talking about. Was she suggesting that Maya work at this clinic of Chase's?

Seanna took a mushroom and two scallops. "Don't be shy. I'm an eater. That's a warning." She smiled at her, and then put the mushroom in her mouth. Her eyebrows drew together. "Mmm. So good," she said through a mouthful.

Maya took a scallop and cut into it, still a little perplexed by their conversation.

After Seanna cleaned her plate, she pushed it forward slightly. "So I hear you've been seeing Bo some this week."

Maya's cheeks heated at the sound of his name. "Um...yeah."

Seanna placed her hand on the table dramatically. "I adore him. He's seriously one of the most incredible men I've ever met. I can't believe he's still single."

Neither could Maya, but she wouldn't share that. "So they're traveling together today, Blake and Bo?"

"Yes, Blake hated to take Bo from you this week. I hope you don't mind."

"No, of course not. We're just hanging out."

Seanna nodded. "Well, that's great. He's a really good hang." She picked up her menu, wine glass in her other hand, a grin tugging at her lips as she perused it. "I'm looking at the shrimp and grits. I know I shouldn't, but they're so good from here. What are you thinking about?"

That was a loaded question. Maya's phone buzzed. "Sorry, I'm sure it's work. I picked a bad week to take off, I think." She picked up her phone and answered a question from one of the production managers, and then set her phone down. It buzzed again right away, a notification about a printer who was upping the price halfway through a catalog job they were running. She pushed her hair back from her face. She should handle this. Andy, who was over that job, was a great production guy, but he was way too nice and he stank at standing up for himself or the company. That was what she was for.

Maya was just about to ask Seanna if she minded if she made a quick call, but then watching Seanna across the table as she breezily stared at the ocean, waiting for Maya, and remembering that Seanna had tossed her phone in her purse when Maya arrived gave her pause.

"Sorry," Maya said, and the phone dinged again. She closed her eyes, willing herself not to look. "I'm just going to turn this down."

"No problem for me," Seanna said. Maya decreased the volume and then gave Seanna her full attention. "So what do you think about the South Walton area?" Seanna motioned at the ocean roaring to the shore beside them.

"It's amazing. We went running over in the Alys Beach area yesterday, Bo and me." She tucked her hair behind her ear and sort of looked down at her plate, feeling presumptuous for using the word we so casually.

"Oh yeah? You're a runner too, huh?"

"Yes, I just finished my first marathon in Nashville."

Seanna pointed at her chest. "I'm from Nashville. I grew up in Franklin."

Maya smiled. "That's where Bo's sister lives."

"I know. I met her when she was here over the holidays, and then I hung out with her when I was home in March." Her eyes widened. "You should see this girl. She wears no makeup, just combs out her hair and it falls perfectly straight, and she's breathtaking to look at." Seanna put the back of her hand to her mouth, leaning in. "If I were gay…"

Maya's neck filled with heat.

"I'm totally kidding," Seanna said. "I mean I'm not kidding about how pretty she is…never mind."

Maya wished she wasn't so uptight all the time. Seanna was loose and casual. How did that come so natural to her? Maya sat up straight, repositioning her fork. "I saw a picture of her, I think, at Bo's house yesterday."

Seanna pointed. "The one where they were at Dale's wedding?" That seemed to fit the description, so Maya nodded. "You know that smile she has on her face in that picture, the one where she's all like…" Seanna cocked her head to the side, lowered her eyelids, and gave Maya a cool, closed-mouth smile that was pretty spot-on with the picture. "That's totally her personality. She either has no idea she's gorgeous or she couldn't care less. I absolutely hate her."

Maya smiled to herself, thinking about how Shayla was on the phone that first night she met Bo. That seemed like a year ago.

"Have you been to Blue Mountain yet?" Seanna asked.

"Um, no. Where's that?"

"It's up the street. There's an ice cream shop there that will ruin you for all other ice cream. Have you walked around the shops here in Seaside?"

"No, but I think we're going shopping tomorrow morning."

"Do you love music or books?"

"Both, actually," Maya said.

"Make sure Sebastian takes you to the bookstore in Seaside. There's a record store on top that I could live in. Oh, and behind that horseshoe, there's this whole other section of shops and art galleries. The cutest stuff ever. Ruskin Place is the name of that area. Oh, and walk around back behind all that. You've got to see the elementary school. It's precious. And it's actually a really good school system."

Maya nodded, feeling a little overloaded with the hard sell. The shopping she got, but the school system comment put her past her limit.

Seanna sat back in her chair. "Okay, I'm totally not getting kickbacks from the chamber of commerce even though it sounds like I am. I just get really passionate about the area."

"I can see why. It's beautiful down here."

The waiter showed back up, and Seanna smiled at Maya. "Ready to order?"

As Maya headed for the public beach access, she couldn't get her mind off of her lunch with Seanna. She'd never flat-out asked Maya if she wanted to interview for a job, but Maya got the distinct feeling that was why she'd been called to the lunch.

She hesitated at the crosswalk, looking both ways. Even though it was clear, she stopped and considered her surroundings. People lived in this paradise, people she knew. Stepping out of the way of two rollerbladers, she re-shouldered her beach bag. She could live near the beach. She could go to the beach anytime she wanted. Not that she was a beach girl, but she could become one.

The powdery sand massaged her toes as she kicked off her sandals and made her way toward Sebastian and Felicity, who were lounging in chairs just outside of Sebastian's cabana. Who had their own permanent cabana on the beach?

Sebastian patted the empty lounger beside him. "All you, sweetie. How was lunch?"

"Good."

He looked worried. "Uh oh."

"No, she was lovely. Really sweet. We talked for like two hours. I felt bad for keeping her so long from work."

"I'm sure it was her pleasure."

Felicity flipped a page of her magazine. "Did she live up to the hype?"

"Yeah, she kind of did. She's really easy to talk to. But I got the feeling the lunch was more of a job interview than anything."

Felicity shut her magazine. "A job interview? What for?"

Maya dropped her bag in the sand and shimmied out of her cover-up "I'm not sure. Office manager maybe? For that clinic they're opening."

"Office manager?" Felicity asked. "Does she know you're a VP?"

Maya waved her off. "It's fine. It wasn't offensive or anything like that, just interesting."

Sebastian eyed her. "Interesting in a you'll consider it kind of way, or just interesting?"

Maya shrugged. "I don't know." Was she considering it? Leaving Indy? Leaving her steady, well-paying job? Rolling the dice on a brand new career when hers was finally paying off? "What am I talking about? No, of course not." Sebastian's eyebrows went up. Maya sat in the chair and pulled her sunscreen out of her bag. "I can't do that. I live in Indy. I'm starting the position I've worked a decade for on Monday. This is stupid."

"Well, it's not totally stupid," Sebastian said.

"Yes it is," Felicity said. "You're not taking her away from me that easily."

Sebastian nudged her. "You come, too."

Felicity gave him a look, and he gave her an understanding smile back. They all knew Felicity couldn't leave Indy as long as her mother was still there. She'd been in a mentally abusive relationship with Felicity's father their whole lives but refused to leave. Felicity stayed for moral support and for the hope that she could one day get her out.

"This is all silly talk. So what have you two been up to today?" Maya asked.

"You're looking at it," Sebastian said. "Did Meade ever get ahold of you?"

"Meade? Did she call you?" Maya asked.

"She texted a little while ago. She was trying to reach you."

Maya's heart quickened its beat as she fished in her bag for her phone. "Is everything all right?"

"I assume so. She just asked if you were with me, and I said you were at a lunch."

Maya had three texts from her and a voice mail. She dialed her number before checking any of them. "That's yours, right?" Maya asked, pointing to the cabana.

"Yeah, go on in."

Maya stepped up through the wide opening and sat on a couch, a finger plugging her exposed ear. Meade picked up on the third ring. "Hey."

"Hey, sorry I've been out of pocket. I was at a lunch, and then I forgot to turn my ringer back up. What's going on?'

"Oh, nothing."

Maya sat silent for a minute. "Meade, you've been texting and calling both Sebastian and me. What is up?"

"I just wanted to say hi."

Maya shut her eyes tightly. For one of the great minds of their country, Meade was the worst liar on the planet. "Okay, what's been going on with you today?"

"Nothing. Actually, I'm going to be late for work. Can I call you later?"

Maya tossed up her hand. "Sure."

"Thanks. Love you!"

"Love you—"

But the line went dead before she could even

finish her sentence. She headed back out to the chairs, where Sebastian was typing into his phone. "Everything okay?"

"Yeah. False alarm I guess."

"So, since Bo and Chase are both tied up tonight, we're having a girls' night," he said. "I've got a reservation for seven o'clock."

Felicity put the back of her hand to her head. "More fabulous food and drink. I'm not sure I can take it."

Maya sat in her chair, watching the waves rolling in. This was a moment to grasp and appreciate. Beautiful beach, close friends beside her, the sun's sweet rays warming her body. But between the job temptation and the call from Meade, she couldn't relax. She checked her phone for a message from Bo. There wasn't one, of course. Not that she expected there to be one. She had no idea how often he texted or called girls he was dating. He could be one of those guys who waited three or four days before calling, or a week. It'd only been a few hours.

She fired off a few work emails, and then resigned herself to relax. She imagined telling Bo that she'd decided to move there. Everything between them now was all desire and heat, but it didn't escape her thoughts that those feelings could easily be due to the fact that neither of them had any expectations past Saturday. She huffed a laugh at the potential look on his face. Surprise! I'm moving here. She shook her head at her own ludicrousness.

Sebastian looked over. "What?"

"Nothing," Maya said. "Nothing at all."

Bo sat at a booth looking at a menu while Blake talked to Seanna on the phone just outside the door of the restaurant. It crossed Bo's mind to wonder why he couldn't talk there at the table, but then he figured he better mind his own business. Catching a glimpse of Blake's guilty smile through the glass, Bo understood Blake was just in love and was probably sparing Bo the stomach ache.

Blake sat down at the same time the server brought their beers. "What'd you guys decide to eat?"

"I'll have the crawfish etouffee," Blake said.

Bo handed her his menu. "Sounds good."

"Can I bring you both a cup of gumbo? Ours is the best. I promise I won't let you down." She gave them both a grin with plenty of innuendo.

Bo shrugged. "I'm never one to turn down gumbo in Louisiana."

"Me, too. I like to conform." Blake smiled and handed her his menu.

Bo gave him a look after the waitress left to put in their orders. "You better be careful with that grin. You're spoken for these days."

"I'm just goddamn happy in general. Can't help it if that comes across like I'm flirting."

Bo would give him a hard time, but he was enjoying his best friend's newfound well-being. He'd been through some dark days in the past few years and was finally starting to pull out of it. Bo didn't want to do anything to rock that boat.

"Doing what you love and who you love agrees with you," Bo said.

Blake shook his head. "I feel like I'm among the living again."

"Welcome back." Bo held up his bottle, and Blake did the same.

"So," Blake said. "How did it go with Maya?"

Bo rubbed his hand over the top of his head. "Good, I guess. I mean real good, actually."

Blake nodded, gauging him. "I can see that." His brow furrowed.

"Don't look at me like that."

"I'm not looking at you any way," Blake said.

"You are, too. I've got this under control. I swear I do. I've flipped the switch in my head. I'm just focusing on right now, this week, enjoying this time, and next week I'll move on to somebody else."

Blake gnawed on the inside of his cheek. Bo noticed he did that when he got nervous. "What?" Bo asked.

"Oh, nothing." Blake moved his beer bottle around in circles.

Bo leaned in. "What's your deal? You look like you're up to something."

"I'm not." He shrugged. "I was just going to say Seanna had lunch with Maya today."

Bo's radar went off, that eerie feeling starting to swirl in his gut. "Yeah, I heard Seanna invited her. How did it go?"

"Good, I think. You know Seanna. She's never met a stranger."

"Mmm hmm. Maya has."

Blake smiled. "Yeah, she's a little tentative, I guess?"

"Little bit. I kind of like that about her though. She's tough to get through to at first, but when you do…" He trailed off thinking about her that first night, and how she stiffened when he touched her arm or hand. Then how after a while she would touch him, but with respect and discernment. Blake cleared his throat and Bo met his gaze, realizing he'd been off in left field. "Sorry. What were we talking about?"

Blake lifted an eyebrow. "Their lunch today?"

"Oh, yeah. Glad they got along."

Blake sort of scrunched up one side of his face in an apology. "Well, yeah, of course they did, but I think Seanna might have had some alternative intentions."

There went Bo's stomach again. "Some what?"

"Um, she may have talked to Maya about a job."

Bo sat up straight. "What are you talking about?"

"Running the clinic from an operational standpoint."

"Are you fucking kidding me?"

Blake held up both hands. "Don't get pissed."

Bo leaned in. "Don't you think that's the kind of thing you might have run past me first?"

"I told Seanna we should talk to you before she set the lunch up, but she swore to me she was just going to mention the job existed and get a feel from her."

Bo glared at him. "I'm guessing that's not exactly how it went."

Blake ran his fingers through his hair, finally meeting Bo's gaze. "I guess she took it a little farther than she should have. She got excited for a minute. You know Seanna doesn't have a mean bone in her body."

"I didn't say she was being mean."

"What's the harm, anyway? I thought you really liked Maya."

"I do. But this is for her and me to figure out together."

Blake cocked his head to the side. "Oh, sorry if you didn't want me butting into your love life."

Blake had him there. Bo and Chase had interfered quite a bit trying to encourage Blake to go for it with Seanna. "The circumstances were different. You were the one who was trying to leave town, not Seanna. Maya's got the job of her dreams waiting on her when she gets back home on Monday. I can't ask her to stay here and neither can you or Seanna."

"We're not asking her to stay. We're telling her about a job possibility."

"Well, quit it."

"All right," Blake said, and they sat in silence for a few minutes.

Bo gauged him. "Out of curiosity, what did she say?"

"Nothing. Just listened while Seanna talked. Apparently that's what had Seanna talking more and more. She said Maya was so quiet that it made her nervous, and she just kept spilling her guts."

Bo shook his head, just picturing Seanna's mouth running away like a locomotive.

"Well, at least it's out there now," Blake said, "and you didn't put it out there, so you're in the clear."

Bo glared at his so-called friend. "She's gonna think I put Seanna up to it."

"I'll tell Seanna to clarify that—"

"You tell Seanna not to say another word about that job. Do you hear me?"

Blake held up both hands. "All right."

They sat in silence drinking their beers, each of them staring at a television over the other one's head.

"I think I'm going to ask Seanna to marry me," Blake said.

Bo couldn't help a smile, his heart warming for his friend. "If you're sure she's the one."

"I don't even have a single doubt."

"Let me know when you're gonna do it so I can cross my fingers she says yes."

Blake smiled down at his beer bottle. "I don't want to wait any longer. I'm ready to go all-in."

"Kids and all that?" Bo asked.

"Someday. Seanna's not ready right now. She loves this job with Chase's company. She says it's like she's finally found her footing in life." He huffed a laugh. "I asked her to come to Kansas with me last November."

Bo frowned. "You did? I didn't know that."

"She came to see me Thanksgiving night. I was leaving for Kansas. She was moving here, and I was moving there. She laid it on the line for me, but I'd already committed to the hospital in Kansas City by then. I had to go, but I wanted her more than anything. Thank God she didn't come with me. Chase would have hired someone else."

Bo stared at his friend, the beer sloshing around

in his gut. "It worked out like it was supposed to, didn't it?"

Blake nodded. "Yep."

The waitress set two bowls down in front of them. "Enjoy."

As Bo ate, he thought about what would have happened if Seanna would have gone to Kansas City with Blake. Would they have even made it, or would Seanna be pissed because she gave everything up for him?

Maya's sweet face was embedded in his brain. It didn't matter how much he wanted her to stay, he couldn't ask her to leave a job she loved and had worked so hard for. He wouldn't do it.

He'd call her when he got back, maybe see her one more time before she left. He couldn't be rude. This was Sebastian's friend after all. He couldn't end this cold turkey. Besides, it was poised to end that way naturally on Saturday. He just had to ride out the week as planned.

Now, if only he could figure out how to quit falling for her.

Chapter Fourteen

The host seated Maya, Felicity, and Sebastian at a round table for five outside by an infinity fountain. Felicity nodded at the empty chairs. "Who's meeting us?"

"Seanna and Marigold. Ashe and Desiree are caught up tonight."

It wasn't that Maya minded seeing Seanna again, it was just that lunch had been a little awkward as Seanna was clearly trying to sell Maya on the area and possibly that job. But Maya had been thinking about it all afternoon.

"Hello," came Seanna's voice to Maya's right, and then Seanna's hand was on Maya's shoulder. "Long time no see." Seanna hugged Maya to her, kissing the top of Maya's head. It was such a sweet and familiar gesture that Maya didn't know what to do with it. She lifted her hand to touch Seanna's shoulder, but she was already off to the next hug.

"Maya?" a blond girl asked, giving her the onceover. She held out her hand formally. "I'm Marigold."

"Oh, hello." Maya said, taken aback a little. For some reason, she wasn't anything like Maya had pictured. For starters, she was almost glamorous, sort of a young Sophia Loren. Her dress clung to her thin frame, her ears dazzled with decent-sized diamonds, shy of gaudy though.

She took the seat next to Maya and leaned in. "So, you and Bo, huh?" Maya blinked, taken aback by this woman's candor.

"Move," Seanna said. "I'm sitting next to Maya."

"Why can't I sit here?" Marigold asked.

"Because she doesn't know it, but she's going to need a buffer."

Marigold took a resigned sigh. "I'm told I'm a lot." She air quoted, but dutifully moved to the other seat.

Maya smoothed out her skirt, getting herself prepared for the night. She wasn't sure what lay ahead.

"Have you ordered drinks yet?" Seanna asked, and then a waiter showed up.

After they all gave their orders, Marigold rested her elbows on the table, leaning in. "So I've heard you and Bo are spending the week together."

Seanna rolled her eyes. "Marigold."

"Um, where did you hear that?" Maya asked.

Sebastian's expression contorted into something resembling apology. "You know I'm a sucker for a great romance. I can't keep these things to myself."

Marigold squeezed her thin hands into fists. "I love this. This is huge!"

"It's not huge," Seanna said. "Don't say it's huge. That's a lot of pressure. It's nothing." She glanced over at Maya with a deer in headlights look. "I mean, it's not nothing. It's something. It's just not huge. It's medium." She gauged Maya as if looking for an answer, like Maya had a clue. "Shit, I don't know what it is. Where are those cocktails?"

Maya looked at Felicity, who gave her a comforting grin in return. Being the center of attention wasn't something Maya relished, typically, but with the enthusiasm this group was showing for her love life, she sort of didn't mind it for once.

Marigold leaned in. "So, what's he like?" she asked, waggling her eyebrows.

Seanna opened the menu. "I'm thinking about a salad. Maya and I had a big lunch today."

"I mean," Marigold said, "we all know he's huge, but does he know how to use it? Ow!"

Seanna glared at her. "Marigold, I swear."

Maya's ears heated up like boiling eggs.

Felicity put her menu down. "She left that part out this morning. So what are we talking about here?" She directed her question to Marigold, presumably knowing Maya would kill her if she put her on the spot like that in front of this group.

Marigold sat back. "Well, I've not had firsthand experience with it, of course, but I did see it on New Year's Eve."

Maya shifted in her seat, resting her elbow on the armrest to look as casual as possible, brushing the hair back from her forehead. "Oh, yeah?"

"We were at Sebastian's on New Year's Eve," Seanna said.

Sebastian and Marigold exchanged smiles. "I know," Marigold said.

"You know about this?" Seanna asked Sebastian.

"I had to tell somebody," Marigold said.

Sebastian held up both of his pointer fingers. "Let the record reflect that I can keep a secret when asked."

"So what happened?" Felicity asked.

Marigold inhaled a deep breath. "It was stupid, I mean, even for me stupid. We'd been back and forth all night, giving each other crap, just for fun like we always do. But of course I had too much to drink and not enough to eat, and I had to take it too far."

Sebastian put his hand on her arm. "Of course you did, sweetie."

She gave him a look, and then went on. "So he goes to the bathroom, and I pull the key from the top of the doorframe, and I open the door, just as he's getting ready to zip up."

"You were going to intentionally walk in on him peeing?" Seanna asked.

"I told you it was stupid."

Seanna rolled her eyes and shook her head.

"So I snapped a picture of it with my phone."

"You did not," Seanna said.

"Oh, I totally did."

Seanna looked around the table for someone to be stunned with her and landed on Maya, except Maya couldn't even blink at the moment, fascinated to hear this stranger tell a story about something that happened with Bo before Maya ever met him.

"Do you still have the picture?" Felicity asked.

Marigold pursed her lips. "No."

"I think there's more to this story," Felicity said.

"Oh, you bet," Sebastian said.

They all stared at Marigold, waiting for her to keep going. She clearly enjoyed holding court. "So I join everyone in the living room like nothing happened. And in a minute, he walks back into the room and just stands there waiting on me. I tried so hard not to look at him. I swear, I was determined not to look, but I could feel him right there, and my heart was pounding like the devil. So I finally look up at him thinking I've got this major poker face on, and he just stares at me and then walks into the bottom floor guest room."

"Did you follow him?" Seanna asked.

"Like a lamb to the slaughter."

Maya's stomach quivered, imagining what was coming next. Marigold had said she didn't have firsthand knowledge of Bo's body, but this woman was talking about walking into a bedroom with the guy Maya was currently sleeping with. She didn't know whether to be fascinated or horrified.

"So he closes the door behind me, and then turns to me and says in that low, Southern drawl of his, 'You like what you saw?'"

Sebastian looked heavenward. "Yes!"

Marigold rested her forearms on the table and leaned in. "He backs me toward the bed. I know he's up to something because I've been trying to get in his pants for years, and he's never allowed as much as a kiss."

Maya's neck filled with heat. Marigold was gorgeous. Why hadn't he slept with her if she really had been trying to get him to?

"But since I'm a glutton, I let it play out."

The waiter arrived with the drinks and passed them out. "Have we decided yet?"

"Bring us your three favorite apps, and we'll order in a little bit," Sebastian said, leaning toward Marigold on the arm of his chair.

"Will do," he said, and was off.

They all stared at Marigold, and she picked up her drink, casually, and then looked around, wide-eyed. "Oh, did you want me to keep going?"

"Yes, queen, please," Sebastian said.

She wiggled in her seat, settling in. "So, he steps toward me and puts his hands on my waist, staring down into my eyes. Now I've known Bo a long time, and he's never looked at me like this before. So I'm thinking, it's New Year's, we're both single, maybe he's finally decided to give me a try. So I sort of just sink into it for the moment."

"Mmm hmm," Sebastian said, lifting his eyebrow.

Maya didn't think she'd been more interested in a story in her life. She found herself leaning toward the table and forced herself back into her seat. Hearing Marigold talk about Bo like this gave her both an odd tweak in her gut and a little tingle in her belly.

"So he moves in a little closer, leaning down like he might kiss me. I waited there for it, but he kept lingering close, teasing me like it was going to happen any moment."

Maya bit her bottom lip, her stomach warming.

Marigold stared off at the roof of the restaurant. "He moves slowly across my cheek, sort of walking me toward the bed, and I'm thinking, oh shit. You know I talk a big game with Bo and Chase, but it's only because they never take me seriously. But now, I've got to put my money where my mouth is."

Seanna holds up a hand. "So you're thinking you're getting ready to have sex with Bo Harrison."

Marigold sat up straight, her expression dead serious. "I was preparing for anything."

Felicity and Sebastian shared a conspiratorial glance, and Maya couldn't help a little giggle. The theatrics were too over-the-top not to have fun with.

Seanna gave Maya an eye roll, but she had a little grin on her lips. Seanna made a circular motion with her hand. "So…"

"So, I fall back on the bed, and he moves down on top of me, hovering over me. He's so close I can smell that woodsy aftershave he wears."

Oh, Maya knew the one. She could almost smell that subtle earthy scent right then.

"His fingers tug at the waistband of my pants, and my body is going ballistic at this point. I'm like full-on ready."

Seanna held up a hand. "TMI."

Marigold mirrored her hand, continuing. "So, just as I let out this little sexy whimper and sort of settle in, he's off of me, leaving my body in a heap of frustration on the bed."

Maya blinked. "That was it?"

Marigold nodded, sitting back in her chair. "He had my phone and was out the door. By the time I got myself together and met him in the living room with everyone else, he handed me my phone back with this triumphant little irritating grin and said, 'Good try, darlin'.'"

"What about the picture?" Felicity asked.

"Gone."

"But your phone had to have been locked," Maya said, always with the details.

Marigold waved her off. "I didn't keep it locked back then. I do now, of course."

"So what'd you do with all that buildup inside of you?" Felicity asked.

"Not a damn thing. I just sat there for the rest of the night horny as a jackrabbit." She rested her forearms on the table. "So, what's he like, Maya?" This time, Maya didn't feel so trapped with the question. She felt...looser.

"How do you mean exactly?" Maya asked.

Marigold gave it some thought. "As a romantic."

Maya liked the word. Bo, the romantic. "He's very thoughtful and kind. Interested in what I have to say. That hasn't been a common thread in men I've dated in the past."

"Join the club," Felicity said.

"He's so confident in the way he presents himself, but I don't find him to be the least bit arrogant one on one," Maya said.

"So you like him, don't you?" Marigold asked, but she wasn't teasing. Her tone was matter of fact and earnest.

Still, Maya wasn't sure how to answer. She

tucked her hair behind her ear. "Yes. He's really nice."

Marigold smiled at her. "Well, I think I can see why he likes you."

Maya smiled back, understanding the reason they all took to Marigold so well. The ringing of Maya's phone woke her back to reality. She checked it, and her heartbeat sped up.

"I'm so sorry. I'll just be a minute." She walked over to the patch of grass behind the patio. "Hey!" She couldn't help a giggle as she answered.

"Sounds like you're having a good time," Bo said. "I'm not interrupting anything, am I?"

"No, you actually called just as Marigold was finishing a story."

"Ah, okay. Anything good?"

She smiled into her phone. "Sort of. It was the one from New Year's Eve? About the phone?" she asked, and then cringed as she waited for his response.

"Aww, shit. Just ignore her, okay?"

"It sounded pretty intense."

"I just needed to get the phone from her. I figured that'd be the easiest route."

Maya bit on her lip. "She's really pretty. How come you never dated her?"

"I don't know. I just don't see her like that, I guess. She's always carrying on."

The name Angela laid heavy on Maya's mind. Of course he'd had relationships in his past, but putting a name on one and seeing how agitated he was talking about her last night piqued Maya's curiosity. "Who do you see like that? I mean usually."

He hesitated before answering. "Why are you asking me this?"

"You're delaying response."

"Maybe I don't want to think about other girls when I'm talking to you, or at all."

She was grinning now, like an idiot no doubt. "Good answer."

"How you feeling?"

"Great, why?"

"You said you thought you might be walking funny today."

"Oh, yeah. I totally am." She laughed. "Seriously, I'm fine."

"I can be home in five hours."

She giggled. "That'd be nice, but stay put."

He cleared his throat. "So how did your lunch with Seanna go?"

Maya glanced at Seanna, who was looking at Felicity and laughing. "Good. I like her."

"What did you all talk about?"

"Oh, just different stuff, our families, restaurants in Nashville we'd both been to, endangered sea turtles," she said with a smile.

"Did she talk to you about work a lot?"

"A little, yeah. She's hiring for a position at Chase's company. I think she was looking for a little advice. She's new at hiring, I guess."

"Did you give her the advice?"

"Yeah, as much as it was worth. Hiring's always a crapshoot. I've hired people who were excellent interviewers but weren't so great at showing up for work or getting anything done. I think you just have to go with your gut most of the time. You know. You must do the hiring for your company."

"I've got a guy for that."

She smiled. "Good for you. Must be nice to be the boss man, have the buck stop with you."

"You ready to start your new job Monday?" he asked.

Her heart twisted in her chest. "I am. It's going to be quite the culture shock though, assimilating back to reality from this life. It's weird for me to think this is your reality."

"Maybe I'll come up to Indianapolis and check out your reality sometime, after you're settled into your new job, of course."

A blanket of warmth came over her at that idea. "I'd love that. I'd take you to St. Elmo Steak House and show you how we do shrimp up north."

"Oh yeah? Is it good?"

"Let's just say it will definitely clear up your sinuses." Silence sat between them, and she didn't want to hang up. "What are you up to tomorrow, when you get home?"

"Coming to see you."

She couldn't get the ridiculous grin off her face.

"Can I call you later?" he asked.

"Tonight?"

"Yeah. Maybe we can get each other to bed."

Her face was starting to get sore from smiling. "Are you and Blake sharing a room?"

"I'll kick his ass out."

"Don't do that. I think we can manage a night apart." Her heart sank at the thought of having to spend every night apart after Friday.

"I'm not sure I can make it," he said.

"Be strong, Bo," she whispered into the phone. "And I'll make it worth your while tomorrow."

"Aww damn, I hate I'm here, and you're there."

"Just a few more hours," she said, and then glanced at the table where the server was delivering the appetizers. "I should go."

"All right," he said, his voice low and gravelly. "Have a good time. Stick with Sebastian so it scares off the guys who want to hit on you."

She huffed a laugh. "You're sweet, but with this bunch, I don't think you have a lot to worry about."

"Why would you say that?"

She loved that he saw her in the same way other guys probably saw Seanna, Marigold, and Felicity, all three of them being such attractive women. "Never mind. Have a good night in Baton Rouge. Eat some gumbo for me."

"You like Cajun food?" he asked.

"It's a huge vice. It's impossible for me to resist."

"Good to know. I'll talk to you later."

"Okay." She bit her lip. "Bye."

"Bye."

She ended the call, and then held the phone to her heart like it could somehow make him closer to her. When she got back to the table, someone had made a plate for her with something from each of the three appetizers. "Thank you," she said.

"We didn't know how long you'd be," Sebastian said. "Wanted to make sure you got something before they cleared the plates away."

"I wasn't gone that long," she said.

"I can't believe you're not in a car on the way to Baton Rouge with the way you were smiling," Seanna said.

She scratched the back of her neck, which filled with a tingling sensation.

"Dang," Marigold said, finishing a bite. "What are you going to do when you have to leave?" The table was silent for the first time all night, and everyone looked at Maya. "You're from Indianapolis, right?" Marigold asked.

"That's right," Maya said, her hand a little shaky as she pushed the food around on her plate.

"Why don't you move here?" Marigold asked.

"Marigold," Seanna said under her breath.

"What? They've spent the whole week together haven't they? She's nuts about him, and he never dates the same girl consistently. If he called her from the road and had her smiling like that, then it seems like he's into her. They should be together."

Maya's heart felt like it was being squeezed like a sponge with Marigold's simple and logical summary.

"Maya got a big promotion at work," Felicity said. "She starts Monday. VP job."

"Oh," Marigold said. "Congratulations."

"Thanks," Maya said, dabbing her mouth with her napkin, her hands still a little shaky.

"That definitely changes things," Marigold said. "Bo's got his business down here and all."

Seanna's shoulders fell. "Marigold," she said, this time without even trying to hide it.

"Okay, I'll shut up." She did, and so did the rest of the table, everyone gaining sudden interest in their food, but Maya's appetite had withered.

Seanna set her fork down. "That was really good. Are you done, Maya?"

"Oh, yes." She pushed the plate forward a bit.

"Can I steal you for a sec? This place has got a fabulous rooftop bar."

"I want to go," Marigold said.

"Give me ten minutes with her, okay?" Seanna said.

Marigold pursed her lips and then sucked down the rest of her cocktail.

"Order me a crab cake salad, please," Seanna said to Sebastian.

"I'll take the goat cheese one," Maya said and then gave him a smile. "Thanks."

"Sure thing."

Maya followed Seanna up the stairs to a rooftop bar that overlooked the hustle of Seaside nightlife to her left and the serenity of the sea to her right. She had to pause for a minute to really appreciate the beauty of this special nook of the world. "God," she said, stepping up to a bar table and setting her clutch down on it, "it's hard to believe this is where you all live. Do you just get used to it after a while?"

Seanna huffed a laugh. "No way. I sit outside on the back porch pretty much every night and just watch the waves roll in. Not to sound new age-y, but it sort of puts the world into perspective for me. It can be cathartic at times."

Maya nodded, imagining having that as her nighttime scenery. Maya's house was in a trendy part of Indianapolis where young professionals populated the area, so her backyard was a postage stamp-sized, fenced-in affair, and most of the surrounding sounds were of the traffic sort. To sit on a patio or a balcony and watch waves roll in every night was something that sounded as fantastic as it was unimaginable for her.

Seanna put her hand on Maya's arm. "I want to apologize for earlier today at lunch. I came on really strong, I think, talking about the job and this place. I get a little overeager at times."

"Oh, don't worry about it," Maya said.

Seanna opened her mouth to speak, and then closed it, seeming to be choosing her words carefully. "Bo did a lot for Blake and me this past year. Blake had been through something that was really tough, and he was having a hard time. Bo's been the most incredible friend to him." Seanna's eyes started to water. Maya took her hand, her heart expanding in her chest. Seanna smiled, wiping back tears. "I'm so sorry. I'm trying really hard not to cry."

Maya gave her what she hoped was a reassuring smile. "You can cry if you need to."

Seanna nodded, pulling herself together. She blotted her eyes with a beverage napkin. "Bo's probably one of the most special and dearest people I've ever known. He saved Blake's life." She teared up again and then shook her head, standing up straight. "He was there for Blake when he was in the darkest hole of his life, and he pulled him out of that. Then when he saw Blake had serious feelings for me that he was trying to push aside, Bo went to great lengths to push us together." She laughed at the memory. "God, he even tricked us into this really romantic evening cruise on Chase's boat." She waved her hand dismissively. "It's a long story. Point is, he's a fantastic guy. Blake's known him going on four years now, and he's never seen him this happy with a woman."

Maya's throat threatened to close with emotion.

"I know this is an impossible situation, and I need to mind my own business." She held up her hand like she was stopping traffic. "Blake made that very clear to me on the phone earlier. And I'm totally going to. But I'm just going to say this one last thing about it. Bo's awesome, and you seem really kind and elegant and wonderful, and the fact that Sebastian adores you like he does already puts you on a pedestal in my eyes." She took a moment to look into Maya's eyes. "And Bo's a really good judge of character. He sees something in you that he doesn't see often. I can promise you that."

Her heart pounding like a stampede of horses, Maya forced a smile, trying desperately to calm the chaos in her chest.

Seanna hit the table with finality. "Now that's done. Let's get a drink, on me."

"Oh, no—"

"Please, let me. I've done enough damage for one day, God knows. What would you like?"

Maya smiled. "May I hug you?"

Seanna held her arms out wide. "Yes, please." She took Maya in, crushing her large chest against Maya, hugging her so tightly Maya had to hold her breath, but that was fine. In the absence of her being able to express her feelings in words, this would do.

When they pulled apart, Marigold stood beside them. "I swear I waited ten minutes. Even timed it on my phone."

Maya and Seanna both busted out in laughter and then brought Marigold into the mix.

Chapter Fifteen

"Love-forty," Sebastian called out with plenty of irritation. It'd been at least a decade since he and Maya had played a match, but they'd easily fallen right back into their typical competitive spirit without missing a beat.

He served the ball right to her, and she sent it back to him, starting a volley that lasted several shots. When he hit one short, she rushed the net with her tennis instructor's voice echoing in her head. Catch the ball with your racket. Don't swing at it. It's not about power, it's about placement.

Maya raised her racket with all intents of placing the ball at the corner of the ad court, but at the last minute, with the intensity and abandon with which she'd treated the rest of the week, she swung at the ball like she was hitting a homerun, sending it soaring near Sebastian, who swung and missed as the ball bounced squarely on the line then jammed itself into the fence. Sebastian walked over to it and pointed with his racket. "Are you serious with this?"

She laughed and turned to walk back to the baseline to start the next game, but froze in her step as Bo Harrison came into view sitting next to Felicity in the grass.

Her heart pounded as she approached the fence. "Hey."

He sat on the hill of Sebastian's neighbor's yard with his elbows resting on his knees, his legs apart, strong hands dangling. It was like he'd been infused in Baton Rouge with a double-dose of steaminess.

"Don't mind me. I just came to say hi. But this is better. I want to watch you play."

The past day and a half apart from him had seemed easily like a month. It was silly, she knew, because a day was nothing to be apart from someone she'd just met. Still, now that he was right here in the flesh, the idea of spending another half hour away seemed completely out of the question, even if she was spending that half hour whipping Sebastian's butt on the court. She glanced at Sebastian, and he rolled his eyes. "Go. I'm sick of getting killed out here anyway."

Felicity stood and wiped off her shorts. "I'll play." She opened the fence gate and leaned in toward Maya's ear. "We'll keep away a good long while. Go." She gave Maya a wink.

Maya's stomach did a little dance at the possibilities. "Thank you." She scooted off the court and made her way to Bo.

He wrapped his hands around her waist. "Man, I

missed you."

His touch was so natural on her body but still made her core light up. "Me, too." He pressed his lips against hers, and she let out a moan as her heart filled with the connection she shared with him.

Seanna's words had been lying heavy on her heart since last night, though nothing she said had come as a surprise. Maya already knew Bo was an incredible person. She just couldn't believe she was lucky enough to grab his attention, even if it were for just one week.

"Get a room!" Sebastian yelled from the court.

"Come on. I need a shower." She hooked her fingers into his belt loops. "Wanna join me?"

"Damn, I'm glad I decided to stop by."

She pulled him toward the house and led him up the stairs to her room. She locked the door behind them and then headed to start the shower. As the water rushed down, she turned to find him standing in the doorway. She had been trying to picture his face for the past day and a half, and she thought she had it down—his dark eyes, skin deeply tanned from working in the sun, hair buzzed short but still thick. But she'd left out a few key components—his jaw peppered with a day and a half worth of scruff, that little scar on the side of his eye that she guessed was from a particularly determined chicken pock, the set of his jawline forming a perfect diamond.

She brushed his cheek with her fingertips, taking in every inch of his face, committing it to her memory so she'd never forget, like she could. "I really missed you." She took a step backward and peeled her tank top off. He moved to her and kissed her shoulder. "Sorry, I'm sweaty," she said.

He ran his hands appreciatively over her shoulders and arms. "I love your body." His words made her heart melt.

She grasped the bottom of his shirt and pulled it over his head, admiring the rippling muscles in his chest and abs as she went. "I've never been with a man as perfect as you."

"I'm far from perfect, darlin'."

"Your body is pretty perfect. And your lips." She ran her finger across them. "I really like your lips."

He cupped her breasts. "I like these." She gave a huff of a laugh. "I'm serious." He pulled her sports bra over her head and admired them. "They're perfect."

She let out a breath, getting comfortable with him looking at her naked breasts in the bright light of the bathroom. She'd never had a problem showing her body in a bathing suit, but her breasts exposed in the glaring light was a different thing. However, the more she was with him, the more she found herself warming to the idea of him seeing the most intimate parts of her.

He laid his mouth on one, teasing her nipple with his tongue, sending tingles throughout her body. The bathroom was starting to steam up, and she wasn't sure if it was from the hot water or from him.

She nodded toward the shower. "Let's get in."

He pulled her tennis skirt and underwear down to the floor, and then she did the same with his shorts and boxers, releasing him with a smile. She remembered exactly what his cock looked like and was pleased to see it make its ready appearance.

They stepped inside the shower, and he moved her under the spray, the water washing away the sweat from the tennis match. She scooted around to let the water wash over his hard body in turn, savoring the droplets of water rolling down his muscled chest and arms. He pulled her close to him back around under the showerhead and poured some shampoo into his hand, lathering it into her hair. She closed her eyes and let his touch on her scalp flow through her, the water and soap cascading down her body.

"You're so beautiful," he said.

She couldn't remember ever having heard those words before from any man, not even her father. She wasn't a beautiful girl. She was plain, cute at best. Those had been the words used to describe her in the past. Never beautiful, at least not said by a man and with that sort of conviction. But he had used that word with her often now, and every time he seemed to put more meaning into it with his tone. He had no idea how much she treasured his words.

He poured her coconut body wash into his palm and lathered it between his hands. He rubbed up her waist over the sides of her breasts, pulling her arms up and rubbing up the full length of them forcing them straight up into the air, exposing her body to him. He worked his way back down, past her underarms and to her waist, giving her one of the more sensual moments she had shared with him yet, and he hadn't even touched an intimate part of her.

His cock brushed against her leg, sending a bolt

of anticipation through her core. She gathered some body wash from his chest and moved it down south, switching places with him and letting the water wash down his body. She played with his most sensitive parts, causing him to close his eyes and groan, loving the expression of satisfaction etched over his features.

He braced himself against the shower wall, his face washing with color. "You better quit that or I'm going to ruin it for us," he said.

She wanted to watch him this time so she could see exactly what she could do to him. "I want you to come this way."

"You're going with me then."

He pulled her closer and ran a hand over her ass, finding her core and letting himself inside. She gasped as he took the breath out of her. They pressed against each other, their bodies moving together in their own unique rhythm.

He covered his mouth over hers, so much sensation moving between them that she didn't know which way was up and which was down, but what she did know was that she'd never experienced any moment more erotic in her life.

His body quaked with release, which excited her more than anything. She let go of him and allowed herself to focus on her own release, his fingers working magic inside of her that made her come apart in his arms. She wrapped her arms around him, their naked bodies melding underneath the water pouring down over them as emotions consumed her that she never knew existed.

He held her tightly as he trailed sweet kisses

along the back of her neck until he rested his head in the crook of her neck, and they held each other there, naked to one another, without a single word.

He finally pulled back from her and quirked an eyebrow up. "How do you know what I like?"

"Call it a good guess."

He smiled and poured more body wash into his palm. "Is it okay if I touch you again right now?"

She surrendered, both hands in the air. "I'm all yours."

He lathered up again and washed her belly where he had left his mark on her, then moved one hand over her ass, and the other through her front, and then down over the top of her, rubbing gently. She let her head drop back as she exhausted a deep breath.

"You like that?" he asked.

She grinned. He knelt down on his knees and rubbed the body wash up and down her legs. She wondered how she was ever going to go back to showering alone after this.

He stood up, and they switched places again. She knelt before him rubbing the wash all up and down his strong legs. She giggled a little as she couldn't seem to stay clear of his massive manhood hanging down. Even with his erection gone, he was still enormous.

He gave his own chuckle. "Don't laugh at me."

She laughed again. "I'm sorry. It's just so big."

"You weren't laughing about it night before last."

She stood up and met him face to face. "I'm laughing because I'm just really happy." She realized how content she sounded and shoved her guard up. "I mean, how many girls get a chance with a guy who could be a porn star?"

"If you come home with me tonight, darlin', we'll live out every porn fantasy in the book."

"Will you dress up like a pizza delivery guy?"

"Would the fantasy be me or the pizza?"

She giggled. "How about a plumber who's come to clean out my pipes?"

"I'm up for anything you want anytime you want it."

She widened her eyes as a thought popped into her head. "Pool guy! That's a porn thing, right? You've come to clean my pool."

He smiled, and her heart surged with heat. She kissed him before she slipped up and said something she would regret. She turned off the water. "Hold that thought until later tonight."

He moved his hands over her ass. "I don't know if I can wait that long."

She grabbed the towel and dried him off with it, wrapping it around his penis and giving it a good squeeze through the towel with a laugh.

"I'll be sure and come by more often," he said, and then the smile dropped a little from his face as a weight pushed against her heart.

He put his clothes on while she dressed in her closet, the sound of Felicity and Sebastian coming in downstairs in the background. She shook out her hair, and then walked over to where Bo was waiting for her on the edge of the bed and straddled him.

"Thanks for coming by," she said.

"Thanks for the shower. By far the most fun I've

had in a bathroom."

She grinned. "Me, too."

He looked deep into her eyes, making her typically organized emotions a complete mess. "Will you come home with me now?"

She nodded. "I'd love to."

He patted her on the ass. "Pack an overnight bag. I want you for the rest of the day."

Sweeter words had never been spoken. "Okay."

He brought her in for a kiss, and then pulled away. "Damn, it's good to see you again."

"You just saw me yesterday," she said, her voice quiet.

"I want to see you as much as I can before you go."

She nodded, her heart reaching a level of vulnerability that scared her to death. This wasn't control. That had flown away with the seagulls the second she saw him at the tennis court. This was something primal that she didn't understand and wasn't sure she could even comprehend fully. But she was sure of one thing—there was no ripping herself away from him, not a second before Saturday morning.

Chapter Sixteen

If Bo had his way, he'd take Maya home to his bed, and they wouldn't leave the room again until Saturday morning. But there was time for that, the little bit that was left.

He put on his turn signal. "Do you like gardens?"

"Like botanical gardens?"

"Yeah." He pulled into the parking lot. "This is a place that belongs to a client of mine. It's a venue for parties, weddings, that sort of thing. It's usually empty during the week when there's not an event."

"Sure," she said, giving him a curious look.

He took her hand and led her to the front door. He punched numbers into a keypad and watched the expression on her face when he opened the door.

"Oh, my gosh," she said, scanning the room filled with every flower Bo could and couldn't name. "This is like the Opryland Hotel or something. Have you ever been there?" she asked.

"No, but Shayla says it's something to see."

She walked over to the waterfall on the back wall. "So you take care of all the water in here?"

"Yeah. I'm selfish. I do this job myself."

She followed the running stream walking in the direction of the current. "You said people get married here?"

"So I've heard. I've never been to a wedding here, but I imagine they're pretty nice."

She held out her arms. "You wouldn't need any flowers." She twirled around and let out an uncharacteristic giggle. "How do we have this whole place to ourselves right now?" He hoped she would like it, but he was pleasantly surprised she was this into it. She pointed at the pool. "Can you swim in there?"

"It's safe enough for it. Come on. You haven't seen the tropical room yet."

She grabbed her purse off the wrought-iron bench as he led her to the separate room behind the waterfall with elephant ears and palm trees galore. She glanced around, shaking her head. "This is amazing. I want to live in this room."

"I take my time when I'm here, trust me."

She slid up to him. "This place is doing odd things to me."

"Like what?"

She grinned and then got an excited look on her face. "Hang on." She opened her purse and pulled out a small bag. "I got these for you."

He peaked inside the bag. "Aww, damn. I love chocolates."

"Those are no ordinary chocolates. They're mint

chocolate truffles."

"Even better. How'd you know I like these?" He popped one in his mouth and held out the bag to her.

"It was kind of a selfish gift. The first night you kissed me, you'd just eaten that chocolate mint and you tasted that way."

He gave her a closed-mouth smile, still chewing. "You like that," he said through a mouthful of mint.

She kissed his lips. "I'm ruined now for chocolate mint." She waited for him to swallow and then kissed him again.

He pulled her closer, and let her keep kissing his lips until she finally nudged his mouth open. "Mmm," she said. She dropped her purse and ran her hands over his hair. She pulled back. "I swear, I feel half-buzzed and I haven't even had alcohol today."

He pushed the hair out of her face. "That's how I always feel when I'm around you."

She kissed him again, this time hungrily and full of passion he was afraid he wouldn't be able to stop if they kept up at that speed. "Fuck, Maya. Let's get home."

She smiled. "Did you lock that front door behind you?"

"It locks automatically."

She glanced around at the ceiling. "Are there cameras in here?"

He liked where this was going. "Not in here. Just ones aimed at the doors in the front room."

She lifted his shirt and found his fly. "I dreamed I did this to you last night." She dropped to her knees, and tugged down his pants just far enough to release him. It took about two seconds for him to get rock-hard. His chest filled with a flood of heat as she made him forget anything in the world existed except her sweet mouth around him. He rested his hands on her shoulders as she squeezed him tightly, making him lose his mind with the sensations she was giving him.

"Maya, you've got to stop," he said through heavy breaths. "I don't want to…"

She didn't stop though, she just worked harder, her tongue doing things to him that sent his body to the sun and back in the best way fucking possible. He squeezed her shoulders as he let himself go. "Goddammit," he said, catching his breath.

She stood and stepped away from him, holding the back of her hand to her mouth with a sneaky smile as he zipped himself up. "Come on," she said. "Let's go back to your house."

"You've got to try it with the butter," Bo said, offering Maya a piece of popcorn saturated in the stuff.

She rested the back of her head on his shoulder, holding up her own piece. "I've got my own, and it's very good without butter."

He reached into her bowl and took a piece. "Ah, that's so dry. How are you not choking on that?"

"Shh, we're missing the movie." She grinned, not even knowing what the heck they were watching. She wiggled a little, settling into her spot in front of him. His sectional had a chaise lounge on the corner that couldn't have been more perfect for snuggling. She sat between his legs and could still stretch her long legs out in front of her. She could so get used to this, but she needed desperately not to. His hand snuck around her, holding a piece of buttered popcorn.

"If I eat that, will you quit bugging me about it?"

"Deal," he said.

She opened her mouth and he put it in, but not without her biting at his hand.

"Oh, you're getting it for that."

He tickled her sides, and she squealed like a little girl. She hadn't squealed since she was ten. "Okay, I give up."

"Damn, you're easy."

She wiggled into his cock. "You haven't been complaining about that this week."

He reached around for a kiss, and she gave him one. As soon as it started to get intense, she stopped. He was due for a little teasing. "The movie? Do you mind?"

"All right," he said, pulling her back to rest against his chest again. "So, what motivates you to be so disciplined with your eating? I can't do it all the time like that."

She inwardly winced, thinking about her overbearing mother. "Honestly, it's just easier for me when I keep everything in order." Jake wagged his tail from the other end of the couch, and she was glad for the distraction. "Do you want some attention, Jake?" she asked, and he wagged harder, crawling toward her on his belly.

"Don't encourage that mutt," Bo said. "You get him over here, and we'll never get rid of him."

"Come here, boy," Maya said, patting her leg. "Come here. Isn't that a handsome boy."

Jake's long tail thumped against the couch as he crawled some more and got within petting distance.

"That's it," Bo said. "You pet him behind his ears, and we'll never be alone again."

Jake whined and laid his head on her leg. "He's so sweet, and he doesn't stink. Big dogs usually stink."

"The guy who comes and lets him out when I'm gone gives him a bath. He usually stinks."

"Mmm," she said, stroking Jake's fur. She couldn't imagine a place in the world she'd rather be at that point in time.

"You had fun last night with Sebastian and them?" Bo asked.

"Oh, yeah."

"Uh oh," he said.

She grinned. "Nothing you wouldn't approve of."

"Mmm hmm. I bet."

Maya had never been in a relationship that included jealousy on either part. The sorts of guys she dated weren't exactly the type that had other women lining up to steal them, and, in turn, her partners didn't seem to fear anyone romancing her away from them. She always considered that healthy and normal.

With Bo's looks and the way women responded to him everywhere they went, Maya suspected jealousy had played a part in Bo's past relationships, possibly on both parts if he dated women who were used to getting plenty of attention from men. She imagined these comments at their core were designed to make her feel desired. She appreciated it, but she didn't need it, especially since while sweet on his part, she wasn't sure if they were authentic.

"You don't have to do that, you know," she said.

"Do what?"

"Act like you're jealous."

"I'm not acting," he said.

She turned her head so she could see him looking all innocent. She shook her head and turned back around, focusing her attention on Jake. "So how many girls have you taken to those botanical gardens?"

"Including you?" he asked.

"Mmm hmm," she muttered, gritting her teeth.

"Oh, I don't know. I lost count around three hundred and eighty." She elbowed him in the ribs, just barely. "Well, it's not like you'd believe me if I told you the truth."

She looked him in the eye. "Of course I'd believe you."

"Really?" he asked, lifting his eyebrows. God, his eyes were so deliciously dark. She kissed his perfectly dreamy lips in response. He nudged her waist. "Just one."

Her default was not to believe men as beautiful and desired as Bo. Her main experience with guys like this were the ones who Meade hooked up with. They couldn't be trusted further than Maya could toss them out of Meade's life. One was as useless as the next, draining Meade of her money, her emotional energy, and her self-esteem. One appropriately named Chaz had even cornered Maya in a bathroom and tried to kiss her with Meade in the kitchen making his dinner.

But Maya wanted to believe that Bo wasn't bullshitting her. Could it be true, that he'd been sitting on such a gorgeous place that literally had brought her to her knees in front of him, just waiting for the right woman to bring there, and that she had been that exact perfect woman? Could she let herself believe it, even if just for the rest of this dreamy week?

"Why haven't you brought anyone there before?"

He shrugged. "I don't know. That place is special to me. I know it's not mine, but when I'm there alone, it can feel like it. The sound of the water flowing in the stream, the natural smell of all those flowers, the ridiculous amount of beauty condensed in that one place. I didn't want to make that place about some girl who I didn't really care about."

She stared at him, her heart so swollen it pained her. She grinned. "You care about me?"

"I thought that was obvious." He moved the bowl of popcorn from her lap and set it on top of his bowl on the end table. He took her hand. "I wanted to take you there, so when I go back it'll always make me think of you. And I know that's depressing because at some point I'm going to have to try to stop thinking of you, but you're special to me, just like that place is. You make me feel good like that place does."

A sensation rained down over her body like

she'd never felt before. It was too early to be in love. It couldn't be that. She'd only known him a handful of days. But she'd never experienced these feelings before, not with Al or David or any other meaningless relationship from her past that was entered into with the expectation of security and safety, discarding lust or passion or anything resembling what she felt looking into Bo's eyes right now.

She searched his gaze. "You make it so hard to distrust you."

He huffed a laugh. "Good."

His lips met hers, and there would be no more teasing tonight, not on her part. She turned around and melted into his chest, her hands feeling their way up his strong arms.

He pulled away. "Hang on." He nodded at the end table. "There's a rawhide bone in that drawer. She pulled it out and showed it to Bo. "Toss it onto his bed over there." She did, and Jake shot across the room and settled in with it.

"How long do we have till he finishes?"

"As long as we need. There's more where that came from."

He stood up off the couch with her attached to him and she wrapped her legs behind him. She was thin, but she was a tall girl. She couldn't be light, but he didn't seem to flinch. She'd never dated a man who could pick her up. She let the idea of his strength sink in and heat up her core like a lightning bolt.

He tossed her onto the bed then straddled her, pressing his lips against hers hard and opening her mouth, winding her tongue into his. She wrapped her legs around him and pulled him down on top of her. His weight lay heavy on her, and she drank in every ounce of it.

Sitting up, he ripped his shirt over his head, tossing it aside. She sat up as well and did the same, pulling her bra over her head at the same time. He moved his hand down to her pants, unbuttoned and tugged at them. She helped him, wriggling out of them. He sat up off of her and pulled them all the way off, tossing them on the floor, adding his own pants to the pile.

He climbed back on top of her, kissing her mouth again, hands all over, just like the name of the song they'd heard that night in his truck that would always remind her of him when she heard it. He moved to her neck, leaving trails of his tongue everywhere he went and waves of passion-filled emotion through her chest. He moved down between her breasts, and then farther down her body, kissing her flattened belly. He moved down some more.

She clenched her jaw. She'd denied him the first night, but she doubted he'd be derailed tonight. She might as well settle in and see if he could redeem her past experiences. If ever there was a man who could...

Nudging her legs apart, he lay before her at her center, and she had to close her eyes from the rush of want and intensity that ran through her just seeing him there, knowing what he was there for. Tingles fanned throughout her body as warm and wet sensations registered in her brain. How did this act she'd always steered away from feel like the most natural thing in the world and altogether unlike the stiff, darting tongue of her first boyfriend in quite the wrong spot?

She squirmed, grabbing fistfuls of the sheets as she went on this ride with him. Just when he had her settled into one pattern, he started another, working his tongue in a way she couldn't even figure out, and honestly, didn't care to. When she thought it couldn't possibly get any better, he slipped a finger inside of her, and her body quaked with a variety of sensations so powerful she wasn't even sure who she was anymore.

No longer able to contain the sensations coursing through her from the inside out, she let out a wail as the heat crested in her core and tingles flooded through her arms and legs, all the way to the tips of her fingers and toes.

She lay there still for a moment, her eyes shut, processing what he'd just done to her, what he'd allowed her to experience. She thought she'd be there a good thirty minutes waiting on an orgasm, but the whole thing felt like it lasted seconds instead.

He lay beside her, leaving kisses on her shoulder and the top of her hand. She opened one eye and tried to contain her smile. "Thank you."

He laughed. "You don't have to thank me for going down on you."

"Oh, yes I do. I had no idea what I'd been missing out on all these years."

He turned toward her and moved his hand around on her stomach. "I've been waiting all week for that."

A million butterflies leapt to attention in her belly as he climbed back on top of her and took both of her hands. He pulled them up beside her head, staring into her eyes.

"I'm so ready for you," she whispered.

"I'm so glad." He lifted off of her and pulled a condom out of the drawer. Losing his boxers, he readied himself and found his way to her.

She squeezed his arms. "I think this will work best if you just really go for it hard."

He pushed inside her, the length of him reaching to her chest, seemingly. As he kept pushing, the pain subsided, turning into intense, full-on, filling-her-up pleasure. Every push of him into her intensified her passion, her body's need for him. He lowered himself down farther onto her, holding himself up with his elbows, their bare bodies melding together as one as they fell into sync with one another. Her hands rested on his ass and she pushed him harder into her, needing him further inside her though it was physically impossible.

He buried his face in her neck, kissing her a few times, still moving hard into her, and then he lifted up off of her and sped up his pace, her body filling with the familiar rush of heat and sensation so strong she thought she might detonate right there on the bed. She pressed her hands against the wall behind her, holding herself in place as his movements got stronger and faster. Her breaths came short and stilted as her body hit its crescendo, and she let out a wail that could be heard throughout the Greater Panama City Beach area.

He let out his own groan as he slowed down and ultimately collapsed on top of her. His heart pounded against her chest, their bodies so full of heat, damp from their workout, their bare skin mingled with one another's. He pulled off of her slightly so he could see her face. "I don't want to get up."

She gripped his shoulders, and then pulled his body back down on top of hers. "Just stay inside me, Bo."

He kissed her neck and then guided her arm over her head, running the backs of his fingers down her arm and across the side of her breast. "I've never known anything as gorgeous as you." She smiled at him, her heart swelling like a balloon. He ran his hand down her side and gripped her thigh. "Don't move. I'll be right back."

He made his way to the bathroom while she covered her face with the pillow. She'd never felt happiness and contentment like she did at that moment. How was she going to leave him? What was she leaving him for, a stupid job?

She stared at the ceiling while trying desperately to organize her thoughts. Her job was not stupid. It was the job she'd been poised to move into for years. It was a VP job. She'd be the youngest VP in the company's history. And all it took was an amazing orgasm for her to think it was stupid. Jeez, she was turning into her sister.

Bo shut off the bathroom light and walked toward her, his body still entirely exposed, penis that could be in porn hanging down between his legs. He handed her a washcloth. "Do you need this?"

She took it from him. No man had ever brought her a towel after sex. The simple gesture was so earnest that it made her eyes water. "Thanks."

He sat on the bed next to her. "Are you okay?"

"Oh, yeah," she said, using the clean washcloth to dab at her eyes. "I'm totally fine. It's just, you're very unexpected, Bo Harrison."

"Well, if you think I saw you coming, you're nuts."

She sat up, pulling the sheet over her lap. "So, be honest with me. How many times have you done this?"

He lifted an eyebrow. "Had sex?"

"No, please, I don't need to know that. How often do you spend the week with a girl down here on vacation?"

He frowned, repositioning himself in front of her. "I'm not gonna lie, darlin', I've done this a lot. But I thought I'd sworn off week-long relationships." He met her gaze with half a smile. "That's why I didn't ask you in on that first night. I wanted to. Goddamn did I want to, but I knew you weren't someone I could sleep with and forget about."

She huffed a laugh, her heart full of bittersweet irony.

"What?" he asked.

"I just can't believe my luck. I finally meet this unicorn of a guy, and you're four states away."

"You're calling me a unicorn?" he asked.

She gave him a smile. "Mmm hmm." She took his hand. "Have you ever done the long-distance thing?"

"Oh yeah."

"How does that usually work out?" she asked. He gave her a look, and she nodded, already having known the answer. She narrowed her gaze, her curiosity getting the better of her. "Tell me about Angela."

With that, his soft expression toughened, and he let out a resigned sigh. "What do you want know?" He said it like a suspect who'd been worn out and was reluctantly ready to spill.

"She was someone important to you?" Maya asked, not necessarily wanting the answer but needing it.

"Yeah, she was."

"How long were you together?"

He adjusted himself on the bed, moving to sit next to her, his back against the wall. "A long time." She lifted her eyebrows, waiting for his response. He let out an exhausted breath. "Nine years."

She blinked, turning her body toward him. "Nine years?" He winced at the look on her face, and she grabbed his arm. "I didn't mean anything by that. I'm just curious why you haven't mentioned her. That's a long time to be with someone."

"We've been apart since before I was thirty. Honest to God, I don't know why Jennifer had to mention her the other day. It's not like they were good friends."

"Did you know her from high school?"

"No, college."

"Is she from here?" she asked.

"No, she's from a little town about a half hour outside of Tallahassee. We were at Florida State."

Maya narrowed her gaze. "So she moved here with you after college?"

"More or less."

She wanted details, the whole story, but she could tell she was going to have to drag this out of him piece by piece. "Did you meet her in class, or at a party, or..." she trailed off, hoping he'd finish that sentence.

"I met her at the library of all places."

She smiled, lifting her eyebrows. "Most people study at the library."

"I was there studying, if you can believe it. Grad school was kicking my ass. She was a few years younger than me, but as far as school went we were both in study mode. So we sort of settled in with one another. It was like a whole different life for me. I'd been drinking and chasing tail for four years, and now I was studying and hanging out with a girlfriend."

"How much younger than you was she?"

He thought about it, squinting. "Three years. I was twenty-two when we met, so she would have been nineteen."

"So did you graduate around the same time?" She knew that couldn't be right, but she was still trying to figure out the story. Not only did she want to know, but she sensed that he wanted, or needed, to tell it.

He pulled the sheet over his lap. "No, she was behind in school. She hated it. She threatened to quit all the time. I was always encouraging her to keep trying. When it came time for me to graduate, I was ready to leave Tallahassee. I couldn't get home fast enough. Shayla was already back, most of my good friends had already graduated, and I'll just tell you, I was homesick. I'd been working on my business plan all through grad school. I couldn't wait to get home and get started."

"So what happened?"

He frowned, picking at a fold in the sheet. "She wanted to come back here with me. I wanted her to stay and finish, but she was commuting from home, and she had a horrible home life. Her mom was hooked on drugs, always had men around."

The look of disgust on his face told her there was more to that story, but she would definitely not push him there.

"I went home with her one Saturday and that was all I needed to see. I never wanted her to go back there again." He shook his head slowly. "I couldn't leave her there, knowing she'd have to move back into that hellhole. I was the only stable thing she'd ever had in her life. Goddamn, it made me thankful for my family."

Maya took his hand in hers and kissed the top of it. As he smiled at her, she was overcome with gratefulness for this time with him.

He looked at the wall in front of them, seeming like he was drifting off to a past world. "I kept trying to get her to finish school online, encourage her to start building a career, but she had no interest. She said she was fine waiting tables."

"So did she work with you to build the pool business?"

"No. We kept everything separate from one another. We were together, but after a while it felt more like a roommate situation than a romantic one. She was always private, so I respected her keeping her distance, and, hell, I was always working, building the business during the day and working construction or bartending at night. It was nothing for us to go a few days without even seeing each other. I kept telling myself it was the hours I was keeping, and once things calmed down, I'd remember why we were together."

"Did that happen?"

"I finally got the business to a point I could quit the side work and started focusing on her more. But she wasn't focused on me."

Maya's gut churned at the possibilities. "Was she with another guy?"

"No, but she'd picked up her mother's prescription drug habit. I was just too in my own world to see it until I really started looking at her."

"That's so tough, Bo."

"Man, have you ever seen anyone go through that?"

She shook her head, realizing just how insulated her life had always been.

"It was heartbreaking. She'd go through rehab, and then just when I thought she was going to make it, she'd slip back away, and we'd be right where we started."

Maya hadn't known anyone with a drug problem, but she did understand feeling out of control. "Did she ever pull out of it?"

He let out a deep sigh, his face turning even

more solemn than before. "She'd been clean for ten months, which was encouraging. But she started talking about wanting a baby. There was no way I was bringing a kid into that life. She wasn't even a year clean, and besides that, we weren't in love. Hell, I don't know that we ever had been."

"You must have loved her though to stick with her through all of that."

He shrugged, shaking his head. "I'm not going to say I didn't." He turned to Maya. "But I didn't have a clue what being in love was."

Maya's hands trembled with the intensity in his eyes. She fought tears that she couldn't allow. She didn't want him to think she was reading too much into his words.

"So, the baby?" she asked, needing to return to the story before she said something she couldn't take back.

He adjusted himself on the bed. "She started wanting to have sex again." He glanced over at her. "I'm not trying to give too much information here, but we hadn't had sex in at least a year, hell, probably longer than that. She was wanting a baby, and I just wanted out. Hell, I wanted out as much for me as for her. Neither one of us was happy. But I couldn't leave her until I knew she was stable enough. I kept putting her off, the talk of babies worrying me. I got suspicious and found her pack of birth control pills. It was a Thursday, and the last pill she had taken was on a Sunday, who knew which Sunday."

Maya's hand went to her mouth. "Oh wow."

"Yeah," he said. "That was a wakeup call like

nothing I'd ever had."

"Did you confront her?"

"I ended it. I'd had all I could take. I packed a bag and headed over to Shayla's apartment to think straight. She texted me and told me she was headed home to see her mom. She was baiting me, I knew it, but I couldn't sit still thinking about her going there. They hadn't spoken in years, and as badly as I wanted out, I didn't want her back on those drugs or way worse. So I jumped in my truck and drove down there. When I pulled up to her mom's trailer, I was sick at my stomach to see Angela's car was already there. I was praying the whole way that she was bullshitting me, but I knew she hadn't been. Other than hiding shit from me, she rarely lied to me. I opened the truck door and heard screaming, so I ran inside. I found her mother passed out on the couch and some greasy old man pinning Angela to the floor, trying to unbutton his pants one-handed while he held her wrists with the other hand."

Maya held one hand over her mouth, squeezing his hand with her other one. "Bo."

He shook his head. "I knew right then I'd never be able to leave her again."

Maya felt sick as she imagined the scene in vivid color, the desperation both Bo and Angela must have felt. "How did it finally end?"

"A cousin of hers called one day and said her mother died of an overdose. Six months later I came home from work one night and found a couple of bags by the door. The place looked like it'd been thinned out, but my laptop was still at the kitchen table, and the television was still there. I heard music coming from the bedroom. I opened the door to find her on top of some guy, him about to let go inside of her right there in our bed."

Maya's heartbeat kicked up a notch. "Oh my God."

He gave a humorless smile. "He scrambled off the bed, grabbing for his clothes saying, 'Fuck, fuck. I didn't know she was married. I swear to God.' She hadn't let him in on the game, apparently."

Maya swallowed hard. "Did you know who he was?"

"Not a clue."

She let out a huff of air, blown away by the story. "What did she do?"

"She just laid there on the bed, staring at me, not making a single move. After he was gone, she pulled a dress over her head, walked over to me, and said, 'Now you're off the hook completely.' She walked out the front door, and I haven't seen her since." Maya didn't have a clue how to respond, so she didn't. He turned to her, his brow furrowed. "I've never told anyone that last part, not even Shayla."

Maya blinked, feeling honored that he'd felt okay to share it with her. "Why does she think you broke up?"

He shrugged. "She just thinks Angela left, which is true enough."

"What did Shayla think about her?"

"She'd wanted me to end it for years. She always felt bad for her, but when I told her it was finally over, she cried she was so relieved. I hadn't seen

Shayla cry since we were little."

Maya's heart warmed as she wished so badly she could stay one more day so she could meet Shayla on Saturday, but that was just silly. Bo needed to spend time with Shayla when she got here, and Maya would need to be out of the picture by then, because who was Maya going to be to this family? Nobody.

Maya slid her arms around his waist, and he brought her into his chest. "Thank you for trusting me with all of this," she said.

He huffed a laugh. "Damn. I know how to bring down a mood, don't I?"

She kissed his chest, wondering how she was ever going to let go of him. "I wanted to hear it. I hope I didn't push you too hard."

"I've been needing to get that out for six years."

She squeezed him harder, understanding so much about him now. "So I take it this has something to do with why you've never settled down into another relationship." She sat up so she could see him.

"I've been scared as shit. But I can't let my past keep me from what could be a great thing. Not anymore." He gazed into her eyes, and she'd never felt closer to anyone in her life. She nodded, words failing her. He took her hand. "We've still got tonight and all day tomorrow. I want to spend it all with you. I know you're here to see Sebastian, but—"

"I want to spend it with you, too."

He smiled at her. "Good."

She hiked her leg over him, straddling him, and

then taking him into her hand. She moved up and down on him, watching him grow before her very eyes. When she had him ready, she pulled a condom out of his nightstand and held it in front of him. "When's the last time you had sex without one of these?"

He huffed a laugh. "I'm about to round a decade with that record."

She smiled at him, hoping she could get her words out correctly. "I don't want this to sound like a bad joke, but I'm on the pill and I promise you I don't miss a day."

He chuckled, shaking his head. "I can't imagine that you would, darlin'."

She lifted an eyebrow. "Despite what it might seem like this week, I don't sleep around, even with condoms. I'm on the pill for other reasons." He nodded, staring at her. "Are you game?" she asked.

He took the condom from her and tossed it away, his mouth on hers, his hand cradling the back of her neck. She pulled herself up on her knees and then lowered herself down onto him, closing her eyes as his skin slid over hers, the sensation of direct contact impossibly eclipsing all the other times he'd been inside of her. He filled every inch of her as she moved up and down on him, her hands rounding his broad shoulders.

She relaxed backwards, and he took the lead, cradling her back as he laid her on the bed and then drove into her. She wrapped her legs around him, needing every part of her to be engaged with as much of his skin as possible. She fell into his rhythm, her body becoming one with his as was so natural now. How she'd never known closeness like this was unfathomable to her.

The pressure snuck up on her, building quicker than she anticipated as she squeezed his back. She let herself go as he continued to pump hard into her, and a moment later he was collapsing onto her holding his weight from crushing her. But she almost wished he'd just let himself cover her from head to toe. He pulsed inside of her, and she closed her eyes, savoring him there. She wanted him to never separate himself from her.

Chapter Seventeen

Jake's whine woke Maya up with a smile. She wanted to be awake as much of this day as possible since it was her last day with Bo. It wasn't like she would never see him again. She'd come back to see Sebastian at some point, and she'd see him then, if he wasn't with someone else, or worse, married. She winced, thinking about it. She had to stop. They had one last fabulous day together, and she would not screw it up thinking about tomorrow.

"Mmm," Bo moaned, pulling Maya in closer to him. "Go away, Jake." Of course, that made Jake's whine turn into a howl. Bo kissed the top of her head. "I'm gonna let him out and get his food. Don't move a muscle."

She went to the restroom while he was gone, but slid right back into bed just before he appeared in the doorway. "Didn't move, I promise."

He grinned. "I'll be right there." He closed

himself in the bathroom, and she inhaled a deep breath, running the Angela story through her brain, trying to fathom it all. Nine years. He had to have loved her in a way that transcended romance to keep helping her like he did.

He slid into bed with her, thankfully still nude. She would never be able to get enough of his bare-skinned body. She grinned as she got a whiff of minty fresh breath. She'd done the same. She kissed him and ran her hand over his hair. "I hope I didn't push you last night."

He let out a huff of air while gazing into her eyes. "I feel better, somehow, having told you. I didn't mean to get into so much detail, but I wanted you to understand why I'd been with someone nine years and never married her."

"She was really lucky to have you through that time in her life."

"She could have had better, someone who was focused enough on her to see all the signs. We could have cut the whole thing off at the pass if I'd just paid enough attention."

She took his hand and threaded her fingers through his, pulling it to her chest. "This might sound weird, but there are parts of your relationship with Angela that remind me a little of mine with my sister, Meade."

He furrowed his brow, listening.

"Watching someone you love do something to ruin their life...having little to no control over it but wanting so desperately to fix it for them."

He rubbed his thumb over the back of her hand. "I can see that. But my relationship with Angela's over. You and your sister have your whole life together."

She huffed a laugh, not having thought about that. "God, I'll be worrying about her till I'm ninety."

"You mentioned you've been trying to get her back to Indianapolis?"

"Yes, that'd be my ideal. I really think if I could just get her to move in with me for a little while that we could figure everything out. I'd love to get her in with a good therapist, sort of like Matt Damon's character in Good Will Hunting, except without the rough childhood." She smiled at him.

"You should call her today," he said.

She nodded. "I will. She called day before yesterday, but when I called back she acted like nothing was wrong. It's so hard to know with her."

He nodded, his brow furrowed.

"What do you want to do today?" she asked.

"I could see if Chase will let us take his boat out, or we could lay our asses on the beach, or we could go to the pool I saw you at on Sunday."

"God, that seems like six months ago."

"I know it." He kissed her. "Seems like that long since I've had my mouth on you, too."

His phone buzzed and he rolled his eyes. "Hang on." He picked it up. "It's my mom."

She scooted away from him, instinctively covering herself with the blanket. "Go ahead and take it."

He answered the call. "Hey. All right." He ended the call.

She frowned. "That's it?"

"She's in the driveway."

She shuffled to an upright position. "As in right outside?"

"Yeah, she doesn't like to intrude, so that's her way of knocking. She brought muffins for me to take to the shop. You want to meet her?"

She glanced around, getting her bearings. "Not like this."

"With clothes on, of course."

She put her fingertips to her forehead, trying to think. On one hand, this guy who she had grown crazily close to the past twenty-four hours wanted her to meet his mom. On the other hand, she was in his freaking bed, and his mom likely didn't even know she existed. She met his gaze. "What's she going to think of me?"

He gave her a reassuring smile. "She's gonna love you. Come on. Get dressed."

She got up, grabbed her overnight bag, and then slipped into the bathroom where she quickly got cleaned up and dressed. She could hear voices in the living room but not exactly what they were saying. That was probably for the best.

She checked herself one last time, took a deep breath, and then headed out, her heartbeat racing.

A hearty woman looking about sixty stood in the living room with a warm smile across her face when she saw Maya. "Hello, sweetie. I'm Bo's mom." She held her arms open and wrapped Maya in them like she was her own daughter.

Maya couldn't form words. She just let herself be hugged by the mother of the man who she'd had inside her hours ago. Mortified.

Bo's mom pulled away, holding Maya's hands. "I'm Donna. It's nice to meet you."

Maya nodded, swallowing. "Nice to meet you as well."

She motioned to the kitchen table. "I brought chocolate chip muffins if you're hungry."

"Mama, she doesn't—"

"I'd love one. Thank you," Maya said, going for the kitchen table and taking a muffin.

"I'll take another one, too. I've only had two so far this morning," she said with a chuckle.

They both bit into the muffins, Bo's mom closing her eyes. "Mmm, that's good."

"Mmm hmm," Maya said, chewing, not believing she was standing here in front of the woman who created Bo. She looked a little like him, now that Maya was over the initial shock and could actually look at her. Her hair was graying, but she was still hanging onto some of the same dark hair Bo had, and of course, there were those dark eyes of his. She had to look away.

"You're Sebastian's friend?" Donna asked.

"Yes, from Indianapolis where he grew up."

"Don't you just love that boy? Bo brought him by the house for Sunday supper once and I could have just eaten him up."

Maya smiled, and then took another bite of the muffin when she noticed Donna looking at it in her hand.

Bo cleared his throat, running his hand over the back of his head.

"All right," Donna said. "I'm heading out. I'm sorry to interrupt, but Bo wanted me to meet you."

She held her hand up to her mouth like she was blocking him from seeing her. "I told him I was fine to just drop the muffins and go, but he told me to stay and meet you." She held up both hands in surrender, still holding the half-eaten muffin. "For the record." She winked and then headed toward the door. "See you Sunday, honey," she said to her son and was off.

Maya looked at him, eyes wide, and he flashed her a smile with a shrug. "That's my mom."

They headed out toward Sebastian's house so Maya could get her bathing suit. She was still reeling from having met Bo's mom. Ideally, that would have been done over a dinner at a comfortable restaurant on an even playing field and not fresh from his bed, head hazy from a night full of passionate love-making. Still, she felt honored that he wanted to introduce her. He could have just run out and grabbed the muffins, and his mom would have never known Maya existed. The idea that he cared enough to want them to meet meant the world to Maya.

She glanced over at him, her heart so ridiculously warmed. What was she doing? Setting herself up for misery, that's what she was doing.

She cleared her throat shaking the cobwebs out of her brain. "Are you sure Chase is okay with us using his boat?" she asked.

He drove all sexy-like, laid back with his elbow on the doorframe. "Yeah, we'll just swing by his office for the keys after we get your swimsuit."

"Sounds perfect."

"If you don't mind, I'm gonna run by the shop just a minute."

She smiled, excited that she would get to see it. "No, I don't mind at all."

"I've got to cut vendor checks. It's all in the system. Doesn't take but a minute."

"Sure," she said. "I look forward to seeing where you work."

He pulled into the parking lot of a building with a sign that read HARRISON POOL SUPPLY. When he'd said he had a storefront, for some reason she'd pictured something small in a strip mail. But this was a decent-sized standalone building with its own parking lot. "Wow," she said.

He looked at her curiously. "Was this not what you were expecting?"

"It's just really nice…and big."

He smiled, looking proud. "Thanks." They got out, and he opened the door with a key. The hours on the window indicated they opened at ten, but there were two people inside, one counting down a register and the other stocking a shelf. "Morning," he said, setting down the muffins on the counter.

The girl counting the register did a double take and stopped mid-count. "Hi."

"This is Tracey and that's Andy. This is Maya."

Both of them, each sporting a blue polo shirt with the name of the store appliqued on it, waved and said hello. Maya smiled. "Hi."

This was Bo's business, and it was totally legit. Scanning the room, she couldn't imagine the amount of money he had tied up in the inventory. And this was just the retail portion of his business.

When he spoke about it, he called it a pool cleaning businesses, but this storefront wasn't anything to sneeze at.

He leaned in for a quick kiss. "You can look around in here and come on back when you get bored."

She glanced around the store, moving from aisle to aisle. All of this stuff was his. Bo owned all these pool gadgets and gizmos. He had a section of lawn furniture, a shelf full of beach towels, a display of floats and pool safety for kids. The place was so well-rounded.

She noticed black and white photos on the walls and moved to look closer at them. All Panama City Beach-themed—the Pier Park sign, a big shark's mouth attached to a store, one of a family building a sandcastle on the beach. They were Ashe's pictures, tailored to fit Bo's store. It warmed her heart to see Bo's friendship group represented in his store.

Continuing with her curiosity, she headed back through a hallway in the back and found him at a computer. He loaded paper into a printer tray, and checks came zooming out. She'd seen this done at her work plenty of times, but the buck stopped with Bo. That was his money behind those checks. Of course she understood the concept of business, but it was like she was seeing it from an entirely new angle.

One of Ashe's pictures hung in Bo's office. It was of their friendship group on the beach, holding cans of beer and sort of piled up together, all smiles and laughs. She backed out of his office, that familiar sadness covering her heart. She didn't know how she was going to leave.

A few minutes later, he came out from the back. "You ready?"

"Are you sure you can take the day off?" she asked.

"Of course." He smiled. "Perks of being the boss." He set the checks and a stack of envelopes on the counter in front of Tracey. "Will you make sure these go out in today's mail?"

"Yep," she said. "Hey, I sold the last Davison 115-volt, above-ground pump right before close last night."

"They're coming in on the shipment today," he said.

"And Todd and Pablo are both asking for next Friday off."

"That's fine. I'll cover for them. Anything else right now?"

She shook her head and smiled. "No. Enjoy your day. Thank your mom for the muffins." She turned to Maya. "It was nice meeting you."

"Nice meeting you, too."

Tracey waved and got back to work. Bo helped Maya into the truck, and she watched his shop in action as he walked around the front. He closed himself in and started the truck.

"I feel bad, like I'm taking you away from them for the day."

"You need to get over that. This place runs just fine without me all the time, trust me."

She smiled at him. "I feel like I know a new side of you now that I've seen your business."

"That's just the storefront. It runs like a well-oiled machine. It's the cleaning side that takes most of my attention. I wish I could see you at work," he said.

She chuckled at that thought. "I don't. I stare at a computer in an office all day. It's not in the least bit sexy."

"If you're there, darlin', it's sexy."

She shook her head at him. He was so good at making her feel like the only woman on the planet.

They wheeled into Sebastian's driveway, and Bo leaned over and kissed her. "You sure they won't be pissed at me for taking you for the rest of the day?"

"They'll get over it. We may need to make an appearance at the bonfire on the beach Sebastian is planning for this evening."

"We can do that," Bo said. "Just means I need to get you to that boat faster so we can have the whole day alone."

She leaned over to kiss him, and he cradled the back of her neck with his big hand. He knew how to make her feel so feminine.

"I'll be two seconds grabbing my suit."

"I'll come say hi to Sebastian and make sure he's all right with me taking you today."

She smiled and kissed him one more time. "Okay."

She shouldered her overnight bag and purse and floated up the walk to Sebastian's house, holding hands with Bo like they were teenagers who needed to touch one another to survive. Man she was in for a rude awakening tomorrow.

She opened the door, and stopped in her tracks.

"Meade?"

Her sister stood up off Sebastian's couch and smiled, but her eyes were bloodshot like she'd been crying.

"I was just getting ready to text you, again," Sebastian said, a smile plastered across his face.

Maya realized for the first time that she hadn't even thought about her phone yet that day. That was some sort of record.

Meade let out a huge sigh. "Maya, oh my gosh. Look at you." Meade rushed over and took Maya into her arms.

Maya stood, still as a stone, no clue what was happening. She dropped her purse and her bag to the floor. "What are you doing here?"

Meade pulled back from her, holding both of Maya's hands. "Surprise!" Maya let out a huff of air, trying to process Meade's presence. Meade held out her hand to Bo. "Hi, I'm Meade, Maya's sister. You must be Bo. Felicity and Sebastian have been filling me in."

Bo shook her hand. "It's nice to meet you."

Maya turned to Bo, who was smiling politely but had already taken a step away from her. She turned back to Meade, irritation starting to bubble in her chest. "What's going on?"

Meade let out a huge sigh, glancing at Bo and then back at her. "Well, I came in last night, and I'm here just for the day. I thought I'd hitch a ride back home with you and Felicity tomorrow."

"To Indianapolis?" Maya asked.

Meade got this huge smile on her face. "I'm moving back. I know it takes me a while, but I finally get there. Come, let's sit and talk about everything."

Maya rubbed her forehead, glancing at Bo. He pointed at the door. "I'm gonna head out. It was nice to meet you, Meade."

"No," Maya said, and Meade blinked looking confused. Maya clenched her eyes shut, the ridiculous irony of Meade choosing this one precious day to listen to Maya.

"Come walk me outside," Bo said, his voice resigned.

"We'll see you tonight at the bonfire?" Sebastian asked.

Bo gave something resembling a nod, and then headed outside. Maya followed him, every step they took toward his truck adding more weight onto her anxiety level. When they got to the door of his truck, she tossed her hands up and let them fall to her sides. "I can't believe this."

"Come here," he said, pulling her to his chest.

She pulled away. "This is just so her. So typically Meade. She chooses right now to do this? Right freaking now?"

"She's your sister," Bo said. "She's the most important thing. More important than me or anyone else."

There was nothing more important on the planet at that moment than Bo. But her relationship with Bo was ending in less than a day. Her brain told her to focus on her sister, but her body was having a really hard time falling in line.

He rested his hands on her hips. "I've had a lot of fun this week."

A tidal wave of nausea came over her. "You're saying that like this is the last time I'll see you."

He exhaled a deep breath. "Maya, I'm nuts about you, I don't think that's a secret, but there's nowhere this can go. I want you to stay here, hell I want you to move here, but I would never ask that of you. You've got your big job you're starting Monday that you've worked your whole career for, and now you've got your sister who needs you. You said you'd been asking her to move home for a long time, and it sounds like she's doing that." He squeezed her hips, giving her a smile, his eyebrows lifted in encouragement. "That's great, right?"

She swallowed hard, looking at him, hearing his words, but not wanting to agree with any of it.

His expression dropped, and his brow furrowed. "I don't want to be in the way of whatever's going on here. We were gonna be doing this tomorrow morning anyway. It seems like the right thing for us is to go ahead and say bye now. Don't you think?"

She didn't think. She didn't want that at all. She wanted to get back in that truck and pretend Meade wasn't inside, her eyes clearly bloodshot from crying over some asshole piece of crap who meant nothing. Her throat filled with dread. If she spoke, tears would come, and she wasn't going to cry, not right here in front of Bo.

"Maya, talk to me," he said, but she couldn't. There was nothing to say. She needed to get inside to her sister. This was ending, now, and as much as it felt like her heart was being mutilated by a bear, she had to accept it.

She nodded, trying to force a smile, but there

was no way.

He pulled her in close and held her there against his big body. It seemed impossible that she'd never feel his arms around her ever again.

He pulled away. "Good luck with your new job. I want you to be so happy, Maya. I mean that." He leaned down and kissed her, closed-mouthed and cold.

As he got into his truck, her mouth filled with cotton. She had so much to say, but he was just leaving, done forever. How had he done that? He'd gone from having her in his bed an hour ago to telling her goodbye forever on the spot. She didn't care if he thought he was doing it for her benefit. It hurt, like hell.

She stepped backward at the sound of his truck's engine, watching him put the truck in gear and back out of the driveway, not even giving her so much as a backward glance. As his truck rolled out of sight, her breaths came quicker and stronger. It'd been decades, but that old familiar anxiety flooded into her chest and her breaths. She was hyperventilating.

The door to the house opened, and Sebastian was there by her side. He walked her into the house. "Felicity, get a paper bag. They're in the pantry on the top shelf, right-hand side." He turned back to Maya. "Come here. You're okay." He rubbed her back. "Shh, you're okay. Shh."

He kept rubbing her back and helping her quiet down, just like he'd done in high school the time she was falsely accused of cheating on her trig quiz.

"Oh, my God, Maya. You still do this?" Meade said.

"Meade," Sebastian said, his voice stern but calm. "Please do me a huge favor and take my car to the market on the corner of my neighborhood's street and 30A. Can you do that and get her a bottle of ginger ale?"

"You go. I'll stay with her."

Maya's breaths got faster and harder. "Meade, please. I'd really appreciate it if you could do that for me, okay?" His voice left no room for argument.

He led Maya to the couch where they sat down. Felicity showed up with the bag, and Maya breathed into it, vaguely aware of the front door closing.

Felicity sat on one side of her and Sebastian on the other as her breaths got slower and steadier. Sebastian kept rubbing her back until she calmed down to her regular breathing pattern, the two of them providing more comfort for her with their mere presence than either of them could know. Finally, Maya looked at Sebastian, searching for answers she knew he didn't have.

"I know, sweetie," he said. "I know."

"He's gone," Maya said, her voice flat and dull. "We were supposed to have had this last day together, but he went ahead and said goodbye now."

He shook his head. "I saw it in his eyes as soon as he assessed the whole situation."

"Why's she here?" Maya asked, her voice betraying the frustration in her chest.

"She walked in on Luke fucking some girl in her bed," Felicity said.

Maya rubbed her aching head, her sisterly connection kicking in, the pain slicing through her heart on Meade's behalf. She thought about Bo walking in on that same situation, and thinking about how hard it'd been for him ever since.

She clenched her fists. "Goddamn asshole. How's she been?"

"Crying," Felicity said. "A lot."

The sound of Sebastian's car pulling up in the driveway had Maya sitting up and pulling herself back together.

"Sweetie—" Sebastian said, but she cut him off.

"No, I've got this. I'll be fine. We're gonna just deal with this one step at a time. Why don't the two of you go somewhere, and I'll stay here with her."

"We want to help," Felicity said. The car door shut and Meade's footfalls sounded up the walk.

"No, it's fine. I've got this. I'll talk to her. We'll do a whole wallow day and figure out the next steps. You two go." She took Felicity's hand and forced a smile. "Enjoy your last day here, okay?" Felicity gave her a look. Maya shook off the episode she was now fully embarrassed to have let herself have. "We may join you somewhere. I'll text you. Just go about your day, okay?"

Felicity smiled at her as Meade came through the doorway. "I've got your ginger ale." Felicity moved from her spot and Meade took her place.

Maya forced a smile. "Great. Thanks."

Meade handed it to her and rubbed her shoulder with a concerned look. "You okay, yo-yo?"

Maya nodded, cringing at Meade's baby name for her. As much as she loved her sister, she couldn't help the deep resentment she felt toward her at the moment. It was stupid, senseless really. She was going to have to say goodbye to Bo tomorrow anyway, but she couldn't help equating Bo's one-hundred-and-eighty-degree turn out there with Meade's being here. No talk of texting to make sure she got home from the drive, or trying for a long-distance relationship, nothing. Just gone.

"Was he an ass to you?" Meade asked.

Maya gritted her teeth and shook her head. "Nope, not at all." Meade looked confused. For a girl with a genius IQ, she was certainly clueless. Maya forced another smile and patted her sister on the knee. "Tell me about what happened with Luke."

Meade had looked about as rough as Maya had ever seen her look. Meade had always been the prettier sister. She'd been the older, wiser, better, more attractive one. She'd always been heavier than Maya, but it suited her. She looked healthier than Maya. But she'd not been taking care of herself. She'd lost more weight than looked healthy, and she looked like she'd aged five years since Maya saw her at Christmas. Her hair was frizzy on the ends, and she'd been bleaching it to be platinum blond like Maya's natural color. Meade's natural color was a beautiful, golden blond. The idea of bleaching it was incomprehensible, but probably some stupid guy wanted it that way.

Meade started in with the story, and Maya nodded and listened, trying desperately not to think about the fact that what could have become the great love of her life had just faded away.

Chapter Eighteen

Bo swung hard and made contact with the baseball, sending it soaring into the net. His shoulder would pay for this tomorrow and the next day, but beating the hell out of baseballs was all he could think to do right now. He needed tomorrow morning to get here quick, because as long as she was here in this same area as him, all he wanted to do was go and steal her away from her sister and bring her back home to his bed.

But it had been his time to walk away, that'd been as clear as crystal when he set his eyes on her sister there at Sebastian's house. He'd not understood it at first, this woman who looked like a slightly different version of Maya, but she was nothing like Maya. She seemed outgoing and emotional, so different from Maya's reserve, keeping everything around her in check.

But there was no mistaking the connection Maya

had to her sister. She'd talked so much about Meade and how she wanted to get her home and on the right track. Bo guessed she was getting that wish now, and that was a good thing. He needed to step out of the way and let Maya get to work helping her like she needed to.

Bo waited for the next pitch, but the machine was empty. He wanted to go another round, but there was a line, so he slid the bat back in its slot and headed toward the truck. He didn't want to go home. It still smelled like Maya. As much as he wanted to preserve that smell, he couldn't be around it, not right now.

He turned into the rear lot of his business and snuck in the back way. He didn't want to answer any questions, but it wasn't long before Tracey was at his door. "I thought you were taking the day off."

"I wanted to be there when they delivered that shipment."

"How come?"

He exhaled a deep breath. "I just do."

"You okay, Bo?" she asked.

"Yeah, sorry. I'm fine. Just, weird day."

"Mmm hmm," she said, eyeing him. "I've had a few of those, too."

He closed his eyes as she shut his office door behind her. Putting his head on his desk, he counted the seconds till this day would be over. Shayla was coming tomorrow for a few days. That would help get his mind off of Maya, if that was possible.

Bo sat staring at the guys on television analyzing the leagues' best baseball players. They were on his nerves. He'd finished his beer a half hour prior, but he couldn't be bothered to make his way to the refrigerator for another one. The crunch of gravel in his front yard had Jake's ears up. "Sick 'em," Bo said, but Jake just gave him that look where he cranked his head to the side.

The doorbell rang, and then a heavy knock sounded. "It's Chase. You home?"

He rolled his eyes. "No."

"Let me in. Come on." Bo hauled his ass up off the couch and lumbered to the door. He opened it and then went back to the couch. Chase put his hand to his chest. "Why, yes, I'd love a cold beverage. You need one?"

"Mmm hmm."

Chase found two beers and popped both caps. He handed one to Bo. "You missed the bonfire."

"So I did." He looked Chase up and down. "Shouldn't you be home with Felicity right now?"

"Ah, no. You fucked that up for me. Thanks, by the way." He plopped down on the sofa.

Bo frowned at him. "What'd I do?"

"Since you're not in the picture anymore, they're planning on getting an early start tomorrow. Felicity kissed my ass goodbye about half an hour ago."

Bo considered him. "You okay?"

Chase gave him a curious look. "Of course I'm okay. Why wouldn't I be?"

"She's leaving."

"Felicity?" Chase waved him off. "I'll love again."

Bo eyed him. "So it's that goddamned easy for you, huh?"

Chase set his ankle on his knee. "We were just hanging out. Trust me, she's not losing any sleep over being separated from me. Besides, I think we're gonna be friends, like actual ones. I told her I'd call her later on this week after she'd gotten settled back in."

Bo turned to face him. "So how's that gonna work, huh? You're gonna call her and talk into the wee hours of the night sharing all your stupid stories? Tell each other secrets and get to know her real well knowing you're never gonna have the real thing in the flesh?"

Chase looked off into the distance and then shrugged. "Pretty much. I just like her and want to be her friend. If I never get to have sex with her again, I'm okay with that. I'm sure she's the same way."

Bo thought about what it meant to have Maya in his arms, watching her expression morph into a genuine smile when he said something she thought was funny, the scent of her hair when she was lying against his chest, the feel of her bare skin against his as they made love. "I can't do that."

"Do what?"

"Turn it off like that. Not with Maya, that's for damn sure."

Chase slapped his own leg. "All right. That's enough of this shit. Put on a decent shirt. We're going to Alligator Alley."

Bo glared at him. "Isn't that how I got into this mess?"

Chase held up his big hands. "No women this time. Just you and me. We're gonna shoot some pool, throw some darts, play Pac Man, and drink enough beer to numb the pain."

"I didn't think you felt heartbreak."

"Your pain. I'm gonna be the responsible one this evening."

"That's scary as fuck."

Chase nudged him. "Come on. Go get on a shirt you haven't drooled on."

"It's Alligator Alley."

"True. You're good like that. Let's go."

Bo sat in his usual spot at the bar at Alligator Alley, avoiding making eye contact with Jennifer who was playing pool with some people they'd gone to high school with. He didn't like her comment about Angela the other day or the way she eyed Maya. He had no doubt she was working on something shitty to come say. Whatever it was, he didn't want to hear it.

His phone rang, and Shayla's name came across the screen. "Your sister's calling," Chase said.

"I know, nosey." Bo answered it. "Hey."

"What are you up to tonight?" she asked by way of greeting.

"Sitting at Alligator Alley with a buddy."

"Which one?"

"Chase. You haven't met him." Chase lifted his eyebrows. Bo frowned. Chase was one of his closest friends, but he damn sure didn't want him anywhere near his sister. He was girl-crazy and couldn't keep his hands off anything with a set of boobs. "And you don't want to. What are you doing?"

"Getting off at the Montgomery exit."

"Dammit, Shayla. You know I hate you driving those backroads in the dark."

"I've done it plenty."

"I didn't like it then either. I thought you were driving down tomorrow."

"I was ready to come on tonight. It's fine, baby brother. Will you relax?"

"Get a hotel there in Montgomery and drive the rest of the way tomorrow," he said, knowing his words were futile.

"I'm coming in tonight. Just making sure I didn't need to crash at Mama and Daddy's for the night. I know you've been seeing that girl this week."

"That's done," he said with a churn in his gut. "Come on to my house. You've got your key?"

"Yep," she said.

Bobby put another beer down in front of him. "I've got a seven o'clock tee time with Roy," Bo said. "I didn't think you'd been in till later."

"I think I can manage a day without you. Drink your beer and be careful getting home."

He hung up, and Chase was looking at him. "What?" Bo asked.

"How come you won't introduce me to your sister?"

"You've never been around when she's been here."

Chase eyed him, and Bo gave it right back to him. "Is that the only reason?" Chase asked.

Bo took a sip of his beer, watching the television. He gave Chase the side-eye. "She's not available."

"For what?"

"For your flavor of the week."

Chase huffed a laugh. "If you seriously think I'd try to sleep with your sister, you're more paranoid than I thought." He pointed at his chest. "I don't have a death wish."

Bo pursed his lips at him. Chase was about six inches taller than him, but the idea of Chase in a fight was about as likely as a gorilla crashing through the ceiling.

"I guess I'll miss her this time, too. I'm headed out tomorrow morning for Minneapolis."

"Damn shame," Bo said.

"You want something to eat?" Bobby asked from behind the bar.

"I'm not hungry," Bo said.

"I am," Chase said. "Bring us some greasy ass bar food. A bunch of it."

Bobby nodded. "Coming up."

Bo and Chase sat in silence for a while, and then Bo said, "Why do people live up north anyway?"

"Don't fucking ask me. I can't figure out why anyone would live anywhere but here. White, powdery beaches, salty ocean breezes, warm sun shining down most the time. Hell, I get a chill when it drops below seventy degrees. I'd shrivel up and die if I tried to live up there."

Jennifer cackled from across the room, then glanced at Bo with that look in her eye. No doubt she was coming his way soon. Bo frowned down at his beer. It didn't even taste good.

"You want to go play pool?" Chase asked.

"Nah."

"Well, I'm gonna hit the head. When I get back,

you're getting that ass up out of that seat and we're doing something, so just get ready."

Bo stared at the television screen, but he saw her coming out of the corner of his eye. "Too good to come say hi?"

His stomach coiled at the sound of her voice. "You can walk across a room as well as I can."

She sat next to him, still holding her pool cue. "Your girl-of-the-week go home?"

Bo didn't want Jennifer even thinking about Maya, much less talking about her. He chose not to respond, hoping she'd get the hint.

She looked him over, running her fingers up and down the pool stick. "There was a time you were chasing me around like that. Remember when you took me to Capt. Anderson's?"

Bo tried hard not to roll his eyes. He was fifteen years old, and Jennifer had driven them. He'd really thought he was something back then, taking out the hottest girl in the junior class, him being a sophomore.

She moved closer to him. "You remember what we did later in the passenger seat of my Camaro?" An evil grin widened her face. "You didn't even make it out of your Levi's."

He wondered if it was possible for this day to get worse.

Jennifer's attention went to the door behind him. "Well, looks like your desperate tourist is back for more. Just take your ass back home, bitch."

Bo turned to find Maya walking through the doorway followed by her sister. His stomach flopped around like a fish out of water. Maya marched up to him, glancing between him and Jennifer. Finally, she held out her hand. "Hello, I'm Maya. I believe we met earlier this week."

Jennifer blinked, looking taken aback, and then glanced her up and down. "You're still here?"

"Yep, for…" She looked down at her wrist, which was bare, and then patted her pockets, coming up empty. He held his phone up so she could read the time. "Eight more hours. Thank you," she said with a polite smile that quickly turned into a glare.

Jennifer moved even closer to Bo, making his insides itch. "Well, we'll sure hate to see you go."

Meade walked over to Bo, arms out wide like they were old friends. "So good to see you again," she said, hugging him and sort of inching her way between Bo and Jennifer, then she turned to Jennifer and held out a hand. "I'm Meade." Jennifer reluctantly stepped backward, looking caught off guard. "You want to do a shot?" Meade asked her.

"Okay?" Jennifer said like it was a question.

Meade turned back around to Maya. "What are we having?"

"Red hot shots," Maya said, not missing a beat, but with a little sway. She steadied herself with a hand on his knee.

He hadn't seen her like this. Even the night at Sebastian's when they'd done shots, she maintained her collected and in-control demeanor the whole night. "You want to sit?" he asked.

She pulled her hand off his knee like she suddenly realized it was a hot burner. "No. I'm fine to stand."

Chase walked up. "There's my favorite northerner, well, second favorite."

Maya went to hug Chase and sort of fell into him. He held her up steady though, and didn't let go. Meade turned around, and blinked. "Hel-lo."

"Meade," Maya said, looking like she was blinking herself awake. "This is Chase. Felicity's guy, so don't even think about it."

"Damn," Meade said, handing him a shot. "Red hot?"

"Trying to quit. But don't let me stop you."

Meade handed the shot to Maya, gave one to Bo, and then passed the last one to Jennifer. "To those who wish us well." She smiled at Jennifer. "And we all know where the rest can go."

Jennifer took the shot, the whole time eyeing Meade, who didn't back down an inch. Bo liked her already. Maya took the shot from Bo's hand and knocked it back. He looked at Chase. "Did she just do both of those?"

Maya put her hands on her hips. "Yes, she did." She pointed at him. "I came here to say something to you, Bo Harrison."

Bo glanced around for somewhere they could talk, preferably near a trashcan or bathroom in case Maya needed to puke. "Bobby, give me the key to the storage room."

"It's open."

He took her hand and she snatched it away from him, so he motioned the way so he could follow behind her in case she needed help staying on her feet. Two shots of red hot on top of what she'd clearly already had were a recipe for disaster.

He opened the door to the storeroom and stepped inside, stopping short as she turned back toward him. He held her in place before she could fall backward. She stepped back, holding up both hands. "I'm fine."

"Okay."

She glared at him, her blue eyes glassy and red. "You're an asshole."

He couldn't keep his lip from quirking up in a grin. It was just so uncharacteristic of her. He wondered if being around Meade all day had tweaked her personality a little. She seemed to be Maya's polar opposite. Maya pointed at him until her finger was touching his bottom lip. "Don't do that cute smile. I hate that thing." He tried to straighten his expression, but, of course, now all he could do was smile. "Stop it," she said, but without conviction, starting to look defeated, or real drunk, he couldn't tell which.

"Okay," he said. "What'd you come here to tell me?"

"You can't do what you did earlier today."

"What'd I do?"

She pursed her lips, blinking hard. "You took yourself away from me, just like that." She tried to snap, but it was a misfire.

"I didn't want to get in the way of you and your sister."

"You just can't do that. You can't decide for both of us when this is over. We should decide that together."

He put his hands on her waist, his heart breaking all over again. "I'm sorry. I thought I was helping."

She shoved his hands away. "You weren't helping. You could have come to the bonfire at least." She blinked hard, her eyelids becoming droopier.

"It was too hard. I needed to make the break, clean."

She stepped closer, hands on his chest. "What was so hard about it?"

He looked down into her sleepy eyes, the emotions of the week building in his chest, the attachment he had to her seeming unbreakable, the idea of losing her making his insides crawl. Her head dropped to his chest and he ran his hand up and down her back, taking in the scent of her hair like it was his last breath before being locked in a cell for the rest of his life.

She made a noise resembling a snore and he let a huff of air out. "Because I fell in love with you."

Chapter Nineteen

"Maya," a soft but deep voice said. "Maya, darlin'."

Bo. It was Bo's voice, except it wasn't.

"Maya, sweetie." A touch on her arm had her blinking awake. She sat up straight at the sight of woman with dark, straight hair sitting on her bed. Maya grabbed for the covers, but a glance downward revealed her to be completely dressed, in Bo's T-shirt and boxers.

"I'm Shayla. Bo's sister."

Maya glanced around the room, Bo's room. Flashes of the prior night's catastrophe at the bar populated her aching brain, and her stomach felt queasy, her very empty stomach, which chose then to let out a roar. The noise was so loud that they both looked at it.

"Are you a coffee drinker?" Shayla handed Maya a steaming mug.

"Um, not usually."

"Now might be a good time to start. Felicity and Meade are on their way."

Maya searched the nightstand and bed for her phone. "What time is it?"

"It's nine-thirty. They were trying to give you as long as possible, but Felicity needed to get on the road. She's got her mother's party tomorrow, and you've got a company picnic. If you'd like to sleep in, we can look at flights, but—"

"No. I mean, no thanks. I um. I just need to..." Maya had no clear thought process at the moment. She narrowed her gaze at Shayla, who was quite possibly the most beautiful woman Maya had ever laid her eyes on outside of television and movies, even sitting there with wet hair and not a stitch of makeup on. Her skin was olive like Bo's, her eyes dark like his, her cheekbones high and prominent. She looked so much like Bo and sounded like him as well, and she was here, sitting on his bed. Her confused brain started to register some sort of minor attraction level that made heat rise through her chest and up through her neck. Maya drew her hand there to cover the color. "Is Bo here?"

"No, darlin', I'm sorry. He had a seven o'clock tee time. He wanted to cancel but I told him I'd wake you up when it was time."

Maya forced a smile, tugging at her neck. "Thank you."

"You're a good two or three sizes smaller than me, but I've got this T-shirt and leggings you can wear home if you want some clean clothes."

Maya glanced around. "Um, do you know where my clothes are?"

"Yeah, they're in a bag, tied up tight on the kitchen table. I was going to wash them, but I guess they're dry clean only?" She gave Maya a curious look.

"Oh, yes. So they're…dirty?"

Shayla tilted her head with a crooked smile meant to be comforting. "Yeah, you puked a bit when you got out of the car here in the driveway, apparently. I missed that part."

Maya dropped her forehead into her hand, her whole body ill at ease. Mortified didn't begin to cover it. She faced Shayla head-on. "Do I need to clean anywhere before I leave?"

"No, we got it already. Most went directly in the toilet in there."

She imagined herself vomiting in Bo's commode. "Bo was here for this?" she asked, knowing and fearing the answer.

Shayla smiled. "Who do you think held back your hair?" She patted Maya on the knee over the sheet. "I'm gonna let you get showered. They'll be here soon."

Maya took the clothes. "Thank you for these. If you'll give me your address, I'll launder them and mail them back to you."

Shayla waved her off. "The shirt's a freebie, and I've got about eight pair of black leggings. I'll be in the living room if you need anything else."

Maya waited until Shayla was all the way out of the room before she allowed herself to fully bask in the humiliation. Fueled only by the fact that her friends were motoring their way to her as she sat there, she pulled herself out of the bed and made her way to the shower.

As she cleaned her body, she considered how different the last shower she'd had in Bo's bathroom was. They'd been lathering each other's naked bodies and giving each other orgasms, and now she was washing puke out of her hair.

She dried off and put on the leggings and T-shirt, feeling as ridiculous as she looked. She'd never owned a pair of leggings, much less worn one, though she was grateful to have them. She stripped the bed and brought the sheets out to the living room. "Are you okay for me to start these now?"

"Yeah, I'm gonna be here for a while." Shayla walked toward her. "Give them here. I'll start them."

"Thank you," Maya said. "Do you know where he keeps the clean ones?"

"I've got it. I don't have anything else to do. Grab some cereal or Pop Tarts out of the pantry if you want to get something on your stomach."

She glanced around the living room, looking for anything else of hers while Shayla started the sheets. If there had been any sort of door open for a relationship between her and Bo, long distance or otherwise, Maya had completely destroyed that possibility. Shayla met her back in the living room with a polite smile.

"Do you know if I have a purse or anything?" Maya asked.

"I don't think you have anything, darlin'. I don't see a purse anywhere, and I'm pretty sure you don't have a phone here."

Maya nodded, the sound of tires crunching

gravel saving her from further embarrassment. "Well, that's them, I think."

Shayla glanced out the living room window. "Looks like it."

Maya swallowed hard and faced her. "Words can't describe how sorry I am about all of this."

Shayla waved her off. "It's nothing. I've been there."

"No, I don't think you understand. I haven't, ever. I'm always completely in control. But this week, I've lost my mind, I think."

Shayla winked at her. "My brother has a way of driving people to drink. Seriously, don't worry about it."

Maya smiled, Shayla's charms working on her. "Thank you, Shayla. I really wish I could have met you under different circumstances."

"Maybe we will someday."

Maya wished like anything that was true. "I hope so."

Shayla opened her arms, and Maya hugged her close to her chest, Maya wishing there was some way for the two of them to become friends, but knowing that was impossible.

A knock sounded at the door, and Maya pulled away. "There's my ride."

"Be safe," Shayla said.

"Thanks," Maya replied and left Bo's house for good.

Walking up the front steps to his house, Bo had the stupid hope that Maya would still be there, but of course all he found in his living room was his sister.

"Don't look so excited to see me," Shayla said.

"How did it go this morning?" he asked. All he could think about all day was Maya meeting Shayla and him not even being there for it.

"Good. She's not at all what I expected."

He smiled, collapsing in the armchair. "Right?"

"How'd you land a woman like that?"

He pointed at his chest. "My Southern charm."

She rolled her eyes. "Your Southern bullshit."

"Hey, my charm is natural."

"So, why are you letting her get away from here?"

"How am I supposed to keep her here?"

"Oh, your stupid charm wasn't enough?"

He messed with a spot on the armrest. "She's got a big job up in Indianapolis she's starting Monday. VP job."

"Mmm hmm. And you helped her prep for that the weekend before by getting her so wasted she had to hug your toilet all night."

"I had nothing to do with her alcohol level." Shayla gave him a look. "Well, not directly."

She picked up her mug and blew on it. "So what's the deal? Tell me all about it, baby brother."

Bo did—from start to finish only leaving out the intimate details, even though they were the best part.

"Well, damn," Shayla said. "If I'd have known all this, I'd never have let her leave or let you play golf this morning."

"You're the one who talked me into going."

"That's because I didn't want to see you put your relationship with one of your biggest clients at risk for some stupid piece of ass."

He pointed at her. "She's not—"

"I know that now. All I knew of her last night was she was puking her guts out in your bathroom. What was I supposed to think? It's not like you've been available to talk to this week."

She had him there. He and Shayla usually talked most days. They'd barely said boo to one another this week, and that was mostly his fault.

"I've never seen you like this," Shayla said.

"I've never been like this. I've never met anyone like her before. She makes me want to stand up straighter and do stuff to impress her. And I'm not talking about back flips off the high dive. She makes me want to grow my business and read War and Peace, and volunteer at a homeless shelter. I don't know. This isn't a girl who's impressed with muscles and a wad of cash on an expensive dinner. This is someone I'd have to work to earn respect from, and goddamn do I want to do that."

Shayla gave him a small smile. "So what are you going to do about it?"

He tossed up his hands. "What am I supposed to do, Shayla?"

She put her mug on the end table. "Come on. Let's go eat. I've got something to talk to you about, and it might factor in here."

"Really?" he asked.

"Just come on."

Chapter Twenty

Two weeks back from her vacation, and Maya's life was still in complete disarray. Between trying to catch up on the week she was gone, starting a new job, and answering questions from the woman who'd taken her old job, she'd done nothing but work and sleep, and she wasn't getting nearly enough of the latter.

She set her tablet down on the desk and collapsed in her chair. The meetings were nonstop, and they only generated more work as a result of whatever they met about, but she couldn't get the work done because she was always scheduled for another stupid meeting.

She checked her phone for messages. There were plenty of them but none from the one person she still so idiotically hoped to hear from. When she first returned from the trip, she'd sat down that next day and wrote out a card to Bo and one to his sister, both thanking them for their help and apologizing for her actions. A text seemed entirely not enough, and there was no way she could bring herself to call Bo after the way she'd behaved. So she'd mailed the cards and closed the subject, except she couldn't seem to extricate him from her brain.

She rubbed her hands over her face as her executive assistant walked into the room. Brenda was the only thing keeping her sanity in check. She was way more qualified for Maya's job than she was, but apparently she hadn't even applied for it. When Maya had asked her why, Brenda had looked at her like she was a space alien and said, "No fucking way." It was the only time Maya had heard her use a curse word in the decade they'd worked in the same office.

"Oh, Brenda. Please tell me it's over," Maya said.

"Your day?" Brenda asked.

Maya dropped her hands onto the desk and met Brenda's gaze, whose hair was still in a tidy bun on top of her head, not a strand out of place, makeup immaculate. "I haven't worked out in two weeks," Maya said. "I've eaten pizza four times this week. I haven't had pizza in two years, Brenda. When do I get my life back?"

Brenda exhaled a deep breath and sat down in Maya's visitor chair. "This is why they pay you the big bucks."

"That's great, but I can't spend any of the big bucks because I'm always freaking here." She splayed out her fingers. "Look at my nails."

Brenda winced. "I'm making you an

appointment for tomorrow."

"I'll be here tomorrow, on Saturday."

"Your nails can't look like that, Maya. I'm not kidding. You've got to look pulled together. I'm making you an appointment for a cut, too. I think I'll bring someone in here to the office tomorrow. The company will pay."

"Are you serious?"

"Of course. You've got a big meeting on Monday with the team of executives from West Coast Burrito. "You can't look like this then."

She blinked. "Is the rest of me as messed up as my nails?"

Brenda exhaled a deep breath. "Maya, you're a beautiful young lady, and you'll get used to the hours, but at first they seem grueling and they put you through the ringer, physically. I've seen too many women buckle under the pressure because twice as much is expected of them as it is with the men in these jobs. I consider your success my success, and, clearly, I've not been doing my job these past weeks if I'm allowing your physical appearance and health to deteriorate. From now on, there will be a salad in that fridge every night at five o'clock. And I'll schedule in your workouts as well. Do we need to bring a treadmill in here?" Brenda glanced around the office, and then finally landed on Maya. She frowned. "Sweetie, is something wrong? I mean something outside of work?"

The tightrope Maya had been balancing on for the last two weeks started to snap. She hadn't been able to talk to Meade. It was important for Meade to see Maya staying strong, and for Maya to show her how easy it was to walk away from the beefcake if you just put your mind to it. Except Bo was so much more than a beefcake.

Meade was looking for jobs, real ones. She'd been in touch with professors and people from groups she'd been a part of before she decided to throw her career and her potential down the drain. Meade was doing too well for Maya to take the risk of showing her that missing Bo was ripping her to shreds from the inside out. But she needed to get it out before it imploded inside her chest.

She gave Brenda an abbreviated rundown of her vacation, and Brenda exhaled a deep breath, studying Maya. "I've known you a long time, Maya." Maya nodded, swallowing hard. "Is this job what you really want?" Brenda asked.

"Yes, of course it is."

Brenda narrowed her gaze. "You know it's okay if you change your mind."

Maya held up a finger, her heartbeat quickening. "I'm not changing my mind. I've worked for a decade for this job."

"Yes, I know you have. And if they'd have hired anyone on the planet other than you, I'd have quit on the spot. Not really, but you get the point." Maya half-smiled. "But things change. Life throws curveballs, and we have to reevaluate what's important to us."

Maya leaned in, elbows on her desk. "Brenda, do you have any idea how many lectures I've given my sister about giving up important things in her life for a guy?"

"I understand that. But possibly a little egg on

279

your face would be worth it to marry a fantastic man."

Maya held up both hands. "Oh, no. We're nowhere near marriage talk. We're over, to be exact. It's been two weeks, and he's not even so much as texted."

Brenda shrugged. "Well, then maybe it's not meant to be. But I think the week with this fellow has possibly helped you see that you're not pigeonholed to a certain type of man. Life doesn't have to be boring, Maya."

Maya pursed her lips. "Boring is safe."

Brenda looked over her shoulder and then scooted forward. "I was engaged to be married when I was twenty-one years old. My fiancé was set to inherit his father's auto parts business. My job was going to be staying pregnant and learning how to roast a chicken. My girlfriends took me on a trip to Myrtle Beach, South Carolina, and I left there married to a bartender I met on the boardwalk."

Maya's eyes flew wide. "Brenda!"

"It's true."

"I never knew you were married," Maya said.

Brenda shrugged. "It was another life."

"How long did you stay married to him?"

"A year and a half. He died in a motorcycle accident on the way to help a friend paint his house."

Maya's hand went to her chest. "I'm so sorry."

"I was on the back of the bike at the time. It's a miracle I survived."

"Are you serious?"

"Point is, that year and a half was the best time

in my life. Until that trip, all I thought I'd ever wanted was to be a wife and a mother."

Maya couldn't help stating the obvious. "But you never married again."

Brenda smiled. "Hector was my husband. Once you experience love like that, there's no settling."

Maya fought the tears that stung at the back of her eyes.

Brenda picked up her legal pad. "Last appointment for the day. You have a five-thirty at Preen."

"The restaurant?"

"Yes. He'll meet you at the bar."

"Who is it with?"

"Nathan Edgefield. He's on the partner track at Madero, Lopez, and Washington."

Maya tossed her hands up. "Who is this?"

"Your blind date from last Friday night. We rescheduled it for tonight."

Maya let her head drop into her hands. "I can't go on a date."

"He may be your Hector," Brenda said.

Maya looked at the time on her tablet. It was already five-fifteen. "Okay."

"Grab your purse, head to the bathroom, and give yourself a quick makeover. Even if he doesn't compare to this guy from Florida, if some form of chemistry is there, who knows, this could be a good guy to have a date with once in a while." She gave Maya a significant look.

Maya wondered if this was standard for single executives—find a counterpart whose life was as swallowed up in work as one's own just so one could have sex on occasion. Was this the life she was choosing for herself? What about a family and children? Where did they factor in? What about soccer games and school plays? Runny noses and homework? Was this sort of life conducive to any of that? And since when was she interested in runny-nosed kids?

She made herself as presentable as possible, trying to ignore the bloodshot eyes because there wasn't much she could do about those, and she called Meade as she walked the few blocks to Preen.

"I've got a meeting at five-thirty that I wasn't expecting, so I won't be home till later."

"Like that's new. Who schedules a meeting at five-thirty on a Friday night?"

"It's a blind date, actually."

"Oh. Okay. What do you know about him?" Meade asked.

Maya hit the button at a crosswalk. "I don't know. He's a lawyer."

"Mmm. Sounds responsible."

"What are you going to do tonight?" Maya asked.

"There's a documentary I've been wanting to watch about Eleanor Roosevelt. Looks like it's popcorn and that for me tonight." Maya couldn't help the bit of relief that flooded her chest. They'd been home two weeks, and Meade hadn't even mentioned any men. It was like her brain was powering back up. "I was going to tell you tonight," Meade said, "but since I may be asleep by the time you get here...I got that job interview in Chicago."

Maya pumped her free fist just as a car horn honked. "Yes!"

"I didn't get the job, just the interview."

"I know, but you're so good at interviews. If you want this, Meade, it's yours."

"I do want it. I can't keep living the way I've been living. I'm looking at forty in two and a half years. Something's got to give."

She had no idea how much this was music to Maya's ears. But Maya also knew all it'd take was one trip to some stupid dance club and this house of cards could topple like an avalanche. "That's great, Meade."

"Don't get too excited yet. The guy told me the process would last about six weeks."

"All right, but I'll still keep my fingers crossed. I just got to the restaurant. I'll see you later, okay?"

"Okay. Love you," Meade said.

Maya smiled. "Love you, too."

They hung up, and Maya glanced around the bar and spotted the guy who matched the picture Brenda had sent her. He wore a suit, the jacket slung across the chair beside him, love handles hanging out of his white, tucked shirt. Oh well, she was dating in her mid-thirties. What did she expect? And the way she'd been treating her body these past weeks, she was on her way to having a matching pair.

"Nathan?" she asked.

He stood up, and she looked down at him. With her three-inch heels, she was a good six inches taller than him. She held out a hand. "Nice to meet you."

They sat down, and he pointed at a half-eaten

plate of appetizers. "Sorry. I skipped lunch today. They're going to squeeze us in at six-thirty. Does that work with your schedule?"

That meant she had to entertain him for a solid hour before they got a table. She forced a smile. "Sure."

"So," he said, swiping the crumbs off his hands. "Tell me about your work."

The minutes dragged by like slugs as they exchanged mundane information about their lives like they were both on a job interview, until Maya's text alert dinged. Her heart practically flew out of her chest when Bo's name came across her phone's screen.

Where are you?

She drew her shaky hand to her forehead and tried to put her attention back on Nathan, who was detailing a courtroom case he'd recently argued.

She nodded, smiling, and he looked at her curiously. "Are you okay?"

"Oh, yes. Please, go ahead. You were saying that the defendant had a second policy?"

He went on, and she glanced back down at her phone, which had gone black. She hit the button and Bo's name populated her screen again, the message just sitting there unanswered, sending a fresh wave of tingles through her stomach.

Where was she? Two weeks of radio silence, and now he wanted to know where she was? She forced another smile at Nathan, running her hand over her forehead and smoothing back her hair. She was in freaking Indianapolis. What did he care where she was?

Nathan's phone dinged, and he checked it. "Sorry, this will just take a minute. We're in the thick of a big case. I'm headed back there after this, actually."

Maya picked up her phone and swiped the message open. Where was she? She'd tell him exactly where she was.

On a date.

There. Not her finest moment, but she felt better, sort of, not really at all, actually. Her breath caught as the ellipses popped up indicating he was typing.

Where?

What did he mean, where?

Downtown Indy. A bar called Preen. Why?

"Sorry about that. I'm all yours." Nathan smiled at her. "Do you need another one?"

Maya's wine glass was down to its last few sips. "Sure."

Nathan waved at the bartender, and then went back to his story. Maya's phone had gone black again, so she pressed the button. No new messages.

"Do you need to get that?" Nathan asked.

She scratched her head. "Um, let me just check really quickly." She swiped open her screen, and there sat her message, the last in the thread, no rolling ellipses. That was great. He dropped this bomb on her, completely throwing her off guard for what could otherwise be a...sufficient date, and then disappeared. "Sorry," she said, putting the phone down. "Please finish your story."

Nathan went on as Maya struggled to focus on him, her mind back in Bo's bedroom in Panama City Beach, her legs wrapped around his back as he pumped into her, his head between her legs as he made her feel like some sort of sex goddess, sensations pouring through her, her on her knees while he—

"Hey."

Maya knocked over her wine glass as she turned to find Bo standing in front of her breathing heavily, his face flushed red.

Nathan picked up the wine glass, which was thankfully almost empty, and dabbed the bar with a stack of beverage napkins. Her mouth was forming the word what, but sound wasn't coming out behind it. Bo held out his hand to Nathan. "Bo Harrison."

Nathan shook his hand. "Nathan Edgefield."

"Nice to meet you," Bo said. "Y'all care if I sit? I just ran three blocks."

"Sure," Nathan said, glancing at Maya for further explanation, but Maya was as mute as a mouse.

Bo pulled a barstool over and sat, each of his knees pointed at Maya and Nathan. The bartender, being a breathing female, was at Bo's service right away. "What can I get you?"

"I'll take your finest pilsner on draft, please ma'am."

The bartender, looking utterly charmed, got right to work. Nathan pointed between the two of them. "So how do you two know each other?"

Bo rubbed his hand over his head. "Oh, well, that's a funny story." He turned to Maya. "Do you want to tell it, or should I?"

She glared at him, not sure what he was up to, but not wanting to miss a second of it. "Why don't you tell it?"

The bartender set Bo's beer down, and he took it with a wink. "Thank you."

"Mmm hmm," she muttered with a look that conveyed he could have anything he wanted from her, and Maya was reminded of exactly why she was here with Nathan and not the beefcake. Except Nathan had cream cheese dripping down the side of his mouth as he shoveled in another appetizer.

Bo took a long drink and then set the glass down. "Goddamn that's good."

Nathan, his patience clearly wearing thin, said, "You were saying how you know Maya."

"Oh, yeah. So she came down to Florida on vacation to visit her friend Sebastian a few weeks ago. Has she told you about him yet?"

"I've just met her a half hour ago." That gave Bo a smile that Maya wanted to smack off his mouth, or flood with kisses, she couldn't be sure which.

"Well, anyway, she was there to see him, but we met and had this fantastic week of passion-filled romance." He leaned in. "Best goddamned sex of my life, and I've had a lot to compare it to, if you know what I mean."

Nathan pursed his lips, his face coloring a bit.

"But then I, of course, had to go fuck the whole thing up by ending it before I should have, but my intentions were good." He turned to Maya. "I assure you of that."

She just stared at him, not ready for a minute to let him off the hook yet, even though he had traveled seven hundred miles to see her.

"So, as you can imagine, I didn't want her to leave, but how can I ask her to stay there in Panama

City Beach with me? She's only known me a week. She's pretty sure I'm not a psycho because her friend Sebastian vouched for me. He's my friend, too. Did I mention that?"

"No," Nathan said, crossing his arms over his chest, but still not leaving, surprisingly.

"And on top of all that, she's got this high-powered job here up north, and I've got a small business down in PCB. But I can't ask her to give up everything in her life to take a chance on me when she's not even sure if what she feels for me is driven by a week's worth of mind-blowing sex, or if it's something that'll fizzle in a month." He turned to her. "But see, I'm sure of my feelings for her."

Her whole body sizzled with heat, tingles running down her arms and through to her fingertips.

"So I moved here," he said.

Her heartbeat thudded in her chest. "What?"

"Just down the street, actually. I sublet an apartment. I figured if I was gonna live somewhere else for the first time in my life, I wanted the full metropolitan experience." He lifted his beer mug and took a drink.

Nathan stood. "Well, this would all seem sweet and charming if I didn't have a brief to write." He dug in his back pocket.

Bo held up his hand. "I'll take it from here."

Nathan pursed his lips and snatched up his suit jacket. "You're getting off cheap. I usually bill my time at four hundred an hour."

"Were you gonna leave her with an invoice?" Bo asked. Nathan held up his middle finger as he left, and Bo pointed in his direction, looking at Maya. "You sure you don't want to chase him down?"

"Bo," Maya said, a million thoughts running through her head. "You can't move here. What about your family? Your nephews? Your business?"

He shrugged. "It's all taken care of, the business at least. Shayla's moved home. She told me Saturday after you left. Already had all her stuff packed on a moving truck and shipped to a storage unit in PCB. She didn't want to tell me before. Said she was a grown-ass woman and didn't need her baby brother trying to step in and help her."

"You're so close with her, and she's finally home, and now you're moving here?"

"It's working out perfect. She's gonna take over the business for me. She worked for me for years before she moved up to Nashville, so I can't think of anyone better to do it. She's even gonna live at my house and take care of Jake."

Jake, his beloved dog. Just one more reason this couldn't possibly work. "What about money? Your mortgage there and an apartment here. I'm not trying to be nosey, but—"

"I paid off my house a couple of years ago."

Her jaw dropped. It was a decent house in what had to be a somewhat expensive area being so close to the beach and all the tourism. "Really?"

He smiled. "Don't look so surprised. My business may be small but it performs well."

"I don't mean to seem surprised. I just…that's great. Will you work from here?" she asked, as if this was actually happening, when clearly it couldn't.

"As much as I can. We've got everything on a system so I can keep up with inventory and financials that way, manage all the schedules. I do a lot from my laptop at home as it is when I'm too lazy to go in. I'll see how it goes. If it's too hard, I'll just step back and let Shayla take on a bigger role and hire someone else to help her, and I'll find a job up here."

"Doing what?"

He shrugged. "I don't know. I've got an MBA, and I've run a successful business for over a decade now. Surely that'll land me an interview somewhere."

"Bo, I can't let you do this."

"It's already done. I knew if I tried to talk to you about this, you'd think too much about it. I'm here. I've signed a month-to-month lease on a furnished apartment. If at any time you get sick of me, you can kick me out of town."

She couldn't believe this was happening. She couldn't let him do it, but he already was doing it. Brenda's talk had meant something to her, but she hadn't had time to process it yet. She had planned to do that later this evening. But here he was, throwing her a curveball. And everything he'd said had made sense, at least to her.

She slid down from the stool and went to him, wedging herself between his legs. "I can't believe you've done this for me."

"It's for me as much as it's for you."

She ran her hands over his head, letting his short hair glide through her fingers. "You're the most incredible man I've ever known."

He cupped her ass and pulled her closer to him. "Give it a few months and see if you still feel the same."

She grinned at him. "Deal."

Chapter Twenty-One

Maya stood in the foyer of Meade's new Chicago apartment, knowing it was time to go, but having such a hard time separating herself.

"I'm going to be fine," Meade said, reading her mind like sisters do.

Maya looked her over. Just in the past two months, Meade's transformation had been unbelievable. She'd gained back some of the weight she'd lost in Las Vegas, she'd had her hair cut short so all that was left was her natural golden blond, and her face glowed from her new skin regime. She looked like her old self, the Meade Maya knew from when they were young, not the Meade who let men dominate her life.

"I know you are, but what about me?" Maya asked.

Meade peeked out the window at Bo, who was standing on the sidewalk, letting them have their privacy. She met Maya's gaze, her expression thoughtful. "Come sit with me a second." She took Maya's hand and led her to the kitchen table. Maya stiffened. It really felt like Meade was turning a corner, but Maya could never be a hundred percent sure.

Meade ran her hand over the back of Maya's hair, cupping her neck, and then letting go. "These past couple of months, living with you, observing you and Bo, it's been really tough to watch and not be able to say what I've wanted to say."

Maya frowned, afraid of where this was going.

"He is a hundred percent crazy in love with you, you know that right?"

Maya tucked a lock of hair behind her ear. "We haven't said that yet."

"I don't care what you all have said. He gave up everything in his life to move to Indy, from the beach, from all his family and friends and everything he knows just for you."

Maya's throat burned. "You don't have to tell me that, Meade."

"No, I think I do. Why are you keeping him in Indy? What's there other than your job? And don't say Mom and Dad, because we both know you are so much better off when you are far, far away from Mom."

Maya's heart pinged around like a pinball machine, just like it'd done every time she saw him and thought about what he was giving up for her. "You are the last person who can understand this, Meade."

"Why? Because I've fucked up my life a

hundred times for men? Forgotten who I was when I saw a handsome face and some abs at the gym? Do you ever think that might qualify me to give this advice rather than detract me from it?"

Maya's eyes stung with Meade's words.

"You're miserable at that job. You know you are. You hate it. You complain about it every night. You aren't taking care of yourself. You haven't exercised in weeks. You're losing who you are trying to hold onto a job you don't even want."

Maya clenched her teeth, trying hard not to cry. "I earned that job."

"Of course you did. You worked your ass off for it, and you got it. Beat out a whole slew of candidates I'm sure. And now you've got this guy who adores you, who's given up everything for you, and you're so damned determined to show yourself, and Mom and Dad, and me that this is how it's done. You don't let a man run your life. You make your own decisions. And you certainly don't give up a job you hate for him no matter what the cost." She tossed up her hands. "I get it! I hear you loud and clear, Maya."

Maya wiped tears with the back of her hand. "You don't get it, Meade."

"Oh, but I do. You have no idea how much I get it." She stabbed a finger at the front door. "That man is not a piece of shit. He's not someone whose bills you're going to have to pay, or who's going to expect you to do his laundry or cook for him without any form of appreciation. He's never even once asked you to move down to Panama City because he would never put you in that position.

He's in Indy for you. And you're there for some stupid job you hate. All you ever do is talk about those people down in Florida and the area and how it was the best freaking week of your life. And you have the chance to legitimately go live there with someone who owns a business there and has a house, and friends you love, and family you're desperate to know. God, Maya, to be the one with the common sense in this family, sometimes it's like pulling teeth with you."

Maya blinked, Meade's words dropping on her head like a ton of bricks. "How dare you."

"How dare you? Open your eyes, Maya, because if you don't, you're going to mess around and fuck up the best thing that's ever happened to you." Meade stood up and walked out the front door, leaving Maya in a puddle at her kitchen table.

Maya walked zombie-like to the front door to find Meade standing with Bo, talking with a smile on her face like she hadn't just cut Maya to her absolute core. She hugged him tightly, and then stood waiting for Maya to come out. She wrapped her arms around Maya, whispering in her ear, "I love you," and then headed back inside.

"Everything okay?" Bo asked.

Maya stared at her sister's apartment. "Let's go."

Chapter Twenty-Two

Ever since they'd moved Meade to Chicago last weekend, Maya had been distant. Bo couldn't be sure why. At first, he figured she was just worried about Meade, but as the days crept by, he was starting to get concerned. She'd had a busy workweek, but he was supposed to spend Saturday with her, all day and all night. He wanted to reconnect with her, because he was starting to get a vibe that she was slipping away from him.

His text alert dinged, and he picked up his phone from the table.

Meet me at Monument Circle when you can.

That was a little cryptic. He'd run past Monument Circle a few times since he'd been there. It was roundabout sort of thing in the middle of downtown with a huge statue. He pulled it up on his GPS so he wouldn't get lost and headed out on foot. It wasn't that far. He texted back.

On my way.

When he got there, he found her sitting on the stairs to the monument across from the chocolate café. He crossed the red brick street, noticing a little white bag next to her as he got closer. "Hey," he said, joining her.

She smiled. "Hey."

"What's this? You have a break in between meetings?"

"Something like that. I quit my job."

She said it just as a big truck crossed by. "What?" he asked, wanting to make sure he heard her right.

"I want to move to Panama City with you."

His heartbeat picked up speed. "Darlin', we don't have to—"

"Of course we don't. But I want to. I've wanted to since the week we spent together there. I want to be a part of your family, and I want to be friends with your sister, and I want another hug from your mom. I want to take your nephews out for ice cream at that place Seanna said would ruin me for all other ice cream and go to your parents' house for Sunday dinner. I want to go to fabulous seafood restaurants with Sebastian and Marigold, and Desiree and Ashe. I want to double-date with Blake and Seanna and make Chase go on blind dates with eligible women I meet, approved by Felicity, of course." She squeezed his thigh. "I want to pet Jake behind the ears."

He tried so hard to contain his grin, because he wanted to make sure this was what she wanted, but it was so hard.

"I want this, for me," she said. "Forget the fact that it's what I know you want. It's what I want."

"Sweetheart, I'm happy as long as I'm where you are."

She smiled, her eyes getting watery. "You're such an incredible person, Bo. You have no idea how much so. Thank you for sticking this out here with me."

"I wasn't sticking anything out. I was living here with you."

"I know. But you better get packing soon, because I've got two interviews set up for next week."

"You've been looking for a job there?"

She nodded. "I have. I need to wrap things up here in Indy, so I may be back and forth some, but my boss is completely understanding about all of this. He's offered a letter of recommendation and everything."

"Where are your interviews?" he asked, trying to imagine where in Panama City a woman as classy as Maya would work.

"There's a publicity firm in Destin and a small marketing company a woman runs out of her house in Watercolor. There's also one in Panama City I applied for today. So, I'm learning that Panama City and Panama City Beach are two different places?" she asked.

"You're catching on." He eyed her. "You're sure about this?"

"I've never been surer of anything in my life." She smiled at him and then picked up the little white bag. "I've got something for us." She shook the bag.

He glanced over at the chocolate shop across from them. "Is that what I think it is?"

She nodded with a sneaky look on her face.

He wiggled his fingers. "Gimme."

She exhaled a deep breath, her expression turning serious. "I love you, Bo."

He let out a huff of air, his heart sprouting wings and flying out of his chest. He'd wanted to say it to her a hundred times, but he was being so careful with her. He hadn't wanted to crowd or rush her, since he'd moved up there without even telling her he was going to. He'd wanted to leave that word alone and let it be on her terms. Let her come to him with that one thing when she was ready.

"God above do I love you, too," he said.

She fell into him, and he cradled her to his chest, wondering if it was possible to soar higher than he was flying at that moment. He couldn't believe she was his. He wished he could go back and tell his twenty-something self to hang in there till his thirty-fifth birthday, where something this wonderful would be waiting for him, but he never would have believed it.

The Next Chapter...

Shayla disconnected the call with her brother, relief flooding through her. Bo was coming home. As much as she didn't want to admit it to herself, she welcomed the peace of mind that came with having her overprotective baby brother nearby.

She'd rather be dragged across hot coals than tell him what was going on with her, but just knowing he was in the same town with her would be a comfort, and just in time, too, because by her calculations, her two month's grace period was ending any day now.

His house was too damn big. She was tired of having to walk through it with a baseball bat every night when she got home and every morning when she woke up. Her paranoia was stupid, really. Jake barked when a squirrel climbed a tree at the next door neighbor's house. If someone appeared inside Bo's house, Jake would let her know.

Her phone rang again, sending her heartbeat back into orbit. Shayla had been laid back her entire life, until this past year. Now she was more skittish than a Chihuahua, but based on the caller ID, she had reason to be. She let it ring, biting her thumbnail. All her nails were down to the quick. Her text alert dinged and her stomach felt sick.

Shayla, please.

She stroked Jake's fur. With Bo moving home and bringing Maya with him, she'd have to leave and get her own place somewhere. She'd have to give Jake back to Bo, as disheartening as that idea was. She'd have to go to the shelter and get another dog, preferably one that had Doberman or German shepherd in it, a dog that was loyal and protective. Her phone dinged again.

I've earned the right to talk to you. We had a deal.

Of course they had a goddamned deal. She'd have said her mother was a whore to get out of that situation. She'd never had any intention of staying true to that deal. The only deal she had in mind was one that got her four hundred miles away from him.

You're leaving me no choice. If you don't talk to me, I'm coming down there.

She clenched her eyes closed. She had to talk to him. This was exactly why she hadn't changed her number. Brian knew where she was. He could come there at any time, and he would if she kept shutting him out. Besides, she needed to end things in a final way. She couldn't keep putting that off just because she didn't want to hear his voice. She swallowed hard and hit his name in her contacts, her heartbeat galloping like a Clydesdale.

"Thank you," he said by way of greeting, his voice calm and steady. She didn't respond. "How are you?"

"I'm fine."

"How's Bo?" he asked.

"Good. He's in the living room, so I can't talk long," she lied. If Brian had a clue Bo wasn't living there, he'd have been down there from Nashville in a heartbeat.

"I've been half-expecting to find him at my doorstep ready to fight me."

If Shayla had told Bo what Brian had done, that's exactly what would have happened. But there was no way she was opening that can of worms. She wanted this to be over and in her past. She just had to figure out how to close it down permanently.

"I finished the rehab," he said.

"Mmm hmm."

"It was eye-opening, to say the least," he said.

She let silence sit between them.

"It's changed me, Shayla."

"Good. That's good."

"Sweetheart, you can't start to conceive of how sorry I am."

She dug her knuckle into her forehead, wanting so desperately for this conversation, and this relationship, to be over. "I forgive you, Brian."

"Oh, thank God," he said, his voice cracking.

"I'm not saying we're getting back together. I'm telling you I forgive you, and that is the end. I don't want to be in a relationship with you anymore. This is going to be the last time we talk."

"But we had a deal." His voice was still calm, but it was starting to turn slightly more urgent.

"I know we had a deal. But I am free to be with whoever I want to be with, and I don't want to be with you." She winced as the silence between them hissed like static.

"Shayla, you said that if I went to rehab you would consider forgiving me."

"I have. Like I said, you are forgiven."

"But this whole time, I've been under the impression that you would consider forgiving me so we could move forward together."

"That's not what I said, and that's not what I intended."

"God—" he stopped himself. "I deserve another chance. I've worked my ass off these past two months on this. You told me to give you time, and I granted you that."

Who was he to grant her anything? She stood up, her face so hot bacon would have sizzled on it. "Brian, this is the end of this. Right now. Do not call again. Do not text again."

"Shayla," he said, his voice stern, taking on that same quality it had…before. That was all she had to hear. She ended the call and dropped the phone on her bed like a hot potato. She stepped back from it like it was a snake ready to strike.

The doorbell rang, and she screamed, jumping a mile high. Jake bounded off the bed and ran into the living room barking at the door, the hairs on his back standing on end, just like the ones on her arms.

"Shayla?" a man's voice said. She couldn't make out whose voice though with Jake barking as loud as he was. She grabbed the baseball bat from her bed and eased into the living room, watching the doorknob like it was going to jump at her any second.

More knocking, which made Jake even more agitated, barking like his life depended on it. The person was saying something else, but Shayla couldn't understand a word of it and didn't really care to. All she knew was whoever was on the other side of that door knew her name, and she had just hung up with Brian.

She froze solid when the deadbolt turned, an icy chill spreading through her veins. She could call 911, but that would mean she'd have to let go of the bat she was double-fisting and there was no way she was doing that, not with the lock on the door handle turning. She pulled the bat back like she was lining up at home plate, the bat shaking uncontrollably in her hand. She'd imagined this very situation nonstop for the past two months, and here it was, playing out like a living nightmare.

The door opened, and a tall, dark-haired man held up both hands in surrender. "Holy shit!"

"Who the fuck are you!" she shouted, the bat ready to go.

"Bo's friend…Chase."

To stay informed of all Melissa's new releases, bonus content, and giveaways, sign up for her newsletter at melissachambers.com.

If you enjoyed this story, please consider leaving a review on Amazon. Your words are so valuable to authors, and even a really short review is very much appreciated!

Find out what happens with Shayla and Chase...

Seagrove Secrets now available at Amazon.

About the Author

Melissa Chambers writes contemporary novels for young, new, and actual adults. A Nashville native, she spends her days working in the music industry and her nights tapping away at her keyboard. While she's slightly obsessed with alt rock, she leaves the guitar playing to her husband and kid. She never misses a chance to play a tennis match, listen to an audiobook, or eat a bowl of ice cream. (Rocky road, please!) She's a member of RWA and serves as the president for the Music City Romance Writers. In addition to the Love Along Hwy 30A series, she is the author of The Summer Before Forever and Falling for Forever (Entangled Teen).

CPSIA information can be obtained
at www.ICGtesting.com
Printed in the USA
LVHW092253220919
631915LV00001B/8/P

9 781732 415614